Praise for *The Witch*

"An enchanting debut, Palmieri's plot
read!" —MELISSA DE LA CRUZ,
autho[illegible] Blue Bloods series

"*The Witch of Little Italy* had me spellbound from the very start. Suzanne Palmieri has created a poignant, beautiful tale of love, magic, history, and family, where all are deeply connected and interwoven." —JOANNE RENDELL, author of *Crossing Washington Square* and *The Professors' Wives' Club*

"A mystical family secret hidden in a spicy Italian stew."

—KELLY SIMMONS,
author of *Standing Still* and *The Bird House*

The Witch of Little Italy

Suzanne Palmieri

ST. MARTIN'S GRIFFIN
NEW YORK

This is a work of fiction. All of the characters, organizations, and events portrayed in this novel are either products of the author's imagination or are used fictitiously.

 Printed in the United States of America. For information, address St. Martin's Press, 175 Fifth Avenue, New York, N.Y. 10010.

www.stmartins.com

ISBN 978-1-250-01551-8 (trade paperback)
ISBN 978-1-250-01550-1 (e-book)

First Edition: March 2013

10 9 8 7 6 5 4 3 2 1

For my husband, William,
who taught me that once I started something,
I could finish it as well

Acknowledgments

There are many people associated with bringing this story into the world, and I'd like to take a moment to give thanks. To my early (nonwriter) readers: Jan Nichols, Tahisha Porter, Kathy Viani, Mary Giannotti, Michelle Esposito, Lynne Hodgson, and Rita Palmieri.

To the writers who read this novel and gave me constructive advice on how to make it better: Lou Florimonte, Loretta Nyhan, Amanda Bonilla, Sarah Bromley, Kari Lynn Dell, Simon C. Larter, Sarah Wylie, and Joanne Rendell.

To my literary agent, the keeper of my dreams, Anne Bohner. You sold four of my novels in one day. Did I win the literary agent lottery, or what? And on that note, to Sally Wofford-Girand, who believed in my stories and encouraged me to keep writing no matter what.

To the entire team at St. Martin's Press and Griffin, your enthusiasm has overwhelmed me and made me, in turn, want to make this story shine as brightly as possible.

To my editor at St. Martin's Press, Vicki Lame. You are made of glitter, Glitter. And you sprinkled it throughout this book. I am so happy to have made a "book baby" with you. Also, I made a friend. And that is *always* a good thing.

To my family: Husband William (I *told* you I would do it and I did), I love you, babe. To my three daughters, frequently referred to as "My Coven" or simply: Oldest Witch (Rosy), Middle Witch (Tess), and Littlest Witch (Grace Louise). You are more than patient with my odd ways. You are magnificent and your mother loves you.

Also, thanks to Richard Denton, who helped with the title.

To the writers I admire: Stephen King, Alice Hoffman, Marge Piercy, Peter Straub, Ray Bradbury, and Anne Rice. All of you helped a lonely young woman (me) feel a little less lost. Thank you.

To both my father figures: Robert L. Mele (my godfather in all the ways) and James Sterling Cooper (my father via biology, charisma, and green eyes). And to the Coopers down south: Kim Cooper, my brother Talmadge James, and my first cousins, especially Lana. I love you.

To the entire Palmieri clan who took me in and gave me a name to showcase my culture. Especially my mother-in-law Margaret Palmieri, father-in-law William Louis Palmieri, Jr., sister-in-law, Amanda Palmieri Linski, and my very favorite great-aunt, Rita (Louisa) Palmieri.

Mostly, though, this book belongs to my mother, Theresa Anne Germanese Cooper, and to her mother (my grandmother), Fay Depaul Germanese Barile. You taught me kitchen magic and introduced me to my great-aunts, Carmel, Anna, The Other Fay, The Other Carmel, Mary, and Annemarie. You raised me to respect my Italian-American heritage and reconcile it with the Alabama in my soul. If I have layers, it is only because you layered me. Thank you.

"I'm a Lost Witch, are you a Lost Witch, too?"

—*Suzanne Palmieri*

Winter

I

Itsy

All the Amore siblings had The Sight in varying degrees, and its fickleness got us into trouble sometimes. Like the time when I was young (and still talking) and I called my friend's husband to give my condolences about her death in a trolley crash, only my friend was still alive and the trolley wouldn't crash until the next day.

It was hard to explain *that* one, and harder still to keep my friend off the trolley the following day even though I knew her life was at stake. Regular people have such a hard time listening to the low hum of instinct. Don't get me wrong, I tire of the magic now that I'm old. But still, if I'd had it all to do over, I'd choose magic ways. Especially now, when another, more precious life is at stake.

She's coming back now, the girl. She's coming back and bringing my memories with her. Maybe *she* won't remember anything. Dear God, don't let her remember. If she remembers, she'll land straight back in harm's way. If she remembers, my promise will be broken. And that'd be too bad because it's one of my best skills, promise keeping. And secret keeping. And cartwheels, too.

I used to be able to do cartwheels. When we were little, my sisters couldn't but I could. I can still feel how the air shifted as I kicked over my head and moved my hands. I liked to do things upside down. It bothered Mama. "All the blood will rush to your head!" she would yell. Not to mention Papa and my skirts. "Cover yourself, child! If I can see your bloomers so can the whole block!"

I cartwheeled through my childhood. We weren't poor, but we lived close together. We all lived here on 170th Street in the Bronx for the better portion of our lives. Mama and Papa bought the building when they married. Well, Papa won it. In a fight. They used to fight for money in the streets back then, and one day the wager was a building, and practical Papa, who'd never fought a day in his life, took off his shirt and threw it into the ring.

When we were very young, in those strange, magnificent years between World War I and World War II, we all lived in apartment 1A. Ten people and two bedrooms. Those were the days. Mama was the magic one. She gave us her abilities to see the future, to grow herbs and flowers that held all sorts of possible magical preparations, but the most important thing she gave us was the gift of each other.

But we're old now, Mimi and Fee and me. We're all that remain of the Amore children. Three children left out of eight, each of us carrying the burden of *that day* in our own way. And as we grow ever older, The Sight grows stronger.

On a cold, dark December night, we woke with the same dream and sat around the kitchen table looking into a bowl full of water. Our old lady hair pinned back, my knobby fingers scribbling on my pad with the pen that's always fastened to my chest.

She's coming, I wrote.

"She's coming," said Mimi.

"On Christmas?" asked Fee.

"Maybe . . ." said Mimi.

She's coming. I underlined the words on my pad twice, for emphasis.

Mimi was afraid to believe, afraid to get excited. Her girls so rarely came to see us. But our Sight is strong. It grew as we grew. She should know better than to doubt it.

The Sight helped us through our darkest days, and our magic gardens made our lives wild like rambling roses. But *our* roses had thorns. Thorns sharper than those who live without magic could ever fathom. Like how Mama knew, even before the fortune-teller told her, that 1945 would be a very, very bad year for the Amores.

In the end, no amount of Sight could prepare us for the trouble that arrived. And those of us who were left carried the burden of "The Day the Amores Died" in our own way. We suffered our own tragedies and kept our own secrets. Secrets that scattered pieces of us into the winds for the sparrows to collect and keep, until the day the girl returned.

2

Eleanor

Eleanor Amore took the home pregnancy test on Christmas Eve in her mother's room at the Taft Hotel. Carmen was in a show at the Shubert Theatre that ran straight through the New Year, so Eleanor had the room to herself. Away from her dorm room at Yale. Far from prying eyes. And, more important, far from Cooper.

The Taft was in walking distance from her dorm, but it was a one-way street. Carmen never came to campus. If Eleanor wanted Carmen, she had to *go* to Carmen.

Crossing the Green, she looked up at the enormous Christmas tree, its lights glowing even though it wasn't fully dark outside. The festive tree set against the remainder of the pink sunset struck Eleanor, making her lose track of her thoughts. Contrasts always did that to her. She sat down on the cold concrete and dug into her large, velvet patchwork bag for her sketchbook and charcoal. Leaning against a park bench she began to move the charcoal over the white paper in soft smudges. The black on her fingers always made her hopeful, giddy with possibilities. If Eleanor hadn't been so immersed in her impromptu piece of art, she'd have noticed the pigeons cooing and clustering all around her. And what they saw through their small, black eyes was a very different girl than Eleanor believed herself to be. Working away, she smiled as her own eyes sparkled under her knit hat. She drew with broad, confident strokes, her fingers moving with freedom and skill. Eleanor wore fingerless gloves so her fingers would be able to move freely when she wanted them to.

Soon the sun set completely, and it was too dark to draw. Eleanor sighed and closed her sketchbook, buried it with the charcoal in her bag, blew on her fingers to warm them up and finished her walk to the Taft.

She'd been to the hotel enough for the doorman to recognize her, so he let her into the suite even though Carmen wasn't home from the theatre yet. He was nice to her, looked at her with those sad eyes. The ones that said, "What's happened to *her*?"

Even at Yale, no matter how impressed other students or instructors were with her artwork, she couldn't paint over her own insecurities. No matter how hard she tried to join the crowd, play pool at the Gypsy, she couldn't fit in. The sound of her own fake laugh made her sick. The ironic nature of this "loner" status wasn't lost on Eleanor. Carmen needed to live inside thronging crowds where Eleanor wanted to live in a submarine. Periscope up, periscope down.

Eleanor switched on a soft lamp and took in the posh surroundings of Carmen's suite. Overdone, but entirely comfortable. She made her way to the marble bathroom and ripped the waxy, white pharmacy bag open with shaking fingers, carefully avoiding looking at herself in the mirror.

She peed on the stick and said a silent prayer with her eyes closed. "If there is a God there will *not* be a pink plus sign."

She peeked through one eye. There was a pink plus sign.

"Crap!" Thoughts ran through her head in odd angles, bumping against one another. A baby? A baby. A life was growing inside of her. She'd known it—somehow felt it—the moment she conceived. And in a way she'd cradled the notion like Golem ever since. Her life would change. That wouldn't be so bad. It was the *rest* of it, the logistics that were an issue. And the idea of telling Carmen twisted her stomach into knots.

Eleanor balled up the evidence and threw it in the trash under the bathroom sink. The cabinet pulls were crafted out of pale, pink glass, like sea glass. *Sea glass* . . . a twinkle of a memory flashed . . . children giggling and wrapping wire around pieces of sea glass. Strange bits and pieces of memory had been coming back like errant drops of water since the moment she felt she might be pregnant. Eleanor didn't know what to make of them, or of anything else. Her world, her lonesome restless world, was turning upside down.

She shook her head and walked slowly back into the living room. Switching off the light she looked out the window at the city below. The center downtown Green glistened, heavily lit with Christmas decorations. "Merry Christmas to me . . ." she said to the glass, fogging it up with her breath and drawing a Christmas tree in the gray mist with her fingertip.

Eleanor sat on the couch to wait for her mother in the dark. She put her hands on top of her head feeling for her familiar knit hat. Eleanor tugged on it, pulling the folded brim over her eyes and then unfolding it again.

Carmen had given her the hat when she was thirteen. The last time she'd been to the Bronx to visit with her mother's family. The first time she *remembered* spending any time with the Amores at all.

Eleanor couldn't remember anything solid from before she was ten years old. There existed a sort of misty haze that lit here and there, mostly in the time between sleeping and waking, and mostly in images and faint whispers. They haunted her, those ungraspable, streaming facets of lost time.

Her first "hard" memory took place on the stoop of their brick building in the Bronx. She'd spent a summer there alone with her great aunts, grandmother, and great uncle. Eleanor didn't remember that summer, she only recalled leaving them standing on the stoop while Carmen scooped her up and deposited her in the back of a checkered cab.

They didn't visit the Bronx again until Eleanor was thirteen. It was fun, that night. For Eleanor at least. Not so much for Carmen, who drank too much wine and became loose-lipped.

"A nice soft green for you, Eleanor. Like your eyes. So pretty," she'd said as she gave Eleanor the hat and a rare compliment from her beautiful, self-absorbed mouth.

Eleanor knew enough about pop psychology to understand her attachment to the hat, but it comforted her, so she wore it. If she had to take it off she'd keep it close. Tuck it into a back pocket, or in her bag.

Keys clattered against the door.

Eleanor took a deep breath and tried not to sweat. Carmen could always smell fear on Eleanor and used it against her. She needed to be strong. Stand her ground. For once.

The door opened. The room flooded with light.

"How'd *you* get in here?" asked Carmen.

"The doorman, Mom," Eleanor sighed. "And Merry Christmas to you, too." *Off to a great start,* she thought.

"Screw Christmas," said Carmen, shrugging off a black mink

coat and kicking shiny black heels across the floor. "And look at you. You're a mess. That hat? Really? Did anyone see you come in?"

"Um, the doorman?" *I'm invisible to her.*

Carmen made her way to an ornate cabinet and opened it, revealing a bar. She poured herself a drink in a chubby rocks glass and then looked at herself in the mirror that hung over the bar. She sipped and stared. Eleanor saw her own face next to her mother's reflection.

Carmen was German Expressionism: bold, angular, exotic, exciting. Eleanor was Impressionist watercolor: softer, rounder, pastel. A washed-out version of her mother. Her nose small—Carmen's Roman. Her hair an ordinary dark brown—Carmen's a jet-black mane. And now? Another disappointment to confess.

Eleanor stood. "I'm pregnant," she told Carmen's reflection.

There was a slight stiffening to Carmen's back, and a shift in her eyes . . . subtle, like a draft . . . a surrealist portrait, Carmen's eyes were windows with sheer curtains moving in the breeze revealing the rooms behind. Empty rooms.

Carmen turned and leaned against the bar. Long and lean. Dark and beautiful. "Have you told Cooper?"

"God, no." said Eleanor.

Carmen took a sip of her drink. "Is he still hitting you?"

Eleanor didn't answer.

"You shouldn't let him do that to you, treat you like that. Call the cops, get a restraining order for Christ's sake," said Carmen.

"It's not that easy, Mom."

"Yes it is. *You* make it harder than it needs to be. Get some self-esteem, Eleanor. It'll do wonders for your love life."

"Look, Mom," said Eleanor pushing through the caustic remarks, "I know this is all *so* out of the blue. And I know you and I don't get along that well, but I'm in a *really* bad position and I was wondering . . ." Eleanor paused, a mistake, she knew. A weak spot that her mother could use as leverage later.

Carmen placed her hand to her temples, massaging them. She closed her eyes and asked, "Wondering what? Please enlighten me."

Eleanor let the words tumble out, "I was wondering if I could come with you when you leave in January. Go back to Europe. I can still go to Florence for my internship this summer." Carmen opened her eyes when Eleanor mentioned Europe. Eleanor knew that was the key. Carmen had been trying to persuade her to come back to Europe after Yale for years. Eleanor knew she couldn't live up to Carmen's expectations, but she also knew Carmen didn't know that yet. With Carmen's false hope on Eleanor's side, she asked the real question. "If you'll help me."

"Help you with what?" Carmen asked, genuine confusion furrowing her brow.

"Well," *Big breath. Go on, you have nothing to lose* . . . "I'd need help with the baby."

The word *baby* fell hard into immediate icy silence.

"How dare you?" asked Carmen through clenched teeth, her eyes on fire.

"Please, Mom?"

"Please? Please what?"

"Please calm down and consider this for a second."

"What the hell do you want from me? What reaction did you expect? You come here, drop this baby bomb, and then ask me if you can come back with me to Europe?" Carmen's hands tightly gripped the lip of the bar behind her. "And I'm like, *sure* . . . and

I almost, *almost* thought you were going to be normal. To react to this thing like a normal young woman would. You know . . . have an abortion and then get on with it. And I thought, just for a *split second,* that we could actually get along again, you know? But, no. You want me to be your fucking nanny?"

Eleanor clamped her hands over her ears. "I don't know what to do. I don't know what to do . . . I don't know what to do," she whispered to herself.

Carmen took a deep breath and smoothed back her hair. She faced the mirror again, pulled a little at her thick eyelashes and regained her composure. Eleanor looked up just in time to see Carmen paste a pleasant, motherlike smile on her face. It felt eerie to Eleanor who could still clearly see through the façade, a rendition of Edvard Munch's *The Scream*.

"Eleanor," she crooned, joining her daughter on the couch, "I know I'm being hard on you, but really, baby—listen to me. Kids are life suckers. They suck up your life and then *forget* all the good things you did for them. All the fun times you had." She reached forward and took a cigarette out of the pack on the coffee table and lit it with a fancy silver lighter.

"Mom. My memory loss is not my fault."

Carmen took a long drag from her cigarette, "You know, I read an article on kids and memory loss. Said sometimes they make the whole thing up for attention." She put her fingers to her mouth to remove some invisible tobacco, a habit she still had from smoking unfiltered cigarettes.

"Are you kidding me?" Eleanor leapt up and paced the room. "*You* are the parent, Mom. You're supposed to know what happened to me." In all the years Eleanor and Carmen had quietly struggled with getting back her lost childhood Carmen was never able to answer Eleanor's questions. *"Did I hit my head?" "Did I fall down a flight of stairs?" "What happened?"* It still aggravated her to no end and a ball of anger bubbled up as she looked at her mother.

Carmen exhaled and squinted through a fog of smoke. "Forget it. Oh, wait, you already did." Carmen laughed, a sound that resembled diamonds cutting glass. "The thing is, you can't come with me if you're going to keep this baby."

"So where do you propose I go?" asked Eleanor.

"I'm not proposing anything. I don't support this decision. Case closed."

Eleanor's knees went weak. Her forehead began to sweat and itch under the hat. *What am I going to do?* she thought, her mind racing. She couldn't, wouldn't tell Cooper. Endangering herself was one thing; her baby was another thing entirely. Carmen was her last, best hope—and now it was gone.

She walked around the room in circles as Carmen smoked and poured herself another drink. Eleanor stopped in front of a photograph propped up on a table in front of her. A photograph she knew well, it was always wherever Carmen was. It was one of two constant things in their vagabond life. The photo and the rocking chair.

The rocking chair—Let me call you sweetheart, I'm in love, with, you . . . Carmen rocked and sang to baby Eleanor. She could feel the love pour out. The sweet satisfaction of chubby hands wrapped in silky hair . . .

Eleanor shook away the stinging tears. Tears from a memory she couldn't place. A feeling she'd never known with her mother. *I swear, I'm adopted,* she thought for the millionth time. She picked up the photo. A younger, overly stunning Carmen, standing on the steps of her family's apartment building on 170th Street, stared back at her. A voice Eleanor had been hearing for weeks now came through stronger than ever.

Come home.

The words echoed through Eleanor's head.

Come home.

"I know what I'll do," she said, her voice ringing loud against the stark silence and startling Carmen. "I'll go back there." She picked up the picture and pointed at it for emphasis. "Back to the Bronx," she said, realizing she'd been thinking about it all along. A dim, lacy notion taking hold.

"You will not," stated Carmen, chain lighting another cigarette off the first.

"Why?" asked Eleanor, forcefully. "You grew up there. And they liked me. That *one* time you took me there. Well, the time I remember, anyway. They liked me, I could tell."

"That Anthony boy sure liked you," said Carmen.

Eleanor blushed. "No, really, Mom. I think I fit in there somehow. Don't you remember? You gave me this hat . . ."

Said I was pretty . . .

"Do I remember?" spat Carmen, standing up to look her daughter in the eyes, her hands waving around sloshing bourbon out of the glass. "I remember how crazy Aunt Itsy clawed at her neck. I remember how *hot* it was in there that Christmas. I remember you playing all kissy face with that boy in the hallway. I *remember* what a fucking mistake it was going back there to begin with."

Eleanor focused on the glass in her mother's hand. How it wove around. How it spilled itself out to punctuate Carmen's thoughts. *Even the glass has more backbone than me,* she thought.

"Your mistake, Mom. Not mine. *I* had a good time that night."

Carmen wasn't listening. Again. She'd turned her back and was pouring herself a third drink at the bar, "Freaking Yogis in India making me believe I had to make some sort of peace with them. God, what I would give to take back that whole bohemian stage. I was a little old for a midlife crisis."

Eleanor had been a "late in life" baby, born when Carmen was on the heels of forty. A fact she never really let Eleanor forget. "*You were lucky I even decided to have you . . .*" she'd say.

"Okay then. It's settled," said Eleanor, slapping her knees and going for the door.

"What?" Carmen dropped her cigarette and then stooped to snatch it up, spilling her drink out onto the floor.

Eleanor felt the panicky rise of nervous laughter crowd her chest and flutter at the base of her throat. "I'm going back. I'll be with your mother if you need me." She knew the last bit would sting and the words felt bitter and acidy as they came out.

Carmen placed her hand over her daughter's on the doorknob. Eleanor looked down at the white knuckles contrasted against long nails coated in "Honeymoon Red" nail polish. The nails dug into Eleanor's hand. There was a moment of complete and utter *still* before Eleanor yanked at the knob, throwing her whole body into Carmen to push her away.

"Don't go. There's something wrong there and you know it!" yelled Carmen as she fell against the wall next to the door.

Eleanor threw open the door but stopped to look at her mother crumpled against the wall. Tears formed in the corners of Carmen's eyes. Just as Carmen could always read fear on Eleanor, she could now read fear all over her mother. The tears met with thick liner and created little congealed black clumps. She didn't even look like Carmen anymore. Her lips were thin and trembling; her eyes open and full of truth. "Don't go," she said. "*Really.* There's something *wrong* there, they . . . those women, they can see things. They can *do* things. Things normal people can't do. Things people ought not to do."

"The only thing wrong there is that *you* left it behind. I'm not you. You know that better than anyone. And . . ." Eleanor hesitated.

"And what? Have you heard anything, seen anything strange?" asked Carmen, perking up even as her voice wavered. "It runs in the blood you know. I don't have it, but these things . . . they can skip generations I guess. What have you seen, Eleanor? Tell me!"

Come home.

"I don't know what you're talking about," she lied.

Come home.

They'd talked, during quieter days, about Carmen's childhood. How the building on 170th Street was haunted and how the women there were witches. But Eleanor never believed Carmen . . . not really. She just assumed it was one more dramatic flair Carmen was adding to her personal bio. But lately, with all the strange things happening in Eleanor's own mind, she wasn't so sure.

"I'm leaving, Mom," she declared as she walked through the door trying to slam it, but Carmen was right behind her.

Eleanor ran to catch the elevator, Carmen chasing after her.

She leapt into the open elevator and sighed with relief as the doors began to close. Carmen threw her arm in between the elevator doors, wedging them open.

"What do you want from me?" yelled Eleanor.

"They'll eat your baby," Carmen said through clenched teeth. "They will. I don't know why I'm alive. Think about it, Eleanor. I'm the only one. The only living child. There were *eight* of them. Four girls and four boys. You'd think there'd be a gaggle of kids, right? That I'd have cousins galore? Well I don't. What does that tell you?"

Eleanor grabbed at Carmen's hand trying to push it out of the way so the doors would close and she could be free. A thought—clear-as-crystal—surfaced in Eleanor's mind as she wrestled with her mother's hand.

"You never belonged there, did you? No matter how you tried, they ignored you, didn't they?" she asked.

Carmen's hand dropped but this time Eleanor kept her own arm in the door. "But me? They love me! And that kills you somehow, doesn't it?"

"Look," Carmen said pointing a shaking finger at Eleanor. "I don't care what you think you know. There's some sort of curse on that building. On that family, Eleanor."

Eleanor pulled her hand back and waved good-bye at her mother. The doors started to close. "Suit yourself then," Carmen said turning around, "They're nuts."

She watched her mother through the narrowing view and saw Carmen sweep back into her suite on stocking feet until the shiny metal closed in front of her face making her mother disappear completely.

✦

Eleanor Amore took the Metro North train from Union Station. It was deserted. The conductor tipped his hat and said "Merry

Christmas, honey." The *honey* made her want to cry. Everything made her want to cry lately. *Damn hormones.*

She got off in Stamford and could have taken a cab, but didn't. She transferred onto the 125th Street train and got off on Fordham Road. Eleanor's legs knew where to go. Her mind did, too. A few months back, Eleanor had flipped through her mother's address book looking for any trace of family that might be there. She looked up *Amore.* Nothing. She looked up *mom,* and then *aunts.* Nothing. Then she went to the "B" section. And there it was, the address, 1313 170th Street, Bronx. Only it wasn't listed under "B" for Bronx, it was listed under "B" for "Batshit, Crazy."

✦

Eleanor stood very still outside her family's building on 170th Street. The night was mild for December but the snow fell anyway, glittery dancing dust. It rested in delicate layers, coating Eleanor's hat and oversized sweater. She kicked the snow and faced her past.

She pulled her hat down close over her ears as she gazed at her grandmother's home. Its smallness made it stand apart. Only two stories sandwiched between larger, more modern apartment buildings. And it had a peaked roof, where the others were flat. The iron grates on the lower-level windows curled and curved into everlasting vines. Two chimneys rose tall and old-fashioned on either side of the roof and stood out black against the purple, snowy sky like sentinels. Eleanor thought she could remember holding onto those metal bars, the coppery smell of sweaty little girl hands when she let go—but then—then it was gone. The building looked surprisingly lovely coated in the fine, sparkling

December snow, with warm lights pouring out. Eleanor *almost* wanted to go in.

Bing Crosby's "I'm Dreaming of a White Christmas" came floating out of a window, propped open just a crack. The building in front of her bustled. Eleanor's artist eyes saw a moving still life; a work of performance art. The majority of activity streamed out in sound bites of laughter and clinking glasses from the window on Eleanor's right. The colored lights from the Christmas tree pooled out through the window and bled onto the white ground in a jewel-toned watercolor wash. The apartment to her left was colder. The light, austere. The inside of the front room was devoid of curtains making the shabby room clearly visible.

Peeping Tom Eleanor always had a love of walking around at night. Especially in New Haven. She'd walk around and peer into the houses. Watch the families gathered together making dinner. Watching television. Being normal, whatever that meant.

Eleanor tipped her head up to get a view of the windows on the second floor. One dark, like a black eye. The other dim, but she could see a figure. It moved, the shadow, and Eleanor knew where it was going. Snow fell in her eyes.

She gave the snow an annoyed kick and crossed her arms as she sat on the front stoop of the building. "Crap! I'm not ready for this!" she yelled at the snow.

The large front doors opened and people poured out like bugs. A priest and some old ladies, all laughing and saying goodnight. Someone brushed against her and said, "Excuse me." Eleanor didn't move. She sat still on the stoop.

Her grandmother, Mimi, stood in the doorway, handing out Tupperware containers of food and saying broad good-byes to her guests. Only when they were gone did she turn her attention to her granddaughter. "Babygirl, you've been out here a long time. It's getting cold now. Come in, won't you? I'm so excited to catch up."

Eleanor craned her neck to look at her grandmother. Mimi looked exactly as she remembered. Short and round. Black hair set against an old face. Old but kind. Eleanor felt torn between the solidness of the stoop and the liquid happy that wanted her to fly into Mimi's warm arms. *Why am I so determined to love it here?* she wondered for the six hundredth time that night.

Babygirl. The name made her heart sing. That's what they'd called her. Eleanor shook her head "no" hard enough to send a layer of snow flying. It was all too much. Carmen was afraid of this place, and Eleanor was increasingly convinced that she was going insane, so she didn't know what to think, or who to trust. A part of her, the sane part, weighed the options. It was either the Gingerbread House from Hansel and Gretel, or the Rabbit Hole from Alice in Wonderland. Either way, it was dangerous.

"Okay," said Mimi. "But the door is unlocked. I'll be cleaning up. You come in when you're ready."

One of the front windows screamed open. Aunt Fee poked her head out and yelled to her, "Get inside! You'll freeze your skinny legs off!" Eleanor sat still. *Fee can't hear well . . .* She remembered.

Stubborn and staring at the snow she marveled over how each individual crystal was different from the next. She remembered reading somewhere that Eskimos had a hundred words for snow. Eleanor wished there were a hundred ways to say her name. She thought, maybe, if her name was howled from all the corners of the world, in a million different voices, that she might explode into a cloud of snow. Light and separate, her parts floating down onto the world in a series of beautiful crystalline moments.

"You know somethin'? The Eskimos have a hundred words for snow," said Anthony sitting next to her.

His voice rumbled like low thunder, echoing her thoughts. She wondered momentarily if she'd thought out loud . . . *How?* It didn't matter. Everything was muted and far away. Eleanor, hiding under her hat, didn't want to come back from inside her dream of being snow. And she certainly couldn't look at him. If she looked at him she was sure she'd disappear. *Don't look at me. Don't figure it all out. Keep me in your memory like I was when we were kids. I'm damaged now. Broken. Please.* Eleanor hadn't considered this part when she was making the rash decision to come back to this place. She didn't think about how it would affect the other people.

Maybe her grandmother didn't want a pregnant granddaughter?

Maybe her aunts didn't need something else to take care of at their age?

Maybe Anthony was hoping she'd be a successful, beautiful, grown-up woman, instead of a hopeless, homeless, cloud of snow.

"It's good to see you," he said. "Or at least it's good to see this person who I think is you." He leaned over and picked up the brim of her hat, forcing her to look right at him.

She held her breath. She'd planned this moment a hundred times in her head since she was thirteen. The big reunion. But in her mind they'd be on a beach, or he'd see her browsing in a bookstore. She never imagined it would be like this. Sitting in a heap on a cement stoop.

Eleanor turned her head and looked at him.

Shocked, she closed her eyes for a moment so she wouldn't

make an even bigger fool of herself. She had to take all of it in. Years passed by under her eyelids. Until the moment she looked at him she was completely, ridiculously, expecting to see a thirteen-year-old boy. And the person who'd just slid in next to her like a cat was no boy. She opened her eyes again to drink him in. His beauty. It made Eleanor want to die. Her artist eye knew this was perfection. The balance of features, hard jawline, full lips, Roman nose. His hair was longer, it fell in his eyes. And he was taller, too. She wanted to paint him.

"Hey, there you are!" he said. "I thought I'd lost you for a second."

"Hey back," she said and pulled on her hat.

He cleared his throat; there was an awkward silence. "Welcome home," he said, finally.

"Do you still live here?" asked Eleanor. *Small talk, that's good. Keep it all small talk* . . . she thought.

"Yep. Upstairs. Next to where Uncle George used to live."

Eleanor felt a knot of sudden sorrow in her stomach, though she didn't understand why. "Used to?" she asked.

"Oh, gosh, I'm sorry. Carmen never told you? He died two years ago," said Anthony, putting a hand on her shoulder.

Eleanor shrank away from his touch. "I don't know why it bothers me. He was just a smelly old man."

Anthony looked away from her. "Not always," said Anthony. "Still no memory of our amazing summer?"

Eleanor shook her head. "You remember that?"

"Do I remember that you don't remember?" laughed Anthony. "That sounds kind of like 'Who's on First—' you know, that Abbott and Costello act?"

Eleanor put her face in her hands. "Ugh! I don't know how to do this! I don't know how to even have this conversation. Aren't you married or something?" she asked.

"Well—no. I guess not at the moment. Do you want me to be?" he asked.

Eleanor stood up, her feet slipped out from under her, and she saved herself from falling by hanging onto the iron railing. *Monkey bars. Lookit me Uncle George! I'm doing it!* She was swinging, her arms burning, summer sweat stinging her eyes. Eleanor's head ached with these echoes from the past. They felt like nuts and bolts clanging around. What would happen when they all found their way together? Who would she be? Eleanor took a large stride backward toward the curb. "I . . . I've made a huge mistake. I . . . I have to go."

"Where are you going?" asked Anthony, standing up and brushing the snow off the back of his jeans.

"I have no idea."

"Do what you need to do, but when you decide to come back—and you will—I'll be here." He went back into the building and shut the door,

Eleanor turned around and walked to the curb to try and hail a cab. A crumpled ball of paper flew over her head and landed in the snow at her feet. It began to unfurl. Eleanor picked it up.

That's right. Move along. Nothing here to see.

Love, Aunt Itsy.

"Itsy," Eleanor said the strange name aloud. It rolled off her tongue and mingled with the snowflakes. Her heart knew the name even if her mind only contained a small recollection. She turned back to see the woman who tossed the paper, but as she turned the door shut tight against her.

Something stirred deep inside Eleanor. Something that urged

her to take the bait. To run toward the secrets, into the unknown. *If there was ever a time to be brave*, she thought . . . And then Carmen's voice from earlier in the evening: *"A little self-confidence would go a long way . . ."*

Eleanor Amore straightened her posture and only tugged on her hat once as she stomped up the stairs and threw open the closed doors of 1313 170th Street.

Once inside she leaned against the double doors and adjusted her eyes.

A semicircle of oldness stood directly in front of her. Eleanor turned pale. The lamp on the hallway table gave a warm glow, and the doorways to both downstairs apartments were open, flooding the hall with dueling Christmas lights. The light flickered off the ruby poinsettia pin on Aunt Fee's housecoat, and the high shimmer of the ladies' hairspray.

"Are you okay?" asked Mimi.

They tightened their circle, coming toward her. Sandwiching her back against the door. Eleanor began to hyperventilate.

Itsy held a pot full of what looked like tomato sauce, but smelled like fish. Eleanor was immediately sick to her stomach.

"Move, ladies! I think she's going to blow!" yelled Fee.

Mimi rushed Eleanor into apartment 1A and closed the door. Fee shuffled across the hall into the apartment she shared with Itsy. But not Itsy. She stayed in the hall, thinking about a day long ago as well as a day yet to come.

✦

"Are you going to be sick, love?" asked Mimi when she closed the door.

"No," said Eleanor, taking in air through her nose. "The smell's gone. What was that?"

"Crab Sauce. The Feast of the Seven Fishes, don't you know?"

"Oh, yes. That's right," said Eleanor, remembering the amazing meal from that last visit. Squid salad drenched in olive oil, stuffed lobster tails, and the crab sauce . . . her mouth watered and a warmth spread through her at the thought of the delicious food, but then the queasiness hit again.

"Will you be all right in your mother's old room? Or would you rather sleep with me? I wouldn't mind sharing my bed," Mimi said as she led Eleanor down a narrow hallway running the length of the apartment. The dim Christmas lights mimicked candle glow and cast long granddaughter and grandmother shadows against the walls.

"No, I think I'd like to sleep in her room," Eleanor said.

You don't want to share a bed with me, she thought, looking at her grandmother's wide yet fragile back, *you're probably going to want to kick me out on my behind when you find out why I've come.*

"Is that so?" asked Mimi, stopping in front of a closed door.

Eleanor held her breath. *Did she hear me? Did I say that aloud?* "What?" she asked.

Mimi smiled. "You'd rather sleep in her room?"

Eleanor relaxed. "We had a fight," she explained. "I'd like to be close to her. It's easier when she's not around. If that makes any sense. When I was little and she left me with nannies I'd sleep in her nightclothes. It always made me feel better."

"Oh yes. It makes a world of sense." Mimi's hand rested on the closed door. She moved her palm against it like a mother who rubs a child's back at night. "I don't come in here much. Only to clean. So you'll find a lot of her in here, or at least the 'her' she was when she was mine." Mimi moved her hand to the doorknob. It was made of cut glass in a deep shade of purple. Mimi stopped for a moment and looked up at Eleanor. There were tears in her eyes. "When she was little she liked to pretend this was the largest amethyst in the world, you know. It was the most marvelous thing, her imagination."

Mimi opened the door, pushing past the squeaky complaints of its hinges.

The room was old-fashioned but lovely, just like Eleanor's memory of the rest of Mimi's apartment. And so much like Carmen's own personal style. Only Carmen called it "Classic Chic."

There was a four-poster bed pushed against a large window, and a beautiful Persian rug under her feet. Against one wall stood a two-door armoire with full-length oval mirrors, etched with misty vines and flowers at the borders. Kitty-corner on another wall was an inviting dressing table. Eleanor sat down on the pink cushioned chair in front of it and took stock of the shiny contents cluttering the tabletop before her. Makeup jars, perfume bottles, necklaces . . . all waiting for a sixteen-year-old Carmen to come home and claim them.

Mimi stood perched at the threshold, her posture unsure. The air between them began to settle into a silence. Awkward, yet softly exciting. Like an unexpected snow day.

"Can I get you something to eat? A cup of tea, maybe?" asked Mimi.

"No, thank you." Eleanor's voice sounded strange in her own ears. Higher. A pitch she was unused to.

Mimi took a hesitant step into the room, sniffed the air, and moved closer to Eleanor. Soon she was behind her and they looked at each other in the dressing table mirror. *So many reflec-*

tions of people all in one night, thought Eleanor. "I looked at my mother tonight in a mirror just like this. When we were fighting."

Mimi took off Eleanor's hat and put it on the dressing table. She picked up a heavy silver brush with soft white bristles and began to brush out Eleanor's long, straight hair.

"Your mother has always liked to have conversations in mirrors. She gets to look at herself while she talks. I'm sure you know how vain she is," said Mimi as she brushed down to the ends of her granddaughter's hair.

Eleanor looked at Mimi in the mirror. It wasn't like looking at Carmen's reflection at all. There wasn't any competition, or tension. Mimi just . . . *was.* She was there, brushing her hair as if she'd done it every night for as long as they both could remember.

A pile of small paperback books caught Eleanor's attention and she pulled against her grandmother's strokes. T. S. Eliot. e. e. cummings. Tennyson. Keats.

"She liked poetry, huh?" asked Eleanor.

"Yes. She doesn't anymore? She used them for her monologues at school."

"I don't think I've seen her read anything but scripts. And beauty magazines. She likes music though." Thinking of Carmen curled up with a new script made Eleanor start to cry.

And she likes to dance. And she smells like India. And she hates me.

"You know how you tell a naturally beautiful woman from the rest?" asked Mimi.

"How?" asked Eleanor, grateful for the detour.

"If she's still pretty when she cries, that's how. A lot of women swell up and get all blotchy. But a naturally beautiful woman will shine. Look at you . . ." Mimi put down the brush and rested her chin on the top of Eleanor's head, placing her hands on each side of Eleanor's face, centering their reflection. "You are shining, my dearest beauty."

Eleanor wanted to say so many things. But nothing came out. She pulled away from her grandmother and put her hat back on.

Mimi took the hint and went to leave. "Will you be okay? Do you need anything?"

"I don't know," said Eleanor, her throat tight.

"No, of course you don't. Well, it might be cold comfort, but I love you, Eleanor, and I'm glad you're home."

Come home . . . she heard again. Was it Mimi's voice all along? How? And then there was the sound of a wailing child. Eleanor put her hand to her mouth to make sure it wasn't her own weeping ripping free again. It wasn't.

"Who's that, Mimi?"

"Who's what?"

"Is there a little child living here? I just heard someone crying."

A shadow flickered across Mimi's eyes. "I didn't hear anything. Are you sure you're okay? You don't want to sleep with me?"

"No, I'm fine. But that was definitely a crying child. Maybe outside?"

"Maybe it's a ghost?" offered Mimi, unaffected by the idea.

"Is the building haunted, Mimi?"

"Isn't every building haunted?" asked Mimi, playfully. "Well, goodnight, Babygirl. I'm glad you are here. If that crying keeps you up, you come and get me, okay? Promise?"

"Yes. I promise."

The door closed. And Eleanor was alone.

She picked up the e. e. cummings paperback off the dressing

table and made her way around the room. Atop the trunk at the end of the bed there was a radio combination record player. Eleanor lifted the blue plastic lid, pushed the on switch, and prayed. The turntable began to spin. She lifted the arm and placed the needle to the black vinyl. *This was the last record my mother listened to in her bedroom.*

Connie Francis' "Where the Boys Are" came singing out . . . .

Where the boys are, someone waits for me . . .

Eleanor smiled. It was so . . . sixteen of her! She sat on the end of the bed and let the book of poetry open to a natural place. A clue to her mother's favorite page.

Anyone lived in a pretty how town
(with up so floating many bells down)

Up, so floating. That summed up Eleanor's mood. Something that spanned comfort and terror. But things that terrified most people didn't scare Eleanor Amore. It was a quirk of sorts, her absolute affection for all things Gothic and dreadful. When she was younger and she'd ask Carmen about monsters in closets or ghosts under the bed, Carmen would roll her eyes and send out smoke rings shooing her away with an If-only-life-could-be-that-interesting look. But Carmen didn't understand. Eleanor wasn't afraid of the common childhood threat. She was delighted.

Her paintings reflected her need for dark themes. Her figures rarely had eyes, only reflections of what Eleanor supposed were their secrets. If there was a vase of roses she'd find the one that was wilted, and examine, with her brush, the potential of decay.

"Morose, doom-prophet, depressed, troubled." These were all words used to describe her and her artwork.

"And we can't forget pathetic," she reminded herself aloud. That was Cooper's favorite insult. "Eleanor, you're absolutely pathetic," he'd say after he hit her. And worse, after they'd have sex.

Cooper. She didn't even want to think about him in this place, in her newfound sanctuary, her sacred space . . . she didn't want to channel his energy. But it was too late. Even just the thought of him barged over her, unwanted and present all the time.

She couldn't block out the memories just like she couldn't protect her body from his fists.

She took off her clothes, all except her hat, and looked at her naked body in the armoire mirrors. She examined her bruises. Some old and yellow, fading. Some newer, red and angry. It bothered her that she knew the lifespan of bruising.

The first few months with Cooper weren't so bad. She wasn't in love, but he was beautiful to look at—and popular. And for a brief moment Eleanor felt like a participant in her life instead of an observer. Carmen paid attention. Her relationship with a rich, good-looking boy inspired Carmen to call Eleanor on a weekly basis to "check in." Other girls at Yale swooned over her. Wanting to know her secret. How the strange girl with the freaky green hat had won the most desirable freshman boy at Yale. If only she'd known the secret herself, she may have been able to avoid the last three and a half years. The secret? Damage. Cooper smelled damage a mile away. He knew she'd never run. She'd never tell.

"Oh God," she said into the air as a wave of nausea washed over her. The thick black of sticky memories sloshed up like oil. The memory of those months. Especially the first night she'd had sex with him. The night she lost her virginity. The night he hit her and put his hand over her mouth so she couldn't scream. When she didn't leave him, or report him the next morning, they both knew she belonged to him. And try as she might, Eleanor couldn't figure out why she stayed. That week, when Carmen called, Eleanor told her mother what was happening. There was a silence on the line and then the question: "What did you do?"

What did *she* do?

"Why didn't you tell me to get away from him? Why?" Eleanor asked the walls. Her chest hurt. A familiar void opening up. The rush of breath leaving her as her peripheral vision went fuzzy. She sat down in the middle of the floor and wrapped her arms around herself willing it all to go away. She searched the room for answers.

On the back of the door a nightgown hung from a metal hook. A permanent hook. Not the plastic ones you find in the newer stores, the ones that go over the doorframes and make life more difficult. Just a simple metal hook and a pretty nightgown hanging from it. White with yellow flowers.

Carmen's, of course. Eleanor got up fast and grabbed for the nightgown hungrily. She yanked it off the hook and pressed it against her face while she did the math. Carmen left the Bronx in 1961 when she was sixteen years old. Eleanor wasn't born until Carmen was thirty-nine, on the cusp of forty. That meant the nightgown had been hanging there for over forty years. And still, the fabric smelled like her mother. Spicy and warm.

Relaxing, Eleanor slipped on the light nightgown. It must have been summer when Carmen left because it was sleeveless with lace eyelet edging and tiny buttons down the front.

The nightgown worked better than any drug. All the terrible

memories took flight. She stood in the middle of her mother's room wearing her mother's nightgown, listening to her mother's Connie Francis record. Calmed, her hands went to her stomach.

"I'm here for you. I don't know who you are, or what's in store for us, but I'm here for you. And I swear—I swear to God that if anyone ever hurts you, I'll kill them."

She turned down the bedcovers like she'd lived in the place her whole life and got into the bed. It felt like a dream she'd had a million times. The comfort. Better than any five-star hotel. The city sounds hummed a soft lullaby, muted by the thick glass window and falling snow outside. Eleanor didn't feel like being that snow anymore. She felt like being Eleanor Amore of the Bronx. Whoever that might be.

Refuge is a subjective thing. It can be found in the most unlikely places. Cardboard boxes, underpasses, subway stations. It can be found in drug addiction, under thick layers of skin, and in churches, too. Eleanor Amore found her refuge in an old brick building throbbing with loss and possibly frequented by an invisible crying child. And as the darkness fell soft all around, each resident of 1313 170th Street went to bed with the knowledge that nothing would ever be the same.

In apartment 1A, next to the room that would now belong to Eleanor, Mimi knelt by her bed and cried soft tears of gratitude into hands folded in prayer. She prayed to the God of her father's family and the Goddess of her mother's. Once Mimi'd felt that a new life was growing inside Eleanor she'd taken out her mother's spell book and cast the Lost Witch spell. She'd done it alone, without her sisters, knowing that a new life opens all the channels of the mind. And her granddaughter had listened to her yearning and heeded the call. Mimi climbed into bed with more joy in her heart than she'd held in many years. More joy than she thought it was able to hold at all.

In Apartment 1B, Fee fell asleep in her worn-out easy chair eating Christmas cookies and watching a rerun of Bob Hope's Christmas special on the Family Channel, her snoring as loud as her voice. But as she fell to sleep her thoughts were of her grand-niece, and the children she'd never had. *How different would it all have been?* She wondered. And in her dreams she was thin and quiet and was running down the beaches with her sisters.

Itsy sat up straight in her bed leaning her head against the hard headboard and rubbing her eyes with her hands. *I need a plan,* she thought. *If the girl is to stay, then I need a plan.*

Anthony, in Apartment 2A, slept on the floor to be closer to his one true love. And directly downstairs, Eleanor drifted into sleep trying to grasp all of her lost memories while the soft snow created a cocoon all around them.

And in apartment 2B, Georgie's old apartment, piled high with all his things packed up in boxes and bags, a child was crying.

3

Itsy

After the day that took half our family, the building went to Mimi. She was the oldest functioning child. It was a wonderful gift. And to be honest, it belonged more to her than me or Fee. Mimi loved every brick of the place, still does. It's harder for me and Fee to forget the ghosts. I don't know if Mimi forgets them, or just blinds herself, but I don't ask and she doesn't tell.

Eight siblings and two parents in a two-bedroom apartment was close comfort. Mama and Papa slept in the front bedroom, the four sisters (myself included) slept in the back bedroom, and the boys slept in the attic. They had a fireplace up there for the cold winter nights, but those boys were a strong lot. They liked it up there. They planned their lives up there. My twin, George, was always supposed to be up there with them, but he usually crept into bed with me or Mama. He said he couldn't sleep with the older boys because they scared him. Said they talked about how they were going to die.

And George was right, our older brothers all knew they would die when they enlisted. *They had some kind of courage those boys.*

I thought of the girl, her back pressed against the door in the hallway. That face. Light, like Mama. Soft features, not hard like Carmen. A softer version of her mother in all the good ways. The last time she was back she was about thirteen or so. She wasn't at all the little spitfire she'd been when we'd first had her. I remember I was so worried that night. Worried she'd remember—just like I am now. But her preteen instantaneous (and mutual) crush on our Anthony trumped all, and even though I kept checking to see if my throat would loosen, Carmen yanked her out of our lives just as fast as she'd walked back in. Our girl was gone. Again. She was lost. And it was my fault.

Babygirl. Well, that's what we nicknamed her when she stayed with us that summer she was ten. Her real name is Eleanor.

"That's a fat girl's name," said Fee, once we'd gotten the scared little duck to bed that first night.

"You should know a fat girl's name when you hear one," said Mimi.

Fee couldn't hear her. But she wouldn't have been hurt even if she had. Fee lost her hearing the day we lost our family, the day I lost my voice. Anyway, it was an honest observation. Mimi's honest to a fault. Fee *is* fat. I keep wondering if she'll get so fat she won't be able to leave the apartment.

In the end, we decided on Babygirl. And Babygirl she stayed, even though she's all grown up now. I wasn't *sure* she'd stay. I should have been. When we see something, the three of us, it happens.

Sometimes I wish we didn't know things, especially now that we're getting on in age. It'd make life simpler, not knowing. And The Sight is fickle. It shows us just so much—and then? Then the rest is up for interpretation. Mama always said that was the most important part, the interpretation. Mimi and Fee just liked Seeing. Me? I'd like to be free of it sometimes.

Don't get me wrong; knowing a bit of the future could be useful in a large family. We knew when so-and-so would be late for dinner, or how to stop a sister from tripping on the church steps moments before social suicide.

But, to keep us sane, we all had things about us that helped keep us apart. Things that gave us space in our brains where we could be alone, even as our bodies were squished together. Most times we couldn't even hide in our brains because all you'd have to do is brush up against someone and know all of their secrets, their desires. *Wow,* were my brothers hot for Carole Lombard. I guess it only made sense. Everyone around them was dark. Dark hair, dark eyes, olive skin. Carole Lombard was like the sun. Like the ladies on the Far Rockaway beaches in the summertime.

Summers in the city were hot. I suppose if we'd lived in a different time we could have had fancy AC units. But really, even if that had been invented, we wouldn't have used it. Mama didn't like anything that wasn't true. Air conditioning lies to you. Makes you think that it isn't hot outside, when it is. "If you fool your body your body fools you," she would say.

If it's hot, you're supposed to be hot. You can cool down enough with fans. Fans over bowls of ice cubes worked well. But sometimes we needed to swim, and for that we had the house in Far Rockaway.

Not so much a house as a cottage, really. One in a row of many lovely cottages. Mama and Papa owned it. Well, Mama owned it. She was Irish. Something we didn't talk much about. Papa made her swear off most things not Italian when they married. Mama grew up in Massachusetts, in a town called Fairview.

And before her own mother went crazy, she spent her summers at their vacation house on Far Rockaway. It was her stomping ground. And the summers, all throughout my childhood, we spent wrapped up in Mama's history, and sand, and sea.

Papa stayed in the city and kept up the accounts for his clients. Papa was good with numbers and kept the books for almost every business in Little Italy stretching from Arthur Avenue to Claremont Park. He took the train in on the weekends. And my older brothers, they stayed, too, and worked when they got older, and when we returned to the apartment building in late August, Mama would always throw open the windows and say, "Gotta get that man smell out of this place!" And it was true, the apartment always smelled different when we'd been gone. Me and Mimi, Bunny and Fee . . . and George. Georgie had his problems. He stayed in Mama's skirts. He didn't stay with Papa or the boys. He stayed with us.

He was the baby, anyway, even though we were twins. I was born first. He didn't come until two whole days later.

I can still remember us girls running down the beach and Georgie following us. We always raced ahead until he cried. And I'd always stop. Not my sisters. They ran faster, farther away laughing, always laughing. I'd stop though. Do a few cartwheels back his way and then hold him tight. He belonged to me. He'd reach up and wrap his hands in my curls. He'd straighten the bow in my hair with a shaking hand. "You look a fine mess," he'd say. I'd take him by his hand and drag him back to Mama, who'd have lunch all laid out for us in the shade of the front porch.

"You're a good sister," she'd say.

I was. Then. And then I wasn't anymore.

4

Eleanor

When Eleanor woke up, it was quiet. And, in those fleeting moments between sleep and awake, she was absolutely comfortable. The heaviness of the blankets felt just right against her skin. The heat was clanging up from the basement and toasting the dust particles on the radiators, making the heat smell pop around in the air. The bed was pushed against a window and there was the tiniest draft trying to make its way in and have it out with the heat. It was clean, and cold, and unforgiving. The mix, like most things dark and light, was magical. Eleanor felt herself begin to slip into that place. The comfort place—part dream or memory—she didn't know, and didn't much care. It was just lovely. She was at a beach. Not a European beach. Not the south of France where she'd learned to swim. A pebbled beach. The seagulls were singing and swing sets in the background were squeaking. The lapping waves touched her hands as she did cartwheel after cartwheel across the beach. The sights and smells of this place always calmed her. Slowed her pulse. Made her happy.

But too soon Eleanor's feet got sweaty and her neck began to pinch. She sat up. She was surprised, then nervous, and finally, excited to be where she was. Her head throbbed. A hangover caused by the enormous amount of decision making the night before. She stretched her arms up over her head and listened for sounds, noises of a busy grandmother she'd have to get to know. But there were no noises in the apartment. Eleanor *did* smell coffee. The aroma hung in the air, warm and inviting. Her hat sat on the pillow next to her. She grabbed it and put it on. *If ever I needed you,* she thought. "Merry Christmas, hat."

Eleanor got up, intending to find something to wear and then figure out how she was going to deal with this crazy decision she'd made when the lingering fish and garlic smells hit her. She ran out into the hallway but couldn't make it to the bathroom in time. She threw up on the oriental runner.

"Fantastic," she said.

Eleanor wanted to clean it up, but the thought of it made her gag again. She'd have to find Mimi.

"Mimi?" she yelled out as she felt her way along the walls and then around the entrance to the living room. Silence.

She walked out through an arched doorway into the living area. It was warm, but Eleanor felt cold in her bones, and she was wearing Carmen's summer nightgown. She took a folded afghan off the couch and wrapped herself. She held the crocheted wool to her nose and breathed in the history. Whose hands made this? Were there babies babbling while it was being created? Meals being made? Laughter? Tears?

As she thought about the history of her family, Eleanor heard the crying again. The same sound from the night before. It was coming from the kitchen.

"Mimi?"

She walked through the dining room and into the kitchen but no one was there. She went out into the back hall. No one.

"That's odd," she said to herself. And it *was* odd, but also thrilling.

The back door was open a crack. The cold air felt good on her face.

She headed outside, the afghan trailing behind her, and found herself in a walled, perfectly square garden. Eleanor put her bare feet in the snow. The cold against her skin tamed the nausea.

She sat on a nearby bench and surveyed the area. The sun was so bright on the snow she had to cover her eyes. She could just make out little walkways here and there. A few religious statues nestled between twigs. Bits of black gardener's plastic peeked out from under the snow cover.

"Merry Christmas!" said Anthony, throwing open the aluminum screen door so that it slammed against the brick wall of the building. A little snow fell off Itsy and Fee's kitchen windowsill. A tiny avalanche for Eleanor to focus on so that she wouldn't get sick again. Not now, out here, in front of *him*.

"Not talking?"

Eleanor cleared her throat. "No."

"Suit yourself. You should get a pad like Itsy. And some shoes. It's cold out here." Anthony began to shovel the few inches of snow off of the walkways, stopping to sweep the remaining snow off of the lower windowsills and the heads of saints with his hands. After he brushed off the saints he made the sign of the cross and pulled a gold crucifix out from beneath his heavy coat to kiss it.

"Religious much?"

"Cold much?" said Anthony with a smile. "You should really go inside. Especially in your condition."

"In my what?"

Anthony stopped to look at her, then scratched his head. He looked confused. "Nothing, never mind," he said and continued shoveling.

He was even more handsome in the daylight. His black hair shined in the sun, falling in front of his eyes. He took off his coat as he worked and his white t-shirt stretched across his perfectly built frame. Strong shoulders, wide masculine back. Eleanor felt her own body grow excited as she watched him move. *What the hell is wrong with me?* she thought. *First I'm puking, then I'm all excited over a boy I hardly remember while my feet turn blue in the cold?*

But it wasn't true. She remembered him well. He was the reason she'd held that night so long ago in her memory like a talisman. The memory of him was what first alerted her something was wrong with Cooper. Her few minutes alone with Anthony when they were thirteen taught her more about mutual affection than a lifetime with Carmen.

The back gate of the yard screamed open.

"Anthony! I told you to WD-40 this thing! It could wake the dead it could!" The three women filed in. They looked like triplet witches from a Gothic fairy tale. All three in long black ladies' trench coats, with black umbrellas, and plastic hair covers tied in bows under wrinkled chins. They stopped in a line in front of Eleanor.

"She's barefoot."

"Out in the snow."

"Like a gypsy heathen."

"We have so much to teach her."

Itsy scribbled a note and threw it. It floated like a feather and hung suspended in the air for a moment until it landed in Eleanor's lap.

You look like your mother out here underdressed. Now go put on some clothes.

The three women moved together into the back hall and while they all removed boots and other snow gear Mimi said, "Child. You *will* meet us inside to exchange gifts. It's Christmas, don't you know!" Lined up and leaning from the screen with her sisters' bobbing heads above hers, they looked like a crazy totem pole. And then they closed the interior door.

"I don't have any gifts for anyone," said Eleanor.

"That doesn't matter. Can I sit by you?" asked Anthony as he put his discarded coat around Eleanor's feet and tucked it under. Then he sat next to her on the cold bench.

"It's a free country," she said even as her mind whispered *Oh yes, sit close to me. Please. I've missed you.*

"What did Itsy write to you?" he asked.

Eleanor handed him the note. "It's not true, anyway. What she wrote. My mother's pretty."

Anthony read the note. "No, it's true. You do look like her. Only you're softer. And your eyes are green, not brown. Pretty." He looked into her eyes, making her heart race. He looked away and pushed his hands through his hair. "Carmen has that look-but-don't-touch thing. You . . . you I could definitely touch."

Eleanor flushed. Those words seemed too intimate. They reminded her of Cooper. "Look, I know we were kids together, but do you think you *know* me or something? I don't know you. Are you really an altruistic guy or just a mooch who lives off my grandmother?"

Anthony laughed and went back to shoveling. *He laughed,* thought Eleanor. *He laughed at those bitter words. He didn't slap me, or make fun of me. He laughed.*

"I'm no mooch. These women are my family. The only family I have left. My mom died last year. She had MS. I'm an electrician. Certified." He puffed out his chest as he said it.

"Sorry," said Eleanor.

"It's okay. I know how it looks. Especially from so far away. You and Carmen haven't been around for years."

"Well . . . Mom's been in Europe."

"Yeah, but you've only been an hour away in New Haven."

"Oh . . . I get it," said Eleanor, "You want to be my conscience all of a sudden?" Eleanor was astounded to hear Carmen coming out of her mouth. She clapped her hand over her cold lips and said a muffled, "I'm sorry."

"No, no. Don't be sorry. I guess I deserved some of that." He leaned on his shovel. "You know, we were friends once. I wrote to you, but you never wrote back."

"We were kids." *Did he write? I never got a letter. Did Carmen hide it from me?* Eleanor's mind did tumblesets. She felt like she was swimming in foreign waters except the water knew *her.* Nothing was familiar and everything was familiar. *Déjà-vu all over again,* she thought, understanding the term in a way she never thought she'd understand anything.

"So? I still consider you a friend. No matter what. Okay? You're gonna need one."

"Why?"

"They're good, but crazy . . . your family here. These Amore women. They may take some figuring out."

"Maybe not. Don't forget, I'm one of them."

Anthony laughed again. It sounded like honey. A ladies' man laugh. "True, true . . . well, in that case, you'll need a nickname."

"I already have one. They call me Babygirl. At least they used to."

Anthony looked at her, walked forward and tilted up her chin with a callused finger, "Yeah, but you definitely ain't no baby. I hereby dub you Elly. Elly Amore."

"Elly," she said, letting the sound roll around in her mouth. She liked it. A new name for a new life. "Hey, Anthony, do you know their real names? Mom never . . ."

Mimi's kitchen window shot open, interrupting her. "Did you throw up on my carpet?"

Elly put her head in her hands.

"Hey Meems." Anthony looked up to the open window, shielding his eyes from the bright winter sun. "I just gave our girl here a new nickname. How do you like *Elly*?"

Mimi smiled. "It'll do nicely. *Elly!* Get inside and out of that cold. *Now.*" The window slammed shut. Eleanor . . . now Elly, thought she could hear buildings rattling all throughout the Bronx.

She got up and stumbled, her feet caught in the coat. Anthony righted her. He smelled like Old Spice. Cheap, but thickly interesting. He fixed her hat. She looked at him and their eyes locked. She pulled away from him. Took her gaze and her body back from what could be unsafe territory. Only it didn't feel unsafe, his arms . . . his eyes, like the safest haven she'd ever felt.

"Hey, Anthony," Elly said clearing her throat. "Were you inside Mimi's apartment earlier, crying?"

"Me? Crying? I don't think so," he laughed.

"Oh," said Elly, walking back inside. She stopped at the door and turned back. "Anthony?"

"Yes, Elly?"

"Why doesn't Itsy talk?"

Anthony gave her a long look and then continued shoveling. "She never spoke a word after The Day the Amores Died. That's when Fee lost most of her hearing, too."

"You know a lot about them," she said, looking straight in his eyes for the first time.

"Like I said, they're my family," he said, not shying away from her.

"I want to know everything, too," she said.

"You will, but go inside okay? It's cold out here. We've got nothing but time, Elly."

Nothing but time. Elly Amore exhaled. It was long and delicious. She felt as if she'd been holding her breath for as long as she could remember.

✦

"He's nice that boy. You could do worse," said Mimi, pulling Elly by the hands into the living room.

"I don't think so, Mimi, he's not my type." *But he is, he's exactly my type.*

"Sit down," said Mimi pointing at the sofa. "Take off that hat why don't you?" Elly sat down. "But don't we have to clean up the mess in the hallway? And I'm not taking off my hat."

"I already did that," said Mimi. "Do you really think I'd leave it for you? And that's fine about the hat. Everyone has to have a quirk, right? Forget about it. We have more important things to do—" Mimi moved from in front of Elly revealing the Christmas tree, beautifully lit with a mountain of presents around the stand, "—like open Christmas presents!" Mimi clapped like a child and then called "*Fee,* Itsy!"

The aunts, who must have been waiting in the hall, burst into the room. Fee sat next to Elly making a deep indentation in the cushions, Elly sunk into her supple side, and Fee hugged her close. Elly didn't move, and that she didn't want to puzzled her. *When in Rome . . .* she thought.

Itsy was piling up the presents, putting them in order. There were already two at Elly's feet. Mimi had quite a few, and Fee had one enormous box. "*Books!*" she yelled, making Elly finally pull away. *"I love getting books at Christmas!"*

"Merry Christmas, Ladies!" said Anthony, coming in from the cold carrying a large bag and sitting cross-legged on the floor like a little boy. Itsy wrote him a note.

"Yours are under the tree," he read aloud. "Well thanks!" He reached into his bag and took out presents for each of them, laying one for Elly on top of her others.

Elly looked at him and cocked her head, confused. "How did you know I'd be here?"

"Come on, Elly! These women are special. They can see things. They told me you were coming this year."

"He's only asked us every single year since you were thirteen," said Mimi, teasing. "I was glad to give him a smile this year." She reached down and pinched his cheek. "Move your fat butt, *Fee!* Let me scootch in next to my granddaughter." And then to Elly, "Open a present." Elly reached down and picked up a rectangular box. She tried to peek at Anthony to see if he was disappointed that she hadn't picked up his first—but he was staring right at her. He smiled. Elly blushed and ripped open the shiny wrapping. "That's from me," said Mimi.

It was a beautiful white christening gown. Crocheted. And booties and a hat, too.

"Mimi," whispered Elly. "How did you know?" Elly remembered Anthony's odd comment outside . . . *In your condition* . . .

"Are you a fortune-teller, Mimi?" she asked, taking a deeper look at the woman beside her.

Mimi smiled. "Well, we all have a little . . . what did that program on public television call it girls? ESP? Extra Sensory Projection?"

"Perception," yelled Fee.

"Yes. That. Every one of us. You, too, Elly."

"They're witches," said Anthony. Fee and Itsy nodded.

"You know we don't use that word!" said Mimi. And then to Elly, "It's a bit of ESP darling, that's all. Nothing to be afraid of. Humans only use a fraction of brain space, there could be magic there, no?"

"I doubt very much that I have ESP," laughed Elly. "If I did, it might have been able to help me avoid my current predicament." *But what about that voice? The one saying, 'Come home?' What about that feeling I had when I touched Mom's hand?*

"Why is it a predicament and not a gift?" asked Mimi.

"So you all know?" she asked softly.

Itsy, Fee, Anthony, and Mimi all nodded.

"Great," said Elly, embarrassed. "You really want me to believe you are all witches?"

"Not me, only them. Probably you, too. Now, open the rest of your presents," said Anthony.

They were all for the baby. A Tiffany's rattle from Anthony. A pregnancy journal from Fee. A music box from Itsy. Elly wound it up. "Let me call you sweetheart . . ." was the melody.

"Let me have your hand, honey," said Mimi, taking Elly's palm and stroking it with rough, cracked fingers.

"What are you doing, Mimi?"

"Well, I want to find out more about this whole situation. Hmmmm. Who is this? A baker? Is the baby's father a baker? That wouldn't be so horrible. Unless he was a Polish baker. Ugh. I hate Polish pastries. And where is this? What? Coopersmith? Is that a town or something? Where, my Elly? In England?"

Elly couldn't help it. She pulled away her hands and began to laugh. She laughed so hard she almost threw up again on the sofa.

"No, no, Mimi! His name is Cooper Bakersmith! He goes to Yale. He's going to be a lawyer."

Mentioning Cooper made Elly glance over at Anthony. He was trying not to look at her. She watched as he pretended to flip through a *Sports Illustrated* magazine. "Itsy gets me a subscription every year," he said.

Mimi, who'd begun to crack a smile, jumped from the sofa, hurtling Elly toward Fee once again. "Damn Anglos! Always mixing me up with those mix and match names!" She paced to and from the Christmas tree mumbling. "Cooper Smithbaker, Smith Cooperbaker, Baker Coopersmith . . . could have been any of those." Mimi walked to the kitchen. "Did you have coffee?"

"No. The smell made me nauseous."

"I'll have some," said Anthony.

"I'll make a fresh pot," yelled Mimi over her back.

"*Well,* I'm taking my books and going!" yelled Fee, winking and motioning her head toward the door at Itsy. Itsy nodded and wrote a note. She gave it to Elly. *Merry Christmas.*

Elly stood up and kissed both her aunts. "Merry Christmas to you, too."

"And God bless us, every one," laughed Anthony when the door closed.

The two sat in an awkward silence, both trying to start conversations and failing miserably. Anthony laughed, "I guess we have to get the hang of this," he said, scratching his head.

The smell of fresh coffee wafted through the apartment. "Mmmm, that smells good now," said Elly. And it did. It smelled like the coffee in the best coffee shops. Dark and rich.

Mimi was back with a tray. Three coffee cups.

"How did you . . . ? Okay, I'll stop asking, I guess," said Elly.

Mimi nodded. Anthony laughed.

"Okay, so if you have ESP . . . who was crying in your apartment this morning?" asked Elly.

"You heard it again?" asked Mimi.

"Yes, clear as day. But I looked around and there wasn't anyone here."

"Ah . . . Maybe you hear the baby in your belly already? Or maybe your Sight is very strong," said Mimi.

"Sight?"

"Didn't you ask how I knew your Anglo's name?" There was a sparkle in Mimi's eyes. "I guess it's the same as what you call ESP."

"Well, I don't think my baby is big enough to cry yet."

"Maybe it was Zelda Grace?" offered Anthony.

"Who is Zelda Grace?" Elly leaned forward almost tipping her coffee.

Mimi sat back into the cushions and sipped her coffee, "Well, Zelda was Bunny's daughter. She fell out the window and died years ago. Your Great Aunt Bunny, our oldest sister, was such a good mother, and such a beautiful woman." Mimi started to cry a little. She made the sign of the cross. "No more, no more of this. It's time to clean up."

✦ Babygirl ✦

Clean up . . . clean up . . . At first Babygirl thought living with her grandmother would be too hard. Like going back into the past and trying really hard just to survive. Babygirl and Mimi did chores every day. It was so different than living with Mommy where there always seemed to be a maid or a mess.

There was nothing modern or magical at all to help out with the cleaning. No garbage disposal, no dishwasher, no dryer. Everything took much more time than necessary. And then there was the bathroom issue. There was only one and it didn't have a shower, only a big old claw-foot tub.

"No shower, Mimi?" she asked while scrubbing Comet against the tub. Enjoying the strong smell of the bleach crystals.

"Why do you need one? A bath cleans you the same way, no?"

"No dishwasher, Mimi?" she'd asked.

"Only lazy, stupid people wash dishes twice."

"No garbage disposal, Mimi?"

"No, I don't want garbage in my sink! Do you? It belongs in the pail, not the sink."

"I love you, Mimi."

"I love you, too, Babygirl!"

✦

"Are you okay?" asked Anthony. He was sitting next to her now and had his hands on her shoulders.

"What happened?" asked Elly, shaking off his hands.

"I don't know, it was weird, like you floated off for a few seconds." He sat back in relief. His concern warmed her from the inside out.

"It's strange," she began. "You know I don't remember anything, right? We went over that when you were all mad the last time we saw each other. Remember?"

"Yep! 'Who's on first,'" Anthony laughed, "No one could believe you couldn't remember that crazy summer. We all had the best time. It really is a shame. Uncle George, he was the one who was the most disappointed. He was looking forward to seeing you that Christmas."

"Ah yes," said Elly. "They must have known in advance about that visit, too."

"Yes, indeed. Can't hide much from these women. So what were you about to say?"

"Oh, right. Well, the thing is—since I've been pregnant, I've had these flashes of memory. Like just now, Mimi went off to clean? And I remembered cleaning the apartment with her. It must be a memory from that summer because I wasn't here before, right?"

"Did I hear you say you remembered something about cleaning with me?" asked Mimi, as she entered the room again.

"Yes! Isn't it great!?" Elly exclaimed.

"Sure is," said Mimi, who threw a white dishcloth into Elly's lap. "Now come help me out with some of those newfound memories."

"I'm out," said Anthony.

"Smart move," said Elly.

"See you later?" he asked.

"Later?" Elly responded, excitement fluttering in her stomach.

"For Christmas dinner," he said, and left the apartment.

Elly stared at the door. *How can I feel so close to someone I don't really know?* she wondered.

"Because you do know him. And you loved him very much, once upon a time," said Mimi, pulling her granddaughter into a soft embrace.

"Now, let's get to cleaning. How can we cook if we don't have a clean house first?" she said, patting Elly on the back. A signal that it was time to get to work.

Elly and Mimi began to clean the already spotless apartment.

Finally, as Elly wiped the invisible dust from the living room windowsills and beautiful antique side tables, Mimi walked in and announced, "Now, come to the kitchen and let me teach you how to make a proper Christmas feast. Do you think your stomach can take it?"

Hungry now, with the morning turning into early afternoon, her sickness had passed. She was ravenous. The galley kitchen was small and the counters already piled high with ingredients. "Here, sit here and cut the beets," said Mimi, who led her to the breakfast nook that was outside of the kitchen but next to the entrance to the dining room and opposite the exit to the back hall. Elly sat down in a well-worn, wooden kitchen chair and began to cut fresh, peeled beets into quarters. The bright red juice got on her fingers. Mimi threw a damp towel to her from the kitchen. "Beets are messy things, but they taste of the earth. And they're the color of Christmas."

"What's on the menu, Mimi? I'm starving."

"Oh, now you are starving?" teased Mimi. "The roast is in the oven. Roast beef is our Christmas beast. The secret to cooking any kind of meat is to salt it well and put it in the oven for a long time at a low temperature. Leave it there, don't fuss with it. It's ready when you can't stand waiting for it anymore."

Elly could smell it cooking. A heavy smell, full of crisped fat and savory meatiness. It made her mouth water.

"Here," Mimi said, putting a bowl in front of her that held the heel of a loaf of crusty Italian bread, ladled with sauce.

"This isn't the sauce from last night, is it?" asked Elly.

"No, of course not. Would I do that to you? It's the sauce for the lasagna. We are having roast beef with roasted root vegetables, lasagna, and then a few leftovers from last night, but not the sauce. We never mix sauces."

Elly wiped her hands with the towel (or mopine, as Mimi called it), and picked up the bread, now softening in the sauce. Warm and perfect. Acidic and sweet. The bread mingled with the perfect sauce and gave it a hearty yeast flavor that Elly could almost taste down to her toes.

The afternoon slipped by in a flurry of chopping, tasting, baking, and setting the table.

When everyone was finally gathered in the dining room, with the flickering candlelight casting warmth across the table, Elly felt a sense of accomplishment as she looked over the meal she'd helped prepare. The roast beef set amongst the roasted beets, yams, fennel, and potatoes. Sprigs of rosemary finishing off the platter. The oblong tray of encrusted cheese that held layer upon layer of light, homemade pasta sheets and a mixture of ground beef and ground sausage browned to perfection. A salad of fresh greens mixed with pears and a crumbling of blue cheese. Broccoli drizzled with olive oil and served with bright lemon wedges. It was perfect.

"Merry Christmas!" said Anthony, who'd picked a seat next

to Elly. He tried to place his hand over hers, but she pulled away her hand. Embarrassed by her awkwardness, Elly picked up a glass of sparkling cider and made a toast. "To family," she said.

Mimi, Fee, and Anthony raised their glasses. But not Itsy. Itsy stared down at her hands. "Don't mind her, Elly. She's always been moody," yelled Fee.

Itsy wrote on her pad. *And you've always been FAT.*

"I have not. Tell her, Mimi. Remind her that I was thin, when we were young!"

Mimi slammed her hand on the table, clattering the gold-plated silverware together. "*Abaste!*" she yelled. "You all stop this nonsense and celebrate with me. Look, I have my granddaughter home, and it's *Christmas*!"

"Fine," Fee said as softly as she could.

"Hey, has anyone heard the one about the three witches and the priest?" asked Anthony, breaking the ice.

Elly stole looks at him throughout what turned into a delightful meal, despite its rocky beginning, thanks to him. How could any man be so kind? It worried her, and it tugged at her. Maybe men weren't all like Cooper. Maybe some could be trusted.

✦

After the plates were cleared and the pots and pans cleaned, Fee, Itsy, and Anthony all went home to their respective apartments.

"We are done. Christmas is officially over. Come, sit and talk to me. I want to know everything," said Mimi.

They sat together on the couch. Mimi put her feet up on an embroidered ottoman and reached beside her into a yarn-filled basket taking out a crochet hook and a small multicolored square. She began to crochet in the round.

"I guess you pretty much have the whole story, Mimi," said Elly, fascinated by the swift movement of her grandmother's hands.

"Maybe. But how are you feeling?" Mimi tapped her head. "In here."

Mimi set aside her yarn and went around the back of the couch, gathering Elly's long hair up and making a thick braid.

"That summer you spent with us, the one you can't remember? We spent a week in the cottage at Far Rockaway. What a wonderful summer that was. We had you baptized. You received your first communion and were sealed into the church by confirmation. Old Father Martin, drunk and senile, petitioned the church so we could do it all at once. But the thing is . . . You felt safe. You told me so. You always felt safe here." Mimi smiled, remembering and laughing, "Babygirl."

"I wish I remembered. Why can't I remember?"

Mimi dropped the braid and tilted Elly's head back with her finger looking into her eyes and seeing the truth. "You will. It's already starting."

"I hope so," said Elly, looking upside down at Mimi.

"Well, let me know when you do. It was the summer Itsy decided to speak. She told you something."

"What did she say?"

Mimi sat down and picked up her crochet again.

"I don't know. All we heard was mumbling from the upstairs room. If you want to know, you'll have to ask Itsy . . . or remember it yourself. It's always killed me, not knowing what made her break her silence that day."

Elly wanted to remember.

She looked at her grandmother. The perfectly black hair in the flawless set, the matronly body covered in a boldly flowered housecoat, the knee-high stockings and sensible black shoes. It *was* safe here. The yarn squeaked across the hook.

Babygirl was in the garden with Itsy and George. "Chain five. Single crochet, single crochet . . ." Itsy sat on a bench behind the little girl moving her hands while George sat at her feet giving the words to the movements. He didn't even have to look. He just knew what Itsy was doing as if he'd heard the same, basic lesson one thousand times before.

Elly put her hands over her eyes trying to capture more of the memory. Mimi squeezed her hand and said, "Don't worry my Elly. It will come back. All of it. Just as you've come back to us, all that you need to remember will come back to you."

Elly shook her head as tears started to flow. It bothered her, this instant crying business.

"What is it, my love? Tell Mimi."

Elly looked at her grandmother again. Yes. It *was* safe here. She let the flood of worry out. "I'm worried my Mom won't forgive me for this. For coming here. For having the baby. It's always been just us, you know? And I'm worried about Cooper." *That he'll find me.* "And finishing my senior year. I'm worried about telling my mentor I won't be going to Florence."

"You were going to go to Florence?"

"Yes, I won a scholarship to restore frescoes."

"That's truly an accomplishment, Elly! And you think you're not interesting! My goodness."

"I don't remember telling you I felt *un*interesting, Mimi."

"I'm sorry, honey. It's the damn Sight. It talks to us with such a loud voice sometimes. And other times it's completely silent.

Itsy calls it fickle. I know there's a part of you afraid of all this. Afraid of being who you are."

"But isn't there a chance that when I remember everything I'll be different? That I'll be fascinating?"

"I can't tell you what you'll find, I only know how you feel. And right now there's a part of you so very afraid that you've made all this up. That you wanted so much to escape and now that you've achieved it you've found there's no escape from yourself."

It was true. Mimi could have disappeared in a cloud of smoke right in front of her and it wouldn't have seemed any crazier than Elly's desperate need to escape her life at Yale. Her life with Carmen. Her life with Cooper. Witches, ESP, mystery children crying . . . all of it was preferable to her other world. A world she worried about.

Mimi put the granny square she was making in her lap. "Don't worry about any of that now. It'll all work itself out. Those kinds of things always do. Carmen will get over herself. We can deal with that Cooper boy in our own way. I'll stand by you tomorrow while you call whomever you need to call about your trip. And school? You will finish. You can drive in. It's not far. You can use Uncle George's car. Anthony can show you tomorrow. *Abast. Finito.* Done."

"Really?" *Could it all be so easy?* Elly wondered.

"Really."

"Mimi?

"Mmmhmm?"

"If you have The Sight and it's so strong why don't you know what Itsy said to me that day?"

"She blocked me, the witch," said Mimi.

"I thought you didn't use that word?"

"Call a spade a spade, Mama used to say."

Elly sat quietly watching Mimi crochet while trying to let the whole bizarre situation sink in.

"Mimi, do you have an extra hook?"

Mimi dug into the basket and found a shiny pink hook and a ball of soft, white yarn. "Here," she said. "Make that baby a blanket or something already."

Elly took the hook and the yarn. Her hands knew what to do. *Chain 100, single crochet, single crochet, single crochet . . . . Oh look, Uncle George! Come see, Aunt Itsy! I'm doing it!*

✦

Later that night, when Mimi was asleep, Elly stole out of bed to grab some cookies and a glass of milk. The cookies were the best she'd ever had. Little round butterballs with almonds and powdered sugar. Surprisingly spicy chocolate cookies dipped in a shiny chocolate glaze. And best of all, the melt-away Genettis. An Italian sugar cookie of sorts. Simple and elegant.

With a handful of cookies Elly opened the refrigerator to get the milk. The light shone on a pile of dirty mopines in a corner on the counter. The one on top was the one she'd used to wipe her hands after cutting the beets. There was a distinguishable red palm print. Red like blood. A memory started to surface, but she pushed it down. *Maybe some of these memories won't be so good,* she thought.

5

Itsy

Papa loved Mama. It was clear to all of us, even though they fought from time to time. And, even though, on closer inspection, they seemed to have nothing in common. Mama had a wildness in her, a scattered beauty. Papa thought in lines and numbers. He didn't pay much attention to her magic. Bunny always said it was a shame. That Papa didn't appreciate her. But Mama would hush her and use the complaint as moments to school us. Mama never missed an opportunity to gather us around her and tell us what she thought. She said every moment was a "teaching moment" and no questions should ever go unanswered. And she let us know, very early on, that though love spells existed, they should never be used. You don't manipulate such powerful things. You simply must understand their secrets.

She taught us the secret of love under the shade of the fiery red maple on a glorious October afternoon. The kind where the sun is still warm but the sky spreads out impossibly blue and hinting at winter. We were closing up the Far Rockaway cottage and eating lunch in the yard. Mama was pointing out how brilliant the red of the tree glowed against the blue, blue sky. She was always doing things like that. Forcing us to stop and look.

In 1938 when we went to see the Technicolor genius that was *Gone with the Wind,* I learned a whole new appreciation for the world Mama created for us. My sisters and brothers and myself, we weren't so impressed. But everyone in the theater was oohing and ahhhing over the bright colors on the screen. I remember thinking *Goodness, so many people living in gray worlds.*

Anyway, we were finished eating and Mama was making us look at that Sugar Maple. We lay down underneath it with her and looked up through the leaves at the sky. She was in the middle and we spread out around her like stars, each of us trying to be the ones closest to her face so we could smell her breath, roses and milk, while she talked.

Bunny sat up. "See, Mama, Papa doesn't notice these things. He's always rushing. Look, he's not even here. So busy back in the city at work."

Mama sat up, too, and leaned her back against the trunk of the tree. Her hair was loose and her eyes bright with the day. I remember her apron. Beautifully cut work cotton. Perfectly white against her brown skirt. She patted her lap and George climbed on top of her. The rest of us gathered. Well, not the older boys. Those three—always connected at the hip. They were playing cards on the screened-in back porch.

"Papa doesn't need to notice," she said, "It's enough that I do. And I teach it to you, and you will teach it to yours, right?"

We nodded. Forever wanting to please her.

"Here is the secret to love," she said. "Always make sure that the man loves you just a breath more than you love him."

"Mama!" cried George.

Mama laughed, "Not you, my duck!" and she rocked him.

"Mama, that's not fair," said Mimi, who was always watching over Papa even when he wasn't there.

"Oh Mimi, I love your Papa more than any woman ever loved any man. And still, he loves me a breath more. It's the only healthy way. If a woman loves too much—if her love is heavier—she won't see anything but him. She'll be blind to the world. Women are made like that. We have to teach ourselves not to become obsessed. True love lies in peace, not torture."

And with those words she looked directly into my eyes. They burned a hole through my heart.

6

Elly

"Rise and shine, sleeping beauty!" Anthony was standing over Elly dangling a set of keys on a rabbit foot key chain.

"Gimme a second. Jesus! How did you get in here?" Elly groaned and pulled a pillow over her head. All she wanted to do was stay in bed. She was warm and sleepy like a cat.

"Mimi. I think she wants me to marry you. You know. Legitimize you." He sat on the bed and bounced up and down as if testing the springs for durability.

Elly sat up and hit him with the pillow. "You did *not* just say that! Oh my God!"

Anthony pulled the pillow away from her but held her hands. He looked at her fingers. "Elly, you have paint under your fingernails."

Elly pulled back her hands self-consciously. "I know, it's the oils. I have to use paint thinner to get them really clean."

"That's right. Mimi told me you were an artist. Do you have any paintings in your room? I'd love to see them."

Her paintings. Cooper. Yale. "I do. And I'd like to get them. Like . . . yesterday," she said in a panic.

Anthony laughed. "That's why I'm here. We're gonna get Georgie's car out of storage and take a drive up to New Haven to get your stuff. Okay?" he asked.

"Okay," she said. And then he left her to get dressed.

"God, I'm a mess," she said to her reflection in the dresser mirror. Her hair was a thick tangle, her face rounder than normal. And the hormones were making her complexion think it was sixteen again. "Yuck," she said to her reflection, sticking her tongue out before she began to look for her clothes. She noticed a folded pile at the foot of the bed, a flowered dress, thick stockings, and a gray cardigan, waiting for her.

She put on the clothes and looked at herself again. Much better. They fit perfectly. "Of course they do. She's a witch don't you know," she said into the mirror. She was trying to run a brush through her hair when the invisible crying child started wailing again. This time, it wasn't stationary. The sound seemed to move through the walls. She pulled her hat onto her head instead, gave up on her appearance, and went out into the hall to investigate.

"Zelda?" *This is crazy,* she thought. Crazy wonderful. Like a surprise party you knew was coming only you didn't know the time—making each threshold a carrier of horrifying delight.

She followed the crying out into the kitchen and then into the back hall, where it got louder. "If you're not Zelda, who are you?"

The sound drew Elly all the way out into the snowy yard, but the crying muted right away so she turned to go back inside when she heard her name.

"Eleanor? Is that you?"

There was a young woman just about Elly's own age standing at the back gate wearing a peacoat and waving mitten-clad hands back and forth furiously. Elly walked into the yard, the sounds of her footfalls crunching as she made her way to the girl.

"Do I know you?"

"Of course you do! Come here quick and let me see you. I'm hiding from Mother!" Her eyes shined with mischievous delight.

As Elly walked toward the girl she tried to place her. Thin, short, dark hair. *I have absolutely no idea who this is.*

"Oh my gosh! You look just the same! I knew it was you. I just knew it."

The two young women stood facing each other and Elly was taken aback as she was pulled into a tight embrace. "I've missed you!"

"I'm so sorry," said Elly into the girl's ear. "I don't know who you are."

"I'm Elizabeth. But you always called me Liz and I liked it. It's okay if you don't remember me. It was a looooooong time ago. All that matters is you are here and so am I. We'll be great friends again. But I have to go. Mother is calling and I swear I'm not doing one more chore. Not one!"

Elly watched as the strange girl ran away down the back alleys between the buildings.

"Who are you talking to?" Anthony asked from behind her.

Elly jumped. "You scared me! Don't do that!"

"How about you start dressing appropriately for winter? Look at you, out here again with no coat and no shoes."

"I heard someone crying, and then I came out here and met a long-lost best friend I can't even remember."

"That's good. Making friends. See? At home already." Anthony put his arm around her shoulder and pivoted her back toward the house. "Let's go, the day isn't getting any longer."

✦

"So, you really don't remember anything?" asked Anthony as he drove Uncle Georgie's 1965 Chevy Cavalier, the same red as Carmen's favorite nail polish color, "Honeymoon Red."

"Nope. My first memory is standing on the stoop with Carmen, only I didn't recognize her. She still hates me for it. I was only ten. But she hates me anyway. There's a little more but it's silly."

"*No.* Come on, fess up." He nudged her as they crept along I-95 northbound to New Haven, caught in traffic of mythical proportions.

"I remember doing crochet . . . and cartwheels," said Elly softly. "Just the beach and the sea air, damp sand and cartwheels." She looked at him and shrugged self-conscious shoulders.

"Well, while we're stuck in the car, push harder, close your eyes. Anything else?"

Elly closed her eyes and let her mind reach back. She tumbled hand over hand, her feet kicking up and out like a starfish, and through the fog it came to her, a boy, a sense of love, and a girl standing behind him holding up rabbit ears and laughing.

"I remember you," she said with a surprised laugh. "And . . . that girl . . . Liz, I think. And that's all."

"Well, hell, if you remember me, then that's enough," said Anthony as traffic began to move.

Driving through New Haven made Elly increasingly queasy. Anthony must have sensed it because he kept asking, "You okay?"

Am I okay? she asked herself. *What does that even mean?* No one ever asked her that question. She didn't even ask *herself* that question. As she looked out the window at the familiar buildings surrounding the campus, Elly took a chance and asked herself the same question—*Are you okay?* She answered as Eleanor: "No. You are definitely not okay." As Elly: "I think so. I think you're on the mend." *And as Babygirl: "Of course you are okay! You are always okay! And you're home now, with Anthony and Mimi and Fee and Itsy. Get on with this chore and get back to the Bronx!"*

"You okay?" asked Anthony. Again.

"I don't know," said Elly, "I have a lot of . . . um . . . mixed feelings."

"Totally understandable," he said.

"At least you think so," she said as they drove around Downtown New Haven. "I'm starting to think I have multiple personality disorder."

Even though most classes were not in session the campus was still lively, and parking was an issue. In the end she made him double-park because she thought if they circled the streets of downtown New Haven one more time she'd just give up and go back to the Bronx. Already Elly felt this life fading. The castle-like buildings with towers piercing the sky. The stuffy professors riding bicycles to and from campus, even through the now slushy streets. She watched couples walking hand in hand, wearing matching Burberry scarves and clutching Starbucks coffee. It all seemed so shallow. How had she survived it for so long?

The art. *Her* art. It was the painting. Her only real escape. *And that's why we're here,* she reminded herself. *To get my paintings before Cooper can destroy them.* And he would, too. He'd waited so long to be given a valid reason to obliterate the last shred of herself that belonged to just her. She wouldn't let him do it.

"We have to move fast," she said.

"Why?" asked Anthony.

"I think Cooper is taking an intersession course . . . he might be around."

"What's an intersession course?"

"A class you can take over winter break. He's down a few credits for graduation." Her words were coming out fast, panicked small talk driven by the fear rising inside her the closer they got to the one-way street where the gate to her dorm quad was located.

"He scares you?"

He sees me.

"Let's just go. Okay? Park here . . ."

She thought she'd get an argument about double-parking, about breaking rules. Cooper would have lectured her as he drove in circles through the maze of downtown New Haven getting more and more annoyed until the traffic actually became Eleanor's responsibility. As if she'd conjured it up just to screw up his life. But she was with a different man now, and he thought double-parking with the hazard lights blinking was a fine idea. "Works for me," Anthony said, throwing the car into park. And then he rushed around to get to her side before she could open the door herself.

"This way, m'lady, your palace awaits you."

"Prison's more like it," said Elly, looking up at the imposing buildings. Elly often thought the rest of New Haven, the neighborhoods flanking the city center, could crumble away and still—the majestic, medieval Yale would rise, untethered to Olympus, back to the cold gods of academia that created it in the first place.

Anthony stuffed his hands in his jean pockets and huddled down in his black leather jacket. "It's cold here! Where to?" His breath came out in puffs of warm mist in the frigid air. His black hair fell in his eyes. Elly fought the urge to push it aside like Barbra Streisand pushed Robert Redford's in *The Way We Were.*

Seeing Anthony up close and center in the world she'd existed in for so long without him was dizzying. She cleared her throat and motioned forward with her arms. "Through these gates and then to the right. It's not far."

Anthony started walking, but Elly stood still. One hand on the hood of Uncle George's car. She didn't want to leave the safety of it. It was cold here. So cold she thought the world would crack and she'd be left behind. All alone. Again.

Anthony turned around and held out his hand. "You comin'?"

Elly walked toward him and hesitantly took his hand. "Don't let me go. Okay?"

"Never." He walked her to the gates and Elly swiped a student card to unlock them. As the gates clanged closed behind them, she held his hand a little tighter.

"You did good, you know."

"What?"

"Coming here. This isn't a small thing. Yale is a big deal. You gotta be some kind of smart to come here," he said.

"Yale is Carmen's idea. Only the best for her," said Elly.

"You didn't want to come to school here?"

"No . . . . Well, I don't know." Now amid the snow-covered trees and high buildings, time seemed to stop. The car and the busy streets a million years away. "This way."

Elly's dorm room at Yale was beautiful. Seniors got their pick and if the outside of Elly's building looked like a palace, her room could have belonged in a museum. Exposed stone walls, leaded windows, wide planked wood floors, and even a fireplace. Anthony marveled at his surroundings.

"It doesn't work, the fireplace. And it's really cold in here in the winter." She opened up a large closet door and pulled out some bins and boxes. "Let's start with the art supplies, canvases, and the books. The rest I can live without."

"You always this prepared?" asked Anthony.

"We never really stay put, Mom and me."

"You must think it's crazy, me livin' in that building my whole life." Anthony was already loading books into boxes.

"No. I think it's amazing," she said, the idea of staying put in one place for so long, of *wanting* to, made hot tears burn behind her eyes.

Anthony sat on the floor next to her and put his arm around her shoulder. "Now, what's all this? Are you afraid still? It's gonna be okay. Trust me."

Elly rested her head against him, his solidity.

"And what, the fuck, may I ask is going on in here?"

Elly turned around to see Cooper leaning into the room by the doorframe. He looked amused and confounded at the same time. She hated that her stomach clenched in fear at the sight of him. Blond, with a long, lean swimmer's body and a jaw that spoke of untold wealth and haughty ways. Cooper embodied a world Elly was leaving. A place she'd never felt she belonged.

Elly and Anthony stood up exchanging glances. Anthony's said: *What should I do?* Elly's responded nervously: *I have no idea.*

Cooper's presence made her blood run thin and cold. She felt immediately fragile. Unpretty. She watched as Anthony held out his hand and took a strong step forward.

"I'm Anthony, nice to know you."

Cooper squinted a bit, as if trying to get a handle on the situation, and then shook his hand. "Cooper Bakersmith."

"What are you doing here over break, Cooper?" asked Elly, keeping her voice strong and calm.

"Taking an intersession class. What are you doing?"

Anthony stepped in between them. "Well, Coop . . . we're gonna gather up Elly's things and then get the heck out of here. Okay?"

"Elly? Who is *Elly*? Eleanor, what's he talking about? You never said you were leaving school. Are you leaving school?" Cooper's eyes were twitching with black anger. He took a purposeful stride in Elly's direction.

Anthony put his hand on Cooper's shoulder. "Whoa fella."

Cooper turned around and belted Anthony across his face with his forearm. Anthony fell back into a bookshelf. He shook the surprise off and charged at Cooper.

"*Stop*!" Elly yelled.

Both young men froze a moment apart. "Anthony, can you give us a second?"

"I don't think so," said Anthony, his nose flaring, his body ready for a serious fight.

"Please? You can wait right outside the door. I'll yell for you if I need you." Elly pleaded with her eyes. He had no idea how dangerous Cooper was. Elly had to protect him.

Anthony smoothed back his black hair and pushed his shoulders back. "You won't even have to call. I'll just know. You hear me, Anglo?" He left, walking backward out the door and glaring at Cooper the whole time.

Elly smiled a little, warmed by his concern. But then turned her attention to Cooper. "You didn't have to do that," she said.

"I know, I'm sorry. Just . . . it took me by surprise. And who *is* that? Are you sleeping with him?" The question came out like a whine.

Elly looked at the ground. Hot tears of rage and embarrassment stinging her eyes. "You were the first. You *know* that," she whispered.

"Well, where are you going then? Why are you leaving school?"

"I'm not leaving school. I'm just moving in with my grandmother. She needs some help. She's recovering from hip surgery." The lie came out surprisingly easy. *I have a bit of Carmen in me after all,* she thought.

"Well, okay. But I have to get to class. Oh, and if you're going to be with someone else, try not fucking that wop. It'll bring down my status."

Hair on the back of Elly's neck rose, but she controlled her temper. And her fear. "Okay, see ya."

He flicked her forehead with his fingers, and then he was gone.

A shock of memory went through her.

✦

"In nomine Patris, et Filii, et Spiritus Sancti."

All Babygirl saw was the painted ceiling of the church. The aunts and Mimi held her body as if they were pallbearers and she was a coffin. Babygirl had been to plenty of funerals, all Mommy's friends who died of the sex disease. Babygirl wondered if she was dying. And it was so hot! But then water dribbled over her forehead and she was being kissed and hugged by soft skin and cotton dresses.

✦

"You okay, Elly? You look weird. Did rich boy say something mean to you?" Anthony came back into the room and started hastily throwing books into boxes.

"No, I'm okay. I was just remembering something."

"Me again?"

"No. A part of that summer Mimi insists I lived with her. I think I just remembered my baptism. Ten's a little old to get baptized, no?"

"Come to think of it, I might have pictures of us from that summer. I'll find them when we get back. Maybe it'll help . . ." Anthony searched for the word, "You know . . ." He tapped his forehead.

"Jar my memory?"

"Yeah, that's it," said Anthony, boxing up more books. "What did that creep have to say?"

"Not much. Wanted to know if we were sleeping together. Then he called you a wop and I almost had to hit him." It felt good, joking away her fear. She wanted to believe she could hit Cooper if she wanted to.

"He called me what? *What*?"

Elly realized her mistake too late. "Calm down."

Anthony banged the wall with the heel of his palm and then went to the window and yelled out onto the quad, "Nice! Hey there, Cooper? You gonna call your kid a wop, too?"

Cooper stopped dead in his tracks halfway across the quad, turned around and bolted back toward the dorm. Elly gasped "Oh! Christ, Anthony! No!"

"What? You didn't tell him?" asked Anthony, sounding panicked, his cool gone.

"*No,* I didn't tell him. God!"

Cooper was back in the room fast and out of breath.

"What did this ginzo say?"

"Okay. That's enough," said Anthony, before he gave Cooper one swift punch to the head and knocked him out cold. "Grab what's important and let's roll. Okay? He'll be fine and I got a bruise on me says this fight was mutual."

Elly leaned down to touch Cooper's face and was hit with the red, throbbing rage from his unconscious mind. There was no softness, no worry. Confusion, blackness, frustration. She saw him for what he was, finally. *ESP?* She wondered, and then didn't care. She couldn't get back to the Bronx fast enough.

Elly grabbed bags of clothes and photo albums, her texts for class and her paintings off the walls. They were packed in record time. Back and forth they went to the car, Anthony stopping her every five seconds to ask, "You okay?" . . . which Elly didn't find annoying.

They were running so fast up the stairs and down, to the car and back that they started laughing. When the trunk of the car was squashed shut and the backseats brimming with her past, the two stole away like thieves into the afternoon.

"You don't seem too upset I toasted your boyfriend," said Anthony.

Elly was laughing. She had the window open and felt light for the first time in months. "He's not my boyfriend. And he hit you first. If anyone had it coming, he did."

"I do like you, Elly. I like you a lot. Always have, always will."

He reached over and held her hand. She didn't pull it away.

7

Itsy

I didn't mean to fall in love with a colored boy. I fell in love with a boy who happened to be colored. It was fate, really. He lived two blocks away from us in the Bronx and his family had a summer cottage on Far Rockaway, too. Henry was the same age as George and me, and we all went to the same school. Our Lady of Mount Carmel Parochial. It went from kindergarten to the eighth grade, but George and Henry dropped out in the sixth. They didn't have to finish. Papa and our older brothers made enough money to support our family, and Henry's family did pretty well, too. They dropped out because of the taunting. It started in fourth grade, the kids being mean to George and Henry. They called George a retard. They called Henry a nigger.

"George is a nigger-loving moron."

"Henry's a nigger boy kisser who goes out with retards."

I'll never forget how cruel it was. People like to glorify those childhood days, the schoolyard fights. People look back and shrug off their meanness. Use euphemisms like, "rites of passage" and "trials of childhood." My ass. They were just mean-spirited kids filled up with the devil right there at Catholic school.

I wanted to drop out, too. I was jealous of their free time, Henry and George. But Mama wouldn't hear of it. I was going to be educated, like the women in her family up in Massachusetts. The Greens. "They may have been crazy, but at least they were all smart enough to know it," she used to say.

He kissed me after my eighth grade graduation. Took me behind an old oak and planted a kiss right on my lips. I'll never forget it. Sometimes I take these old, paper-thin fingers and trace my dry mouth. My mouth that doesn't make words, and I feel for his full lips and if I close my eyes tight enough I can still feel them there. His lips on mine. His words in my ear that day.

"Itsy, say you'll be my girl. My secret. Oh, please, say it."

"Yes, Henry. I've always been your girl."

Mama knew, of course. And she didn't approve. It took me by surprise, her immediate and quiet rage. We sat at the table and she made toast. It was her favorite food. Toast with butter and jam. She had the biggest sweet tooth! She'd eat toast and jam even if she made us a sumptuous roast with all the best side dishes. Papa yelled about it. Told her she ate like "white trash." She always smiled and pushed aside her toast. But when we were alone, toast it was.

The day she told me her fears about Henry we were alone and she ate toast. Toast made of the Irish soda bread she baked—not the Italian bread Papa liked so much—and she took out a jar of her very favorite jam. Rose hip jam. Hard to make, we only had a half dozen jars to last us all year. I remember the knife clinking on the rounded glass lip of the jar as she spoke to me.

"I am not prejudiced, Itsy. No matter what you may think. I am not. But the *world* is. There is no good that can come of it. And I didn't foresee it so I know it can be altered. Are you sure this love is something you must pursue?"

"What should I do, Mama?"

"End it, Itsy," she said.

"I can't," I replied.

Mama hesitated. And I knew why. She was going to suggest magic, and she always meted out her magic sparingly. Honestly? I think it frightened her. "We could try a forgetting spell," she said. "That would work. How about it, Itsy? Do you want Mama to help you forget him?"

"I can't," I replied again.

"You can't or you won't?" The coaxing warmth was gone from her voice. It made me boil with anger.

I still wonder about that anger. The kind only love can produce. Boundless anger coming from love. It doesn't seem right. So I said, "I suppose I can't *and* won't."

"There's a time for stubborn and a time for giving in. Look at me. I give in all the time with Papa but I get things in return. Safety, stability, unconditional love. You are throwing away all of that with this particular devotion."

"Not the unconditional love part. I'll have that," I said without thinking first.

Mama dropped her composed façade. "That doesn't pay the bills. That doesn't keep you warm at night. That doesn't do much of anything."

"Then why did you say it?"

Mama stood and raised her hand. I knew she wanted to slap me. And I deserved it. I'd never back talked to my parents. I crossed my arms in front of my face for protection.

She sat back down.

"Do what you will." The bread was dripping with rose hip jelly. She was maniacally spreading it around with the knife.

"Henry's been a great friend to George. I'm sure you can find some kind of joy. But you won't let this play out in front of your father. You won't bring shame on this house. No matter how silly I think it all is, society is society and we are not free of the burden of hate. I have enough to worry about without this. So I'm done. If you pursue it, pursue it quietly. And you must follow my directions or I will end it. Do you understand?"

"Yes, Mama. What do you want me to do?"

"You will graduate high school and go to teachers college. You won't be able to marry him, so you'll have to have a profession. When you graduate you will move to the Far Rockaway cottage. It will be yours."

"Is that all?" I asked

"Don't you sass me, Itsy," she said.

I got up, eager to escape the kitchen and her disapproval.

"Itsy?"

"Yes, Mama?"

"Don't flaunt this. Keep Henry a secret."

My heart flew into my throat.

"Aren't secrets bad, Mama?"

"No. Secrets are important, and wonderful, and . . . well, secret. Promise me?"

And so I promised her. And I've been a good secret keeper and a good promise keeper too.

I *still* have secrets, you know. Not big ones. Small ones. Sometimes it's the smallest secrets that hold the most hope, the most fun, and the most danger.

Carmen gave birth to Babygirl right here in NYC. In a hospital in Manhattan. She called Mimi, but Mimi was at church. I answered the phone. I knocked the receiver against the wall three times to let the person calling know it was me and that I was listening. The line was fuzzy like always, but I knew what she was saying. I tried to speak, but nothing came out. So I went to her, to Carmen.

"Where's my mother?" she asked. So beautiful with her dark hair cascading over her shoulders. Her face devoid of makeup was simply illuminated by her perfect features. She had the child later in life. Forty, I think, but you'd never know it. She didn't look a day over twenty-five. She held a bundle. My heart hurt and I had to stop my hands from going in between my legs. I scribbled on my pad instead: *She's at church cleaning the pews.*

Carmen sighed. "Of course she is. Does she know? Did you tell her?"

I shook my head *no.*

Carmen turned her head toward the window. I could see her fighting back tears. It broke my heart a little.

"Take her then. Get a good look at her so you can report back to the rest. I'm leaving for Europe in the morning."

I thought about writing her a note telling her not to go. I would beg her. Tell her how much Mimi could use this in her life. But in the end I knew it wouldn't do any good. Damage is damage. I took the baby from her and sat down in the chair by the side of the bed.

She was perfect. She looked right into my eyes and my old lady throat rasped out a sound I didn't recognize. Mama's eyes. Green like the seas her family crossed to come to America. The baby's fist came loose from the swaddling and seemed to reach out to me. I kissed it. I kissed that small fist and saw the child's death. Only she wasn't a child. She was a grown-up woman, pregnant? Yes. Dear lord. No. *Enough.* No more for this family.

I never wanted to speak more since the words took flight, than I did at that moment. So I held her up and placed my lips against her forehead and mouthed the words I wanted to say: *I don't know you, but I love you. I will never leave you. I will think about you all the time, every day. You will never be alone. I will not let the fates have their way.*

Carmen turned back to me and held out her arms. "Give me my baby, old woman. Stop the mumbo jumbo. You people, I swear." She rolled her eyes.

I handed over the incredible bundle and turned to leave. I scribbled, *Come by the building before you go.*

"Sure I will," she answered. But we both knew she wouldn't.

For years, I couldn't get that baby's eyes out from behind my own. Truth is, I still can't. Something was reborn in me the day I held her. A joy and a horror.

And that summer she came back when she was all of ten years old? Well, we all lived again that summer. Such a miracle. Such a gift. It was because Elly came home. It was a bit of unplanned magic. I didn't want her there at first, it's true. I knew the dangers of her being in the building. But in the end? She figured out a way for me to keep my promise and my secret. She's such a sharp, clever child.

And then my spell was tested! Oh yes, it was. When Carmen showed up on our doorstep when Eleanor was no more than thirteen, I thought I'd expire right there from the nerves. But the girl didn't remember anything. Nothing at all. She was awkward and nervous, and there was an obvious chasm between mother and daughter, but she looked at all of us as well as the building with a sparkle in her eyes that told me she was seeing it for the first time. Even though she wasn't. Even though it was as much a part of her as it was of us. Every brick of the place. I remember how disappointed Anthony was that she didn't remember him. But that was nothing in comparison to George. His face just lit up when they swept in. But when her timid hand reached out to shake his, he knew. He knew she didn't have any memories. Because if she had? If she had, she'd have run to him and knocked him over with pure love. Poor George. How I robbed him of that love. I've never really figured out if it was the right or wrong way to go about protecting her. So many were hurt in the process.

But now she's back again and I'm faced with the same dilemma. I wish George were still here. Something tells me he'd know what to do. He'd tell me to keep her safe, no matter what.

I will, George. I will. Third time's the charm, right? She was here when she was ten, then for a moment at thirteen, and now. Three visits.

I've kept Babygirl safe all these years. In the end I failed George, but I refuse to fail this girl. Just plain refuse.

8

The Sisters Amore

"If you're going to live with me, you're going to go to church," said Mimi. All three old ladies were sitting at the kitchen table wearing black and pointing crooked fingers at Elly.

"I will not," she said, her arms crossed in front of her like a child.

"Yes you *will,*" said Mimi with Fee and Itsy nodding right along.

"Every day?"

Mimi snorted. "Don't be a smartass. Just Sunday. You'll have to come on Sundays."

"But I don't believe in all that crap. It will be like lying. I won't go. You can't make me."

"You will go," said Mimi and Fee in unison.

Itsy scribbled a note and gave it to Elly.

You could always just go *you know. Nothing is* forcing *you to stay here.*

The frustration of everything welled up inside of Elly. So much had changed in such a short period of time. And now the perfect refuge was shaken all akimbo with this weird religious twist and one of the aunts actually asking her, in so many words, to *leave.*

"Ah! I hate you! I hate you! I hate you and you . . . You *are* crazy! And I was crazy for coming here. Carmen was right!" she screamed and then ran into the hallway and into the bathroom, slamming the door behind her. She skidded on the bath mat and her knees slammed down hard against the black-and-white octagonal tile. Tears came unbidden and soon she was crying so hard the phlegm choked her. She hugged the clean toilet basin and heaved up a heavy breakfast. She heard the door click and open, and then shut as rubber-soled shoes squeaked across the tile. The water in the tub turned on.

It was Mimi. Elly knew it without even turning around. She recalled the exact same moment years ago. Babygirl, the child she'd been but couldn't remember being, ran away from them. Elly felt her grown-up self rise to the ceiling as she watched the two scenes play out. *Then* and *now* overlapping . . . with Elly stuck on the outside.

Babygirl didn't want to stay in a strange place with strange people. Mimi found her shivering like a little refugee in the bathroom and proceeded to run a hot bath.

"No ill in the world a hot bath can't cure," she'd said to the child.

Elly got into the tub without a fight. The hot water brought her slowly down from the ceiling and back into her body. Soon she was letting Mimi kneel over and scrub her with a white washcloth and Ivory soap.

"I remember this. You giving me a bath," she said with her eyes closed. "I was strong then, wasn't I, Mimi?"

"You still are. I see these bruises, Elly, like I saw them in your palm. Such strength you have."

"I don't feel strong."

"That's how it feels when we are at our strongest. It's when we feel safe enough to notice our weakness. You left him. That took some kind of strength." Mimi was lathering Elly's scalp.

"I remembered being baptized," said Elly, as Mimi's hands soothed the wild pain inside.

"Well, that's good," said Fee, barging in with a booming voice and a pile of clean, fluffy white towels. She sat on the toilet seat. Itsy followed and sat on the edge of the tub. She had a plastic freezer bag full of rose petals and she reached in, sprinkling a handful out into the bathwater.

"She's saying she's sorry," said Mimi.

Elly didn't need The Sight to hear the apology. It was in the scent the hot water released from the frozen petals.

A comfortable silence fell between all of them punctuated by drips and splooshes of water.

"I miss my mother," Babygirl said so long ago.

"I miss my mother," cried Elly in the tub.

"What do you want, love? I'll do what I can to ease this for you." Mimi used the same words in the present that she had in the past.

"I want to cut my hair," said Elly.

"No. You mustn't cut your princess hair!" said Fee.

"There's so much power in our hair, good and bad. It holds onto things don't you know," said Mimi, helping her out of the tub while her aunts wrapped her in the towels. She felt like an Indian princess emerging from a pool of jasmine water.

"I'm relieved you didn't want what you wanted when you were just a little bit of a thing," said Mimi.

"What did I want back then?"

"You asked me to bring you back to your mother. And I couldn't do that." said Mimi.

"Why not?" asked Elly.

She'd lost her mind, wrote Itsy.

Mimi grabbed the note, crumpled it, and threw it in the tin garbage can under the sink.

"Never mind all that," said Mimi. "Instead of cutting your hair, why not let us play with it? Maybe a new hairstyle?"

The women moved her into Mimi's bedroom. Elly marveled at the simple beauty. They sat her at Mimi's dressing table. A replica of Carmen's only not as cluttered. Itsy leaned forward and took some of the front of Elly's hair, twisting it and snipping it with a scissor right in front of Elly's eyes.

"I thought we weren't cutting it?" she asked.

"We're not," said Mimi, gathering up the rest and twirling it into a damp knot at the top of her head.

"If you put it up when it's a little wet, it gets all wavy and nice for the rest of the week!" said Fee.

It's a shame she didn't have children of her own, thought Elly.

Itsy pulled out the new wisps of hair created by the angled bangs.

"Windswept and romantic, that's what Mama used to call this hairstyle," said Mimi.

Itsy moved away and Elly looked at herself in the mirror.

"Yes, windswept and romantic indeed," she said, feeling lovely.

Later she tried to put on her hat, but it wouldn't fit over the bun.

"You don't need it anymore," said Mimi as they were leaving for church.

Elly wasn't so sure about that.

✦

"I think I did it wrong. He gave me a funny look," whispered Elly in the pew after she returned from receiving Holy Communion. The Amores had their own pew, on the "Mary" side of the church up front, three rows in. It had a bronze plaque on it that said, "Amore: 1945."

"Did you spit it back at him?" asked Fee, too loud as always and the priest turned to look at them.

Mimi laughed into her handkerchief.

"They're the most irreverent of religious women. The priest puts up with it though. They give so much money," Anthony whispered from behind her.

The whole experience was tolerable for Elly. Enjoyable, even. It made her feel more than a little silly for throwing a fit and exposing her bruises to Mimi. But Mimi seemed to take it in stride, and having it out in the open was a relief.

The church itself was comforting to her artist's eyes. Unapologetic ornate design, blasts of proud reds and virginal blues. Decadent stained glass windows dappling everyone in moving prisms of color. And people seemed to know her. Waved at her. She even saw Liz walk by in the line to get communion. She held up her hand to the side of her face signaling that she would call.

Elly had a wave of nausea before the Mass ended, and Mimi told her to wait in the front foyer of the church. It was peaceful there with the flickering candles next to the saints. The heavy front doors propped open to let in some of the cold, refreshing breeze.

"Hey!" said Liz, surprising Elly.

"Hey back," said Elly, still unsure about how to react to this "friend."

"You escaped, huh?" said Liz with laughter in her eyes.

"I felt a little sick."

Liz gave Elly a hug and pulled away leaving her hands on Elly's shoulders. "Word on the street is you don't remember much of that summer you lived here. So I guess I'm coming out of thin air, right?"

"Sort of—" said Elly, relieved by the truth.

"Don't worry," said Liz. "We'll catch up."

"Who are you talking to?" Mimi interrupted, the aunts looking accusing on either side of her.

"You remember Liz, don't you Mimi?" asked Elly.

"Oh yes, Liz, of course!" she said with a smile.

Fee put her hand over her mouth to stifle a loud laugh.

Itsy walked out of the church and a burst of wind blew in behind her.

Elly turned back to Liz to apologize for her family's bizarre reaction, but she wasn't there.

On returning from church, the inhabitants of 170th Street walked into the building single file. Mimi first, then Itsy, Fee, and Elly. Anthony brought up the rear. As they entered the front hall, Anthony pulled Elly back against him and whispered, "Hold on," against her neck.

The aunts and Mimi parted like a riptide into their respective apartments, Sunday dinner high on their minds.

Anthony put his arms around Elly's middle and pulled her back into him. He leaned against the wall, holding her close, his head buried in the nape of her neck. Elly pressed against him, leaning her head against his shoulder, his protective arms wrapped around her. The sun dipped and began to pour into the hall through the open front door. Its honey light crept across the gray walls until it coated them.

As Elly melted into Anthony, she shut her now teary eyes, smiling as her body relaxed and began to trust his embrace. Years of pain and doubt began to move away from her as the sun stretched higher on the walls, piercing her closed eyes and bursting tears into tiny spots of glitter.

As the pain left, a hole, deep and black, opened inside of Elly. The pit of her stomach started to hurt. She bent over his arms, tears coming harder now. Anthony held her tighter, talking. He was talking to her, "Shhhh Elly, shhh it's okay. You're okay. *We're* okay."

Elly opened her eyes and stiffened her back. "Get off of me."

"Elly, please . . ."

"*Get off of me,* oh please . . ." Elly begged him as she scratched at his hands. "Let me go."

Anthony refused to let go. "I can't . . . I won't."

"You have to!" She pulled against his hands with full force and freed herself from his embrace. She didn't look back, just ran into Mimi's apartment and closed the door. She pressed her body against the door and whispered, "I'm so, so sorry."

Anthony knocked at the door, "Let me in, Elly. Please?"

"What did you do to him?" asked Mimi from behind her.

Elly jumped. "What? Did I surprise you? It's my apartment you know."

Elly looked at her grandmother and tried to get out the words she wanted to say, tried to ask for advice. Tried to ask for a potion, a bit of magic to stop the dark hole from spreading inside of her.

"I'm disappearing," was all she could manage to choke out before she ran into the back garden.

Mimi got up and opened the door for Anthony, who was knocking relentlessly.

"Where did she go?"

Mimi pointed toward the back. "You might not find her," she said. "She thinks she's disappearing."

"I never wanted to hurt her, Mimi."

"Love hurts. Now . . . now you know what it's like . . . now you get to make the decision."

"What decision, Mimi?"

"To follow her or to run away."

Anthony followed Elly's trail through the apartment.

"That's right," said Mimi to herself. "He doesn't run away, that boy. He stays."

"Elly?" He found her sitting on the bench.

"I'm disappearing. You can't love me, I'm not here," Elly whispered.

He sat next to her. "Elly, *you are not* disappearing. It's the part of you that needs to go that's going. You'll still be here when it's gone."

Elly leaned over and put her head between her knees. "It *hurts,*" she cried. "Oh God, it hurts so much."

Anthony stood up. "Come with me."

Elly shook her head "no" between her knees.

"Come on, take my hand . . ."

Elly looked up, the sun obscured all but his shadow. A dark space just like hers. She got up and placed her hand in his. "Where are we going?"

"We're going back in time."

He walked fast in the late winter sun, her small hand swallowed up by his. Warm. She wanted her whole body to feel like that. They walked for a few blocks in silence and then arrived at a playground. Empty in the early winter twilight.

"We played here," she said.

It was a small square playground surrounded by barren trees. There was a swing set, a massive domed metal jungle gym, a slide, and a basketball court. All of it bathed in slightly muted light as the sun set, too early.

"Princess Babygirl, would you like a ride on the royal swing?" he asked, extending his arm toward the swing set.

Elly sat down on a swing, the cold metal chains smooth against her palms.

"Want a push?" he asked.

And then she was flying, flying into the evening, trying to touch her toes to the tree branches, black against a purple sky. And Anthony was on the swing next to her, flying, too. Laughing.

There was power in the controlled flight. Elly remembered being small and finding the perfect point at which to let go and let her body arc through the sky before landing on the ground. She almost released her grip. Her body jerked back, Anthony pulled on her swing before she had a chance to jump.

"Not today, Elly," he said. "You could hurt the baby."

The baby. Reality slammed back into her.

They swung gently back and forth. A comfortable silence settled between them.

She looked at him with a sideways glace. "Anthony?"

"Princess?"

"He hit me."

"He won't anymore," said Anthony.

"I let him," said Elly, wiping away more infuriating tears.

"You were afraid."

"I'm afraid now."

Anthony pulled her swing around and locked his legs around hers so that they couldn't swing apart. "Yes, but the difference is *I'm* never going to hurt you."

"But what if I hurt you? Or worse, what if I make you hurt me? And then you won't be able to forgive yourself, and then . . ."

"Elly, I'm never going to leave you. Period," Anthony interrupted.

"How do I know that? How can I know for sure? How can *you* know for sure?"

"Because I already stayed. I already did it. I've waited. I've lived through you leaving and then coming back and not remembering me. I've lived through that *traumatic* Christmas when you kissed me and then left me cold," he laughed.

"That's not funny, said Elly, breaking away from him and swinging alone. "I didn't want to leave that night either. Carmen made me."

"Come here," he said, his arms open. "Swing with me."

Elly climbed on his lap, facing him, slipping her legs by his sides. He covered her smallish hands with his large ones.

Anthony began to swing slowly, their bodies moving back and forth, the force of the air pressing them together. He stopped and took her face in his hands, the streetlights washing the park in artificial light glowing against her green eyes. He pulled her face to his and kissed her. His warm mouth reminded her of the ache she felt for him all those years ago. The rightness. The kiss that softly expresses wanting to be as close as two people can be. Not like Cooper's kisses. The kisses that violently established ownership and left her mouth bruised and invaded. Elly felt that blackness begin to fill up with something else. Something real and familiar. *Feels like I'm home . . .*

✦

Back on 170th Street there was a rush to get Sunday dinner on the table and Anthony was sent out for loaves of bread. Elly, lost in the fuss, found herself alone. She wandered through the building, through the front hall that narrowed and then became the back hall. Up the staircase that split the apartment building into an A side and B side. She put her hands on Uncle George's closed door and tried to remember more of him than just a muttering, smelly old man. But mostly, Elly listened closely for the crying but didn't hear it. She heard something entirely different but somehow more unnerving. She heard the mystery child laughing. Muffled giggles now paired with echoes of tiny feet running up and down the stairs and in and out of closed doors.

At dinner, in between courses of steaming pasta, meatballs made with friselles (pepper biscuits), and tender asparagus quickly sautéed in olive oil and tossed with salt, there was a lively discussion about the mystery voice.

"Laughing now? The kid isn't crying anymore, it's laughing?" asked Mimi.

"Yeah. And it's just as creepy as it is curious," she said to Mimi at the table.

"Maybe it's Zelda," Fee yelled.

"No, we've already decided it isn't Zelda," said Mimi.

"How can you be sure?" asked Anthony.

"I guess I can't be sure," said Elly, stuffing another mouthful of pasta in her mouth. She'd never had a meal that tasted so—right. It was made with a special ingredient, or so the aunts had said. Strawberry leaves sautéed with olive oil, garlic, and other greens and mixed with chicken stock. Then tossed with the homemade pasta.

"Have you seen it? Is it a boy or a girl?" asked Mimi.

"No, I haven't seen it. And I can't tell the gender by the voice," said Elly. Then she threw her napkin on the table in frustration. "And see, this is crazy. You're all supposed to be telling me it's in my head."

Itsy scribbled quickly, showing Elly her words. They exchanged smiles.

"What did she say?" asked Anthony.

"*It's in your head.* See, at least one of you is sane."

Itsy nodded and grunted out in raspy agreement with herself.

"This pasta is *so* good, Mimi! What's it for again?" asked Elly, reaching for the large ceramic bowl in the middle of the table. It always seemed full, she noticed. As if five people hadn't already eaten their fair share.

"Strawberry leaves," said Mimi. "It's good for the baby, that's all you have to know." And it was *all* Elly wanted to know—because someone caring about her, cooking for her, keeping her safe . . . these feelings were magical enough. She didn't need to know any recipes. Not just yet.

9

Elly and Liz

That night, when all the pots and pans were cleaned and put away, Mimi brought Elly a fine white nightgown with delicate cutwork around the squared neckline.

"Mama made them for all of us. Fee and Itsy made this one for you last night."

"Last night?" asked Elly, taking the lovely yet sturdy garment from her grandmother's rough hands. "But it's so beautiful."

"What is it? A sheet with a few fancies, not much. But a girl feels like a girl in one. So wear it and have a good sleep, okay?"

Mimi was out of the room so fast Elly said goodnight to the door.

She wasn't tired. She wandered around the room, her mother's room, and traced its features with her fingers. The dresser, the blue paisley wallpaper, the molding.

In the nightgown, with her hair piled high and her body scrubbed, Elly felt like she should be a ghost wandering around in old Scottish ruins. A shadow at Stonehenge. A barefoot priestess lost in the mist, carrying a secret.

The winter window grew moss as Elly fell asleep. A pebble woke her. And then a handful of pebbles. She sat up and cupped her hands together to see out of the window.

"Liz?" She opened the window. "What are you doing here?"

"Want to go for a walk in the winter wonderland?"

Elly yanked on her boots and put on the coat she'd borrowed from Anthony. She climbed out the window.

"You're a big girl, I'm sure no one would object to you leaving out through the front door. Sheesh!"

"You don't know my people." Elly dusted cold snow from the windowsill off her neck and shivered. For a moment she wanted to take down her hair and grab her hat. She fought the urge. "Where are we going?" she asked.

"Let's visit Georgie," Liz suggested.

"Who's that? Someone else I can't remember?"

"You don't remember your uncle? Shame!"

Elly knew she knew this girl. She didn't really know how or why, but she knew the glimmer in her eye, the spontaneous fun. It was contagious. "Uncle George is dead."

"I know that, silly! Let's go to the cemetery."

It seemed the *perfect* thing to do on a cold and snowy night in the middle of a dangerous city.

Liz knew back roads and alleyways. Elly ran next to her new, old friend. Her feet sure on the ground. Soon they were at the gates of Shady Rest next to the Botanical Gardens. "It's so beautiful here, isn't it?"

It was. The landscape, already quiet from its burden of heavy stones, was even more subdued from the blanket of soft white. "Come this way. Your family plot is over here."

"How do you know so much about my family when I don't know anything?"

"I can't account for your memory loss," Liz joked, throwing a snowball at Elly.

"I guess not. I remembered you, though."

Liz ran to her and gave her a hug. "Ooh! I knew you would. What did you remember?"

"You giving Anthony rabbit ears, down by the beach."

"Far Rockaway?" asked Liz.

"I guess so. Mimi said she took me there that summer," said Elly.

"Yeah. We all went. It was a great week. Tons of fun."

"Anthony says he has pictures, too. That might help."

Liz stiffened. "Pictures?"

"Yeah, why, you not photogenic or something?"

"No, not really. Anyway . . . come on! Let's say hi to George."

They stood outside a gated plot under a large tree. Two stones were larger than the rest.

Margaret Green Amore
Beloved Mother and Wife
Born 1895–Died May 8th 1945

Vincent Louis Amore
Beloved Husband and Father
Born 1894–Died May 8th 1945

"The same day?" Elly recalled Anthony calling it *The Day the Amores Died*. And then Mimi made mention of "That Day" as well. *For a Yalie I sure can be obtuse,* thought Elly.

"Yeah, they all died on the same day, more or less."

"All?"

"Your great-aunt Bunny, her daughter Zelda Grace. You don't know the story?"

"No."

"Crazy. It's like mythology around these parts. *The Day the Amores Died.* Bunny and Zelda are around here somewhere. Wanna say hi to them, too?"

"All of them?" Elly felt very sad all of a sudden. "I think I want to go back, Liz. I'm cold."

"Sure. Of course. Let's just say hi to good old George, okay?" Liz went through the gate and dusted off a smaller stone. It read:

George Amore: Always a Child at Heart

"Boy, did he love you, Elly."

"Really?"

"Yes. I hope if you remember anything, you remember playing with George."

Fee. Fi. Fo. Fummy . . .

"But he was an old man when I was little."

Liz laughed. "Your Uncle George was never an old man!"

Elly smiled, and then shivered.

"Let's get out of here. You're cold. What was I thinking taking a full-of-life person to a full-of-death place? Your Mimi would have my head."

Did I tell her I was pregnant? Elly wondered.

✦

Elly reentered the building using the front door, unlocking it with a hidden key Liz revealed between some crumbled foundation mortar.

"See ya later!" Liz called out as she ran down the snowy street.

Standing in the hall Elly decided to try and remember Uncle George. Not the old, senile, grumbly person she recalled from more recent visits, but the playmate Liz assured her existed during that long, forgotten summer. She padded into the main hallway and then up the stairs. Halfway up she could clearly see the second floor doors. Her Uncle George's apartment, 2B, was to her left, Anthony's, 2A, to her right. A whisper of a giggle came from the right. Elly gripped the banister and closed her eyes, a delicious bubble of laughter rising inside her own chest. *"Fee fi fo fummy, I smell a girl and girls are YUMMY!"* Elly let out a little squeal and ran up the remaining steps, but when she turned around, no one was chasing her. She was dizzy as she knocked on door 2A. She heard a muffled "Wait a minute" and locks being undone. And there he was, Anthony, his hair tousled, his face transformed by the happy surprise.

"Come on in, pretty lady. I've been waiting for you to find me since we were ten."

"Don't get any big ideas."

"Well, why are you here if it ain't for my kisses?" There was laughter in Anthony's easy voice.

"I think I'm remembering things," she whispered.

"What kind of things?" Anthony took on a serious tone and helped her into his apartment.

"Did Uncle George play with us when we were kids?"

"Oh yeah, all the time." He scratched his fingers through his thick hair and smiled, remembering, too.

"Can you tell me?"

"It'd be my pleasure. Oh, and I found the pictures."

Elly went inside the dark apartment. It smelled like him, but when he turned on a table lamp in the living room, Elly remembered his mother.

"She was beautiful. You took such good care of her," she said, wandering the apartment, re-seeing it again. Exactly the same floor plan as Mimi's in 1A, yet worlds apart. Smart, low Danish Modern furniture, potted plants, floor to ceiling bookshelves. Anthony's mother had a bohemian flair.

"You remember."

"Yes. I seem to remember things easier if they have nothing to do with me."

"Here, look through these." Anthony handed her a cigar box filled with Polaroid pictures. "We took them, so they aren't great."

Images of elbows and too-close half smiles. An ice cream truck, the beach. "Oh look! This is Uncle George, isn't it!" It was a picture of an old man, but not old like in Elly's recent memory. "He was handsome for an old guy. You know, I swear I felt him chasing me up the stairs before."

"Really? That's a little spooky," said Anthony.

"No, it wasn't spooky at all. It was *fun*. Did he chase us?"

"Yeah, he chased us all the time. You mostly. Boy, he loved you. He used to pretend he was a giant and chase you around the building yelling Fee, fi . . ."

". . . fo fummy. I smell a girl and girls are yummy. I'll eat that girl and fill my tummy," finished Elly, laughing with delight.

Anthony grabbed her and held her tight. "You remember."

"Some things. But not everything. There's so much darkness still there."

"Don't worry, Elly, give it time. It'll come back to you."

"Anthony?"

"What is it?" he asked, his head nestled against her neck.

"What if there's a reason I can't remember? What if it's better left forgotten?"

"Nothing is better that way, believe me, Elly. And whatever it is, bad or good, I'll be here for you."

Elly pulled away from him and leaned her forehead against the window, looking out at the city lights. "Why are you so nice to me?"

"Because I love you, Elly Amore. And you love me. You just haven't remembered it yet."

10

Itsy

I saw her leave the building. Out through the window just like her mother used to. But she's different. Not like Carmen. She reminds me of Mama, she always has. I'm tired and can't seem to get a bit of sleep anymore. Fee snores so loud. I try to pretend the sound is the creaking of a ship at sea. It used to work. It doesn't anymore. My mind is just so full.

The boys were born first. Three in a row. Mama was scared she'd never have a girl. Papa, too. Then came Bunny, then Fee, and Mimi eighteen months later. They called Fee and Mimi Irish twins. Mama and Papa figured God was done with them. Three boys and three girls seemed a fair amount of children, and all healthy, too. Then came me and George. Twins. I came first and no one knew little George was in there. He waited a whole two days to show up. The cord came with his feet and everything was jumbled. He didn't get enough air, the midwife said. Not enough air makes you a kid forever. Isn't that funny? Childhood is all about air. Running with hair blowing out behind, puffs of hot air making fake smoke coming out of your mouth on the first colder days of autumn. But Georgie didn't get enough and spent his whole life a child. It was wonderful, sometimes, and sometimes not so much. But he was mine, George was.

It all went swell until 1945. How can a family lose itself in one day? It just happens, that's how. It isn't God, or destiny, or bad luck. Some crap just happens to you and you have to figure it all out on the other side. We fell into the deep end. The boys died in the war. Boom, boom, and boom. Mama died when she heard the news. And then Papa, Zelda Grace, and Bunny.

We'd all spread out by then. Our own version of urban sprawl. Bunny, married with her daughter, sweet Zelda Grace, was living on the second floor in apartment 2A. George was safe across the hall from her in 2B, pretending to be a grown-up man. Mimi lived downstairs in 1B with Alfred, and Fee still lived in our old apartment, 1A, with Mama and Papa. Me, well, I was living out at the Far Rockaway house. As I'd promised Mama. And Henry was living out in his family's cottage, too. It was the only way we could keep our secret safe.

For a few years we all felt we might be able to survive 1945. That perhaps, Mama and her fortune-teller friend were wrong. But then the phone rang, the damn phone. I should have never got on the train. Just let them deal with it. But I didn't. The call of my sisters is powerful. And then, when it was over, I had to come back from my broken-down palace by the sea and move in with Fat Face Fee. Because we needed to stay close. It seemed that the world had an agenda of killing Amores. It seemed saner to stay close, so close we stayed. And insane.

11

Elly

The quiet, magic life of the Amore sisters proved so pleasant that Elly began to go to church every Sunday without discussion. It wasn't that she had some profound religious epiphany. It was simply the quiet joy it gave her grandmother, and soon Elly began to look forward to it. She liked resting her head against her grandmother's shoulder like a child and taking in the soft scent of her. Garlic and Shalimar. She liked the forty-five minutes of peace where she could forget her fears. She liked the community and the priest. She liked the strong dark coffee in the church hall after the Mass. She liked the constancy of ritual. She liked sitting so close to Anthony. Sacred and profane. His thigh against her leg made her woozy.

And then there would be Sunday dinner. Half prepared the night before, she cooked with them and learned the ways of the women in her family. After church they put the sauce on the flame, fried meatballs, made simple greens and an exceptionally large salad full of pickled things. Put chicken thighs into the oven with potatoes and onions and peas. Ran to the corner store for one last loaf of bread. And then they sat down, usually around two, and usually with the priest, young Father Carter, or members of the parish.

Elly didn't have time to miss Carmen, or fear Cooper. She spent her days synching with Mimi, falling into the rhythm of their ways, like waves and tides, in and out, vast and corralled in by the ever-present horizon line of the day's end.

The mornings were all about magical teas and tinctures and taking inventory of all the tins full of dried herbs in Mimi's kitchen. Slowly, Mimi began to whisper the Amore secrets into Elly's open mind. She learned about protection jars and love spells. She learned of darker things that Mama, Margaret Green, warned them against, but taught them anyway—just in case. Elly looked forward to each new day like a kindergarten student. She saw life from these different angels that constantly amazed her.

The evenings sounded like teacups. Mimi ended her day with a cup of tea and an almond cookie, not homemade, a treat from a package. She'd walk past Elly who liked to curl up on the couch and pick through the cigar box full of old Polaroid pictures Anthony gave her, and kiss her goodnight. Elly stayed up later, straining to remember . . . looking at half-faded photos taken of hands and feet and the long stretch of beaches on Far Rockaway.

"A good day. Today we worked hard," she'd say, and then she'd turn the corner to walk down the hallway to her bedroom, the teacup rattling against the saucer. It usually took a while for the laughing to start. But Elly was learning patience and she was bent on finding out what was behind this mysterious joy. So the laughter would start, and Elly made chase, running through the halls and listening to the walls of 170th Street while the other residents slept.

And it was one of these lovely preoccupied Sundays that Cooper decided to finally make his big debut.

The Amore sisters saw it coming. The night before they all awoke from the same dream and gathered quietly at Mimi's kitchen table to look deep into a bowl of water.

He's coming? wrote Itsy.

"He's coming," said Mimi.

To harm her? wrote Itsy.

"To harm her!" Fee yelled.

"Shhhhh!" said Mimi. "You'll wake her!"

"Sorry," said Fee putting her finger in her ear, trying to clear out a wax that could not come undone.

Itsy scribbled: *We must prepare.*

And so, the Amore sisters made an extra pot of sauce.

✦

"Get ready. Be brave. Don't ask questions," ordered Mimi when they got home from church.

"What?" asked Elly. "Why? What's going on?"

"Just stay calm and be yourself."

"Who else would I be?" asked Elly.

Itsy scribbled and handed Elly a note, *That slouchy, wimpy little girl that showed up here on Christmas Eve, that's who.*

"Nice," said Elly. "She hates me. I swear it!"

"She does not. And don't swear. Hush! He's here!" said Fee.

The doorbell rang.

"He's here," said Mimi.

"I already said that," said Fee, and Mimi shoved her as she went for the door.

Mimi went into the hall and threw open the doors to the building. "You must be Baker!"

"Cooper," he said pushing the door open, pinning Mimi behind it. He stood in the hallway looking from side to side, not knowing what apartment door to approach first.

Elly stared at him from the safety of Mimi's apartment. How could he be here? In this other life she'd painted for herself? He wasn't even real to her anymore. But here he was, anyway.

Anthony stood at the top of the stairs. He walked down in a controlled burn. "Hey man, good to see you again. Sorry about the scuffle at Elly's room. She can make a guy *crazy,* you know?" He chuckled, nodding his head toward Elly at the same time he held out his hand to Cooper for a shake.

He's in on whatever this is . . . Elly thought.

Cooper shook Anthony's hand out of etiquette more than anything else. Elly could tell by the way he licked his lips that Cooper was caught off guard by these strangers. He was nervous. Not a common state for Cooper Bakersmith.

"You must be Elly's young man! How handsome you are!" yelled Fee.

"Yes, well . . ."

Mimi, freed from behind the front door, came at him from the rear. "We were just sitting down to eat. Come, be pleasant. You catch more flies with sugar, honey. Didn't your mother ever tell you that?"

Did she actually say that? Elly wondered. These people were so brave.

Surrounded, Cooper was backed into Mimi's apartment. Anthony was behind him talking.

"I'm sorry we got off to a bad start. Elly's got nothing but nice things to say about you. Don't you, Elly?"

"Eleanor?" His eyes found her and she watched him try to drink her in. Her hair pulled up, her clothes and growing tummy. She knew he hadn't planned on any of this. He was just going to get her. Collect what was his and take her back to New Haven so he could make sure she got rid of the kid.

"Why not sit and have dinner with us, Cooper? Then I'll get my things and come back with you, okay?"

Elly could feel the pride coming off her grandmother and great aunts. She didn't know what she was doing, but whatever it was . . . it was the right thing to do.

They ushered him from Mimi's pretty living room and Elly touched his arm. She felt his surprise by the beauty of this place, that he was expecting matching drapes and wall-to-wall carpets. His class lines were getting blurred. *Serves you right, you uptight Anglo,* she thought.

They sat him at the long dining table. Itsy was scribbling. She tore the paper off the pad and pushed it toward Cooper. Anthony stood over his shoulder and read it aloud.

You must eat with us. It's only fair. Give and take. That's how it works. You lose something you have to get something in return. Loss has consequences until it's found.

"This is all too crazy," said Cooper. "I'll eat, but then she's coming with me."

Anthony sat down and Fee and Mimi placed bowls of pasta on the table.

"Mimi makes it fresh. Nothin' like it in the whole world. Have you ever had fresh pasta?" asked Anthony, tucking a fabric napkin into his collar.

Cooper seemed fascinated by the napkin.

"It's antique, you know," said Elly. "Handmade."

"Yes, of course. I've *lived* in Italy," said Cooper, ignoring Elly's remarks.

"Good, then you'll want some more sauce," said Mimi, ladling more over his meal. It smelled so tempting, that extra ladle. Acidic and hearty. Like hot summer days in Tuscany. Elly motioned for more, too, but Anthony mouthed the word "no."

It took exactly three bites. Cooper's head landed face-first in his bowl of pasta.

"That was fast," said Mimi. "How much pine did you put in the sauce, Itsy?"

Itsy shrugged.

Elly watched in disbelief as Anthony clapped his hands together, rubbed them for a few seconds, then lugged Cooper over his shoulders and walked out of the apartment. The old women followed and Fee grabbed Cooper's keys off the dining room table saying, "Only an Anglo would place dirty keys on a dinner table," as she threw them to Anthony who caught them in midair.

"What the hell was that all about?" she said, following the trio of old women into Mimi's apartment.

"What did you do to him? Where are they going?"

"Anthony's taking him back to school. He'll wake up tomorrow and his purpose for this visit will be forgotten," said Mimi.

"How?"

Fee put her hands on Elly's shoulders and eased her onto the couch. "Oh, a few herbs, some hypnotism. Nothing really harmful."

"It's not right. You can't just do that to people."

"And what about what he did to you? Hmmmm?" asked Mimi.

Itsy scribbled: *And what about what he was going to do to you?*

"What was he going to do?"

Itsy put pen to paper again, but Mimi put her hand gently over her sister's. "She doesn't need to know that, Itsy."

"Why can't I remember anything?" Elly asked them. "Is that what you did to me? Did you put some kind of spell on me making me forget everything? It can't be a coincidence that my memories start the minute I left this building."

"Look at me," said Mimi, turning Elly around to face her and looking into her eyes. "Look at all of us and know this to be true. We never did anything but care for you. No spells, no concoctions. If you can't remember, and that bothers you, try harder. It's starting already, I can tell."

Elly looked at Aunt Itsy. And Itsy averted the stare. Her hands stayed still at her side. Itsy wasn't saying anything.

"What did you say to me, Itsy? That day when you broke your silence?"

Itsy shrugged and shuffled back into her own apartment.

Elly walked to the front window and watched as Anthony drove Cooper away in Cooper's car. "I hope you witches told Anthony where Cooper parks his car. I'd hate for him to be suspicious when he comes to."

Mimi drew Elly away from the window by the hand. "Oh, no worries. We try not to let those little details get in the way," said Mimi.

"Of course you don't," said Elly.

Spring

12

Itsy

I miss Mama's garden. Sure, we keep it up. We do the same things the same way. But it's never the same without her. The gardener is just as much a part of the garden as the soil.

I can still see Mama in her garden. A small square space, but plenty of room for the Eden she created. In the rough, rawness of early spring she'd be there working the ground, the bottom of her skirts and cuffs of her sweaters muddied as if she'd risen from a shallow grave.

We all helped, not because she asked us to, but because she was silent and joyful as she worked. At peace. A peace we rarely felt emanate from her. That peace drew us in like moths to a flame.

As we worked, we asked her questions. She'd sit back on her heels and answer every one. I marvel now, when I look back, at how she always had the time for that. There was never a question too small or too big. And in my memory—clouded now and certainly gilded—she never said, "I don't know." Even though she taught us there was power in that sentiment.

"Are you magic, Mama?" we'd ask her. We already knew she could do things other mothers couldn't, and we already had an appreciation for the genetic abilities we seemed to inherit from her.

"*Magic* is a funny term," she'd say. "There is nothing supernatural about the earth. As long as you know what does what."

"What do you mean?" we'd ask her.

"There are plants that heal, hurt, manipulate. There are ideas to plant in people's minds. There is power in everyone . . . most people don't use it," she'd answer.

"Is Papa magic?" we'd ask.

She laughed at that. "Well, he's magic for *me*. But he doesn't know half of what he is capable of."

One time, George (who was never afraid to ask anything, his inhibitions lost in those days he waited to be born), asked the question we all wanted to ask: "How do we see the things we do? Are we witches?"

I remember Mama was pruning a rose bush. Cutting it all back and explaining that this was the only way to propagate. That if you do the *opposite* of what seems to be the right thing; mostly you get what you want. If you want more roses? Cut back the bush.

Anyway, she pulled away from her task, her hair getting caught on sharp thorns and she put her arms out to him. We must have been eleven or so.

"Come here, my Georgie!" she called to him and he ran to her, their smiles meeting each other and their breath becoming one. She rocked him and called us all from our different corners of the yard to come to her.

"And what, do you think, is a witch, my delicious little ducks?"

We all had different answers.

Bunny said, "A green face and a big nose!"

Mimi . . . who was a daddy's girl said, "A *witch* is a *strega,* like Daddy's Aunt Florencia who gave her husband the *malocchio* and he *died.*"

Fee said, "A fairy." Her voice was so soft then. I can't remember it well, I just remember how soft-spoken she was before all the madness.

Mama then turned her attention to me. I always seemed to be the last one on her mind. "And what about you, Itsy, love? What do you think makes someone a witch?"

"Being mean?" I suggested.

Bunny laughed at me. "That's a *bitch* not a witch!" she said.

I was embarrassed.

Mama hushed her.

"Now listen close," she said. "My family in Fairview, which is your family, too, don't you forget, was considered witches. All it meant was that there was a certain knowledge we had . . . a separate sort of looking through time and space that could help or hurt those around us. We knew what to grow and when to grow it. More importantly, we knew what to *do* with what we grew. And we called *that* a witch's garden. Like this one. It is true—we could see things . . . the past and future in a clearer way than most. But I think they called us witches because there were things we did, things they simply couldn't or wouldn't understand.

I think we were just people who opened ourselves up to the world. And that's what I'm doing for you. So if you need to consider yourselves witches . . . go ahead. Have fun! But in my opinion we are simply . . . Smart!" And with that she tickled Georgie and we all went back to work.

I remember asking her the difference between a witch's garden and a regular one. Mama took a stick and drew in the earth—softening as the spring sun grew stronger in the sky—a square space with intersecting circles, the directional arrows North, South, East, and West in the corner.

"We plant and work the soil the way the earth chooses, which is only right as it is the earth that gives us the permission to use her the way we do. Keep in mind, there should be shadow and light, distinction between plants that heal and those that can make you ill. And perhaps most important, my Itsy, a place to sit." She pointed at the stone bench in the corner of the garden by the back door. "Papa had that made for me. When the boys were young he sat here and watched us for hours."

"Why doesn't Papa help in the garden?"

"Papa has a black thumb!" We laughed together. "Itsy . . . men don't really understand the magic garden."

"What about George?"

Mama's face drew quiet. "George isn't like other men, my Itsy. You of all people know that! I often think I'll take him home to Fairview and to my house and my people. That they would know what to do. That they could right the wrong that happened in my womb. And even . . ." She looked toward the sky and pushed back her hair, "Even change the course of events that haunt me so . . ."

"Why don't you, Mama? Please!" I begged.

"There's no one left, love. I have no people anymore."

"You have us, Mama."

"Yes, sweetling. I do. Don't I?"

And she did. She had us wrapped up inside her. But even so, the idea of fixing George stayed with me. I prayed every night for weeks that Mama could bring Georgie back to the magical place she came from. Heal him of all that was wrong. Give him back all the air I stole from him by coming out of Mama first.

It took a while before I realized I was praying more for myself than him. That I wanted to be free of the responsibility. I'd have to try making magic my own way. It turned out my magic couldn't fix George . . . but the more I learn about our Elly, the more my magic grows. And I can fix *this whole* situation. I surely can. Even if what I have to do scares me. Scares me to death.

13

The Sisters Amore

Spring came slowly to the Bronx with a lot of rain and soft watercolor tree blossoms. As Elly grew more pregnant she also grew wiser with Amore wisdom. Mimi and the aunts showed her more and more of Margaret Green's ways. Protection jars were a new favorite of Elly's. "I wish it was summer already," she said, adding a cat's eye marble to a mason jar already full of cobwebs and sage then screwing the metal cap shut. She placed it among the others on an already crowded table. Anthony would have to reach and put them over the doorframes later. "I hate being pregnant," she said. "I can't even learn the magic right. And *you* won't let me on stepladders to put these things up properly."

"Oh, come now . . ." cooed Mimi from the kitchen where she was frying thick pieces of steak to put together with tomatoes and red onion on focaccia bread. It was Elly's newest craving. "It's your full-of-life time. Don't throw it away."

"But I feel so ugly. And I miss my mother."

Elly hadn't spoken to her mother since Christmas Eve, and it was already April. Easter had come and gone with its delicious dandelion soup and garlic pork roast. Easter pies: rice, wheat, cream, and ricotta spread out on the table and Elly not only eating but learning. She'd absorbed so much tradition in so little time. Sometimes the phone would ring in the middle of the night and Elly would jump out of bed and run to the kitchen, whispering *Mom, Mom, Mommy* under her breath only to find Liz on the other end.

"Well," said Mimi, "I can't make Carmen do anything she doesn't want to, I never could. That child came out determined to keep on going. But I *can* help with the ugly . . . maybe."

"Gee thanks, Mimi!" Elly laughed. She was getting used to Mimi's abrasive sense of humor. Finding solace in it, even.

"Come with me. Your face is so pretty. It's your clothes. You don't have anything to fit your belly."

✦

Mimi took her to the attic.

Elly felt a strangeness wash over her. "I remember this, I think," said Elly. "Is there a hiding place behind the attic door?"

"Not that I know of," said Mimi.

"No," continued Elly. "You're right. It wasn't a straight staircase. I was wrong. I don't remember it."

"Ah, well. Memories are strange and fleeting things," said Mimi climbing the narrow, dark stairs one at a time, holding onto the thin banister for support.

The attic was huge with deep peaks and corners. It was tidy, with one back wall lined with boxes and steamer trunks. A part of Elly held her breath. She really thought she remembered something. Mimi was rummaging through boxes, but Elly was pressing her fingers against her temples. Her heart was racing.

"I know they're here somewhere . . . maybe . . . Yes." Mimi opened a large steamer trunk that looked like a treasure chest with wide metal strips holding together strong, weathered wood.

✦

Downstairs, Itsy, who was stooped over, making Fee's bed because that fat sister of hers couldn't get around the corners properly, stopped. She turned her head up toward the ceiling and slowly creaked open her mouth. She closed her eyes, a tear making its way down her cheek, through her deep wrinkles. *Is this how it would happen? Now? With no meaning? Making Fat Fee's bed?* Itsy wondered.

She waited, stayed quiet—and then tried to make a sound.

No. Not now. It wasn't the right trunk. Itsy shook her head and continued on with her chore.

✦

"I've found it!" Mimi creaked open a second trunk and started shaking out beautiful summer dresses. "These were mine. They'll fit you fine. Want to try some on? We'll wash them, of course. And you could buy new ones if you want."

"No, I want them. I want them all." Elly threw her arms around her grandmother and began to cry. Mimi sat with her on the attic floor. She let Elly rest her head on her lap and she rubbed her granddaughter's back as she cried.

"Everything's going to be fine, love. I promise," said Mimi.

"Mimi? Why did I come stay with you all those years ago? Where was my mother?"

"You really don't remember?" asked Mimi, pushing back the hair from Elly's forehead.

"No. I really don't."

"And you're sure you want to know?"

"Yes Mimi. I *need* to know."

"Okay then, I'll tell you. But do me a favor?"

"Anything, Mimi."

"As I tell you the story, why not flex your muscles? Try out your Sight. Listen to my voice, but see the truth. Can you try that for me?"

Elly closed her eyes. "Tell me, Mimi. I'm ready."

New York City was beautiful in the early summer. Itsy, Fee, and Mimi were glad to make the trip from the Bronx to Fairview, Massachusetts, but troubled by the reason. They hadn't been called yet. The phones were probably ringing throughout the 170th Street building as they drove, but the sisters were already on the road. Awoken the night before they gathered in the dark garden holding hands around the ornate, cement birdbath. Not knowing or caring who was speaking to whom or even if it was a dream, they gathered their thoughts and came to the same, chilling conclusion.

She's hurting.

"She's been hurt."

She's hurt her?

"She's hurt herself."

The smell of Mama's roses, not yet in bloom, told them where to go.

Fairview. The home of Margaret's people, the Greens. Margaret Green who married Vincent Amore and left sweet, seaside vistas for urban decay.

"She never looked back, though," said Fee while Mimi drove George's car and they told each other their mother's story, laughing as if it was the first time, as if it weren't built into the fabric of who they were as a family.

Fairview was a quiet place. It would have been a tourist haven like the Cape if it weren't for the hospital, and that was where the sisters were headed.

Fairview Mental Hospital.

It used to be called Saint Sebastian Lunatic Asylum before the 1960s made everything politically correct. "Call a spade a spade." Mama would have said if she'd been around to see it. They drove up the long driveway and took in the Gothic building. They'd been there before. When they were small and Mama came to visit her own mother, their grandmother. It seemed just as dark and sinister a place as it had all those years ago. As they stood at the base of a wide staircase entry, Itsy wrote: *Why would she come here of all places?*

Mimi read it and passed it to Fee. All three women shook their heads.

"Blood holds onto history. A part of her belongs here. Why would she go anywhere else?" asked Mimi.

The three nodded together, understanding the situation. Inside they met with the doctor in charge who explained the situation. It was a mixture of cocaine and alcohol. Carmen needed time to "detox" and get her life back "on track." And the girl? She was such a brave little thing. They needed to collect her.

She was in a fancy waiting room at the front of the hospital.

Far away from the screaming back rooms where her mother was being treated. The women felt tiny as their shoes squeaked across the polished parquet flooring.

Mimi hadn't seen her granddaughter since she was a baby. The resemblance was striking. *She looks like, looks like, looks like Mama!* they thought and murmured together as they moved toward her. Itsy, Fee, and Mimi went to the child, where she sat straight as a board in a wingback chair with her small, paisley, corduroy suitcase on her lap. Patent-leather-clad feet with pretty little lace-topped ankle socks were crossed daintily and dangling. Mimi knelt by the girl who would not look at them. She stared straight ahead.

"You are wearing a lovely dress," said Mimi, softly.

"Thank you, my mother bought it for me in the south of France," said the girl loud enough for Fee to hear and still staring past them.

"Come on, let's go," said Fee.

They drove straight home and when they got back the apartments were dark except for the lights in George's window upstairs. The girl was asleep in the car, but as soon as she woke up, she ran away . . . deep into the building itself, trying to escape them all like a kitten in a strange new place. And when they found her, they gave her a bath. And they tended to her bruised body, but her bruised mind would need more care.

✦ Babygirl ✦

She didn't like the way it smelled at her grandmother's house. The old aunts pinched her and they smelled funny, too. Not like Mommy. They smelled like kitchens and chemicals. Mommy smelled like perfume, and smoke, and snow.

She ran away from them into the first door that would open and down a hall until she found a bathroom. She backed herself up against a window that looked out on a small but luscious garden illuminated in a pool of moonlight. And that's when it happened. She saw Liz. Not in her mind, but real! Babygirl decided that if being here means she gets to play with Lizzy, real Lizzy, *then being here might not be so bad. And Mommy needs a rest. Mimi said so. So Mommy will have her rest and Babygirl will play with Lizzy and that boy upstairs. Because he is just so cute! Lizzy called dibs, but Babygirl knows he has eyes only for her. Babygirl can tell those things. She can feel them a mile away. Just like she knew it wasn't Mommy who did those things. It was something sad and ill inside of Mommy. Babygirl didn't need the doctors, or the old ladies, or the priest to tell her that. She knew it already.*

She knew something else, too. She knew her Aunt Itsy was hiding something. It was a mystery. Babygirl loved mysteries and if she had to search all summer, she would solve the whole thing. And then Uncle George . . . sweet Uncle George took her to Playland. And there was nothing better in the whole world than doing one cartwheel after another up and down the beaches of Far Rockaway. Old Aunt Itsy did them, too. Babygirl loved watching Itsy do cartwheels. She'd watch from the sand while she caught her own breath. She'd watch Liz and Itsy do cartwheels together, their arms and legs striking out at different intervals like graceful starfish with the sparkling waters of the sea behind them.

✦

Georgie was the one who made everything all right. He thought they should take her to Playland. Mimi arranged to have the cottage at Far Rockaway cleaned up and they all went, took the little boy, Anthony, who lived upstairs with them, too. They went for a week to the beaches of Far Rockaway. It put the stamp of childhood squarely on Babygirl's forehead. It began to heal her. But wounds can be reopened. And get infected, too.

✦

"Oh, I remember, Mimi . . ." Elly said softly, raising her head out of Mimi's lap. "I remember you bringing me here. And I remember why."

"She was sick, Elly," said Mimi.

"I know. I think I knew it then. When I was little, I think I knew she never meant it. Drugs, right? I think it was drugs."

"Yes. Sinful."

"No, Mimi. Not sinful. Weak."

"Are you troubled by all this, Elly?"

"No. I'm more troubled that she never told me."

"It's hard to tell people you've hurt them."

Elly looked around her at all the boxes and up to the rafters. She felt her baby move deep within her. *Mothers and daughters . . . How we dance around each other . . .* she thought. Then she changed the subject.

"I also remembered a bit of that summer! The cottage. The beach! How wonderful! Is it still there?"

"Oh, yes. Of course. We couldn't give up Mama's cottage. But Far Rockaway is a different place now. Damn urban renewal projects. Barren and blah. That's what it's like now."

"How about Playland? Is that still there? Oh Mimi, I'd love to go."

"No, sweet. They tore down Playland."

Elly put her head back in Mimi's lap and started to cry again.

"How do you tear down something called Playland? It's . . . it's . . . it's a sin!"

"It's true. A sin it is. Tell me dear heart, do you remember anything else? The rest of that summer, what Itsy said?"

"No . . . well . . . bits and pieces. Uncle George. Playing with Liz and Anthony. You remember Liz, right Mimi?"

"Oh yes, Liz! Of course," said Mimi, stroking Elly's hair. "How could I forget about her?"

"Yes, it's been nice getting to know her again."

Mimi shot a worried look at Elly. "Love, did you remember anything else?

"No, I don't think so. But I have the strangest notion that all of my memories are tied to what Itsy said to me that day."

"Always follow your notions, honey. That's instinct and listening to instinct is what keeps us Amores different from all the other yahoos in the world."

Elly sat up, laughing. "Mimi? Did you just say *yahoos*?"

Mimi smiled and swatted Elly with a maternity top. "Let's go back downstairs, out of this old attic, and have some lunch. Then the garden, okay? There's a lot of work to be done there."

"Why can't Anthony do it?"

"Elly. Rule number one about a true garden. Men can't do anything but weed it. Nothing will work right if they get involved."

She laughed as the two made their way back downstairs with armfuls of maternity clothes, and as they did, Elly felt disarmed by déjà'vu, again. Not the same as her ever unfolding memories. This was different. Scary.

"Mimi, is there another way into this attic?"

Mimi looked over her shoulder at her granddaughter. "No. Why? Do you remember something else?"

"No. Just a notion."

"Well, take notice, Elly. Take notice of those instincts. Something's trying to come true."

"Well, why can't it just come on then? These memories? *All* of them?" asked Elly later, as they gardened side by side.

"There's only one reason," said Mimi, not looking up from her task.

"And what's that?"

"You. You are standing in your own way. And that means whatever it is scares you. It won't forever . . . but take your time. Nothing good was ever rushed."

"I'd rather hurry all this up, Mimi."

"Rushing through pain tears us. Do you want to break or heal?"

Elly didn't want to think about breaking. She pulled at the weeds and pushed the dimmer memories away. *Not yet, not yet . . .* she thought.

But it was no use. They shimmered there anyway.

14

Itsy

"Let's go to Playland? What do you think? Are you bored of the beach, my lovelies?" asked Mama.

Bunny came out of the bedroom. George and I ran in from the porch. Fee and Mimi slammed the screen door giggling and dropping clothespins from clutched aprons.

"Oh yes!" shrieked George.

Playland was a treat for many reasons. Spending money, sugar, death-defying rides. All things Mama didn't like, but she had a gleam in her eyes that day and we understood. Papa was supposed to come that morning with the boys. It was already afternoon and they still weren't in sight . . . so Playland for us was *his* punishment. We could read her mind: *Oh, so you think you can keep me waiting? You think you can worry me? Well, let's see how you like it, Mr. Amore. Hope you come home and think we've been carried off by gypsies. And later, when I get my hands on you, you'll be eating scones. Yes, those scones you like . . . the ones that make you dizzy.*

As we made our way down the street toward the beach and boardwalk, I looked back for a moment at our summer place. All the cottages looked the same from far away. The street faced the beach and we all had the same view. The neighborhoods segregated themselves. Mama's block was Irish, and we all called our cottage "Mamma's House." Summer belonged to her and her ways. The family of her childhood was gone but the house was still there. It was small but lovely: one large, long room with two bedrooms and a pull-down staircase for storage. Mama left the staircase down on rainy days so we'd have room to play and stay out of her hair.

Her hair.

How could she ever know how much I wanted to be inside her hair? Thick and black but not like our wild Italian locks. Shiny and dense. Straight like silk, her hair. And my Mama had gypsy eyes that glowed green like the phosphorus sea. Like the vistas her ancestors saw. A reflection of lives lived long ago.

✦

Right past the entrance to Playland was the line of tents that housed the freak shows: the baby in a jar, the miniature horse, the Siamese twins, and the fortune-teller.

As we passed her tent she emerged from the multicolored fabric. "Mrs. Amore, how nice to see you again."

Mama went stiff for a moment, and then softened, her body floating toward the jingle-jangle woman. "Willow! Well, I never! How have you been?"

Mama turned to Bunny. "My word! A childhood friend and a fortune-teller, too. Watch the children, Bunny, okay?" And then she was gone, swallowed up into the folds of the tent.

George jumped up and down. "I want a candy apple! I want to go on the cyclone! I want to see the fun house!"

Bunny rummaged in her apron pocket and pulled out some shiny silver dimes. "Itsy, take him away, would you? I can't hear him for one more second without going batty."

I didn't need coaxing. I took the money and my brother's hand.

"One, two, three . . . *you and me*!!!!!!!!" we screamed, and ran from my older sisters free as birds and full of carnival air. It was our own sacred cry. We shared it with Henry, though. I remember wishing he'd been there, too.

But, even without Henry, we had a grand time that afternoon. Just Georgie and me. We ducked through crowds of people—no longer on the outside, like usual, but *inside* the thronging breathing beast of the crowd.

They found us on the end of the boardwalk pier, our mouths sticky with all sorts of pink and red confections, our hearts still racing from the twists and dips of lightning fast rides.

I could tell something was wrong as soon as I saw Mama. She didn't hold her arms out to George for a hug. She stood apart from my sisters and looked past us, out over the ocean into the setting sun.

"Come, children," she said, her voice catching in her throat. "Come, let's go back to the cottage and cuddle up, okay?"

Even George knew not to fuss. We followed behind her like ducklings. And I listened to the whispers of my sisters.

"Who was that woman?" asked Fee.

"Willow Bliss. From Fairview. One of Mama's best friends!" said Bunny.

"What did she tell her, Bunny?" asked Mimi.

"I think it was bad news. Something about terrible things happening to us."

By the time we got home, George, scared by the smatterings of conversation we heard on the beach, started to cry.

"Love, love . . . darling boy! What is it?" cooed Mama as she rocked him back and forth.

"The girls said we are all going to *die*!"

Mama patted the sofa cushions and we sat all around her as the night crawled up the sky and cast shadows on the whitewashed floors of the beach cottage.

"My babies. It is true. My friend Willow saw a very sad day for our family. But to be honest, it's something I've seen from the start. Or . . ." She took down her hair and sat back into the cushions. "Or at least something I've tried *not* to see."

"What is it Mama?" asked Mimi.

"1945. 1945 will be a very bad year for us. I don't know when or how or why. But there will be a war. A war that will take your brothers." Mama turned to face the picture window. She traced her fingers down a pane of glass.

"They know they'll die in a war, already," said George. "They talk about it and talk about it. It's all they ever say."

"I know they know," said Mama, still looking out the window, hoping to see their tall figures walking up the street. "I've just spent too much time trying to deny it. And now I've learned that other things may happen."

"What other things, Mama? You're scaring us," said Bunny.

Mama looked at Bunny. "Oh dear. You're right. Look at me scaring all my ducks. All you need to know is that futures have a way of working themselves out. Some fates can change. Tragedy happens every day." She stood up. "No more of this right now. We'll speak of it some other time . . . or maybe you'll just hear the echo of it in your own hearts . . . but for now? Now, I need to make Papa his favorite scones so he can have a full belly when he comes later tonight."

At this, we all laughed. Papa would eat those scones and be sick for a whole day. Silly Papa.

I remember I slept alone on the screened-in back porch that night. I didn't want to be near my brother or my sisters. I didn't want to hear their thoughts or worries. I wanted to go to sleep listening to the surf against the beach. It worked, lulling me into a soft sleep, and then Mama woke me.

"Itsy?" she asked, sweeping her fingers across my forehead. "Wake up, honey, I need you."

She needed me. And she sat with me that night, just the two of us with the moonlight pouring in. She told me the things she needed to say.

"It's your job, Itsy. You are my very special girl. I know you don't feel like it. I know you feel like your voice is so little it's lost among the rest, but it's not. Mama's going to need you. And you have to swear a solemn vow. Swear to me you will take care of George and Mimi and Fee. Do you swear it, Itsy?"

"But Mama? What about you and Papa and Bunny and the boys?"

"Well, if all goes the way Willow Bliss assures me it will, you won't have to worry about all the rest of us, dearheart."

"Well, I don't like it. But I swear. I swear to you the solemn vow."

And I kept them safe for as long as I could. Mama. I kept them safe. Didn't I?

15

Elly

"Happy birthday to you, happy birthday to you! Happy Birthday dear Elly . . . *Babygirl* . . . *Eleanor* . . . Happy Birthday to *you!*" The aunts and Mimi walked toward the table; their wrinkled, singing mouths illuminated by the candles on the Italian cream cake. Anthony was sitting next to Elly clapping as he gave her a kiss. "Make a wish . . ." he whispered into her ear as the cake was placed in front of her. Elly felt her whole body ache for him. Liz was standing in the shadows, smiling. "Happy Birthday!" she said.

"How does it feel to be twenty-three?" asked Mimi, "It's a good number, you know. Two and three make five. Five like the leaves on a rose bush. Very lucky!"

"I feel very young and very old all at the same time, Mimi."

"Mimi, do you mind if I show Elly her present before we have cake?" asked Anthony.

"Of course not, dear. I still have to perk the coffee; it'll take a while. *Someone forgot,*" she yelled loud enough for Fee to hear.

"So what if I only care about the cake?" asked Fee.

"Thank you so much for the delicious dinner," said Elly.

Mimi had prepared Elly's favorite pasta. Bucatini amatriciana.

Long, hollow spaghetti with tomato sauce made with pancetta and red onions.

"You are very welcome, birthday girl. Now go see what our Anthony has done for you!"

"Close your eyes, Elly," said Anthony. She did as she was told and she let him lead her out of the apartment and up the stairs.

She heard the door creak open, and she smelled the fresh air smell that only comes after you've opened something that's been closed for a long time. Air and dust and bleach. The thankful gift of plaster walls and dusty windowpanes newly awakened.

Colors danced behind her eyelids. "Can I open my eyes now?" asked Elly.

"Please do. Happy Birthday, Elly."

It was Uncle George's apartment, only it wasn't. The space was huge and sparsely furnished. Elly remembered it immediately, the way it was before, and marveled at Anthony's job. George had been a hoarder of sorts. Holding onto everything, his apartment floor to ceiling boxes and bags, baseball cards and soda cans. But now there was a tidy space, with a beautiful worn Persian carpet, a wingback chair and an easel. An easel with all her supplies from school. It looked like there were new things, too. Fresh canvases and brushes. Unsqueezed tubes of acrylic paint. And the work, *her work,* she'd brought home hastily in Georgie's trunk. It was all hanging on the walls.

"Oh . . ." escaped from her mouth as she turned around, looped her arms around his neck, and kissed him. He picked her up, kicked the door shut with his foot and brought her into the bedroom. Elly felt weightless, safe.

He lay her down on the bed, a mattress on the floor, but beautifully made with lots of fluffy pillows stuffed into clean crisp pillowcases decorated with tiny blue flowers. A white chenille bedspread cushioned her with its soft tufts of knotted fabric. It all smelled of lavender. They were the linens of the Amores. Scavenged no doubt from the trunks upstairs. *The trunks upstairs?* Elly's mind started to twist and turn . . . but then Anthony was kissing her again and easing her back against the soft fabric. The window was open, the afternoon breeze blowing in.

"Anthony, stop. Wait. We can't . . ."

"Why?" he murmured. "It's you Elly, it's always been you. You're my girl. You promised me."

All she'd ever known was Cooper's punishing love. His quick movements, his hand over her mouth. She closed her eyes and turned her head away from Anthony, in submission.

"No. Not like that," Anthony said, turning her face back toward him. He kissed her again, softly, nudging her mouth open. He placed small kisses down the side of her neck, by her ear. Elly felt her body open up to him. She didn't exactly know this feeling, but it was all over her. She was lost inside of his breath.

Anthony had calloused hands, but he moved them slowly, sitting her up, supporting her, lifting off her flowered sundress. He caressed her swollen belly.

"This baby is my baby," he said, and with those words won over any part of Elly that was still hesitant. She fell softly underneath him as they became one body. His head to his shoulders to his arms to her side. Her hips to her neck to his waist to the arch of her back.

"We were married you know, on the beach," he said after, tracing her face. Their naked bodies entwined, he was supporting himself on his elbow so he could stare at his prize.

"What?"

"Yep. When we were ten, we got married. Near the end of that summer. I took you back to Far Rockaway on the ferry," he laughed, remembering.

"Did we have rings?"

"No. But we had feathers."

"Feathers?"

"Yeah, we exchanged them instead of rings. It was Georgie's idea. We wrote vows and everything." He nuzzled her neck, "God, Elly, you smell just like you did when we were kids. Like a mermaid."

"What does a mermaid smell like?" she asked, closing her eyes and opening her mind to him.

"Like sunshine and the beach and roses and magic."

Elly closed her eyes and felt the breeze, Anthony's grown-up hands on her torso and his little boy hand on her shoulder.

"I promise by the sea and all that is good in the whole world to love you forever. No matter what and no backsies." It was a gray day that threatened rain. The ocean was wild and the sea spray christened the two children, sealing their marriage.

"I remember," said Elly. And in that moment she opened like a flower. Her body and heart fully opened to Anthony. Her mind opened to the strange ways of the Amores of the Bronx. Her senses opened to the building and to all her surroundings. Elly opened, for the first time, to her silent, aching hopes and dreams for the baby cradled in her womb.

They fell asleep that way. Cake and coffee forgotten and married in their minds. A soft coo and a giggle woke Elly up.

The windows were open and there were two pigeons on the sill. The building was old, and the sills, all the molding in the apartments, were oversized. The birds were grooming each other and cooing. Elly looked at Anthony, still asleep. Her body ached for him again. *Crazy,* she thought. All those years of feeling nothing, and now . . . everything was coming at her, the storm bringing up relics of her life onto the shores of 170th Street.

The smells of the city, good ones, were coming through the window over the birds carried on the air. Baking bread and cool rain on hot tar. The birds were looking straight at her. Elly got up and put her dress back on. She looked at the birds. Surely they'd fly away? Nope, they were still there. Elly put her hand over her mouth to stifle a delighted giggle. She tucked her hair behind her ears. It was just getting long enough for that now, and she walked slowly to the window with one hand outstretched. She got so close . . . her fingers reaching out. Would they let her touch them, and then . . .

✦

Babygirl was in the park with Uncle George and Aunt Itsy, Liz and Anthony. The birds were everywhere. They played a game. George would sprinkle the bread crumbs, gathering the birds in a huge flock, and then Liz, Babygirl, and Anthony ran at the birds yelling "One, two, three, you and me!!!!!!!!" A sacred cry that Itsy and George taught them from their own childhood. The birds would fly up all around them and for just a second, in the heart of the flock, Babygirl thought she could take flight, too. Soar above the rooftops of this amazing city that was her new home. Fly to the beaches of Far Rockaway and back again in seconds. The three spun together like separate arms of a pinwheel and then, when the birds were gone, they fell to the ground dizzy and laughing.

✦

Elly shook her hands in front of the birds and stifled another set of giggles as they flew away. She watched them, leaning on the sill, up, up, up they flew. *All the way back to the beaches,* thought Elly. *I should have woken Anthony to show him. He'll never believe me. They were so close!* A feather floated down from the sky on the breeze and in through the window past Elly's nose. It bounced around a bit before it started its descent. Elly ran to catch it, proof of her incredible moment with the birds. It fell behind a low bookcase. Elly nudged it aside.

"Gotcha," she whispered as she grabbed the feather that was stuck in the hinge of a small door. "What the . . ."

Elly pulled the door open and—

This was the *real* memory. Not the route Mimi'd taken her into the attic to look for maternity clothes. An alternate route. But why was it so important? What was still lurking there, just around the corner?

Elly went through the small door, like Alice into the beautiful garden at the bottom of the rabbit hole.

16

Itsy

At the cottage, Mama held us close on stormy nights. All us girls piled on her iron bed, making the feather mattress dip. Her thick, black braid pulled to one side. George tucked himself like a baby under one arm, Bunny—even though she was the oldest of us—on the other. Fee and Mimi nudged each other trying to get closer . . . but not me, I found space at the bottom of the bed, by their feet, so I could listen to her voice, like the ocean itself, like the storm outside. Her voice told us the stories that lived inside of them. She spoke of passion, of the summer when she was sixteen and met Papa on the beaches of Far Rockaway. Of a summer romance that showed her stability and love could walk hand in hand. That love wasn't really what she'd been taught by her own family. It wasn't supposed to be a Tasmanian devil of insecurity and obsession. "Life gets heavy," she told us, "like hot summer nights. At first you toss and turn, but slowly you learn that if you keep very, very still your body can capture a random breeze that latches onto you and cools you for a moment. Infinite and blissful, your body soars to greet it and holds onto it, but it leaves. And that's love. That's what love does."

She taught us well. Too well. Because that's how I knew I loved Henry. I recognized it right away and wasn't ignorant enough to deny it. And it ruined both of us—that love. And it killed our baby.

✦

On a hot day, sometime toward the end of the summer of 1944, I was sitting on the back concrete step of the cottage looking over the small square yard. So like the yard in the Bronx, only we called that "The Garden" and this, "The Yard." The difference being that "The Yard" was enclosed by lengths of picket fence where "The Garden" had high stone walls and iron gates. The pickets were wide and you could see fractions, strips of other people's lives. I liked it better that way. On 170th Street there was nothing but stone and mortar. Thick ivy. No peeking. I found it suffocating.

But really, they were the same patches of earth in so many ways. Mama planted the same things on both properties and all us kids learned how to garden just like her. The gardens were plotted identically. Planted by moonlight and using the stars to sort out what went north, south, east, and west. The plants themselves came from Fairview and the gardens of Mama's people—nowhere else. Witch's gardens. They came first to The Yard, and then, when Mama married they were split and brought to the Bronx.

The flowers, abundant and hearty: roses, lilac, wisteria, black-eyed Susans, azaleas, rhododendron, hydrangea, simple daisies, phlox, bluebell. And the herbs: echinacea, bee balm, yarrow, feverfew, chamomile, hellborn, foxglove, hemlock, valerian, lovage, lavender, thyme, lemon balm, sage. Oh, yes . . . and belladonna.

The vegetables took the most work each season because the seeds had to be removed and then dried and sealed. Tomatoes, peppers, peas, and beans. All grown generation after generation in Mama's family. Who knows where the seeds originated? It was a mystery. All we knew was that the garden was almost as important to Mama as we were, so we took it to heart and made sure the "Green" herbal ancestry stayed alive and viable year after year.

Mama's garden was magic; we all knew it and she taught us its secrets. We all knew that when Papa was mad he was sure to get her lavender scones. He'd settle down and then get silly. The next morning he'd be sick as a dog and need to sleep the whole day away.

And George with his rages, she made the tea that soothed him and brought down the beast. I made that tea for him every day until that last day. The day he pushed my hand away and said good-bye.

Sitting on the stoop looking out over The Yard, waiting for the sheets to dry on the line. That's where I was when I saw him through the fence. Henry. It was broad daylight but I didn't care. He looked like he'd come straight off the train to *me*. No one else. He was on furlough. Off till Christmas, he said.

I ran to him, the heavy, wet sheets smacking me in the face. He threw down his heavy army bag and lifted me up into the sky so that I blocked out the sun.

"You still my girl, Itsy?"

I couldn't talk. The tears were choking me. I nodded like a lunatic and cried. He brought me down slow so that our faces met and he kissed me through salty tears. In his kiss I was home. I found my real home. All throughout that fall of 1944 we were reunited, George, Henry, and me. I barely saw the rest of my family at all. I don't think I went into the Bronx once. Sometimes I wondered if Mama missed me, because I didn't hear from her. But I also knew Mama favored Bunny and George. We all knew it. Bunny because she looked like a Green. Not one bit of Italian at all. She had Mama's stormy eyes. "She sees the world the same way," Mama'd say. And George . . . well. He came from God. Sometimes I felt like Mama blamed me for being born first. For tricking her into thinking she was done . . . for ignoring the other pains. Sometimes I really thought I wasn't meant to be born at all.

I just know that's the reason why it was so easy for her to push me away when she found out about Henry. So easy for them all to push me away. All of them but George. My sweet, sweet brother.

Anyway, I was glad to be away from her that overlapping time of 1944. None of the real-life magic that occurred would have been possible under Mama's nose. But now, now that I'm thinking about it, she must have known all about it. It was probably part of the future read to her by Willow Bliss. Ah . . . things make so much sense when we look at them from far away, hindsight *is* a wonderful thing. So she knew. She knew all along. And she gave me that gift. Because no matter how it turned out, it was a gift. If I had to look at a life where I'd never known Henry. Never been touched by him. Never to run on the beaches with freedom and sea air blowing all around, holding hands in between George and Henry? I wouldn't want to live that life. I choose the pain. I *chose* the pain.

Henry had to ship out right after Christmas, so Christmas Eve we spent together, just the two of us in our little world. George was with Mama, of course.

I strung up paper lanterns I'd bought at Woolworths, and I made us a fine dinner. Roasted chicken, mashed potatoes, red wine. I used up all my rations for that one meal.

Sitting at the table, our favorite song came on the radio. "Dance with me?" he asked.

"Forever," I said. Henry was a wonderful dancer. He literally swept me off my feet. We danced while Bing crooned:

I'll be seeing you in all the old familiar places
That this heart of mine embraces all day through . . . .

I stared at him while he twirled me around and hummed along. I could never get enough of his face. The deep brown eyes, lighter than mine. The color of his skin, soft and supple, an invitation to touch like velvet on a bolt. The defined chin, his eyebrows, always arched and playful, guessing I was up to some sort of trick. But it was his mouth. From that first kiss against the Oak tree. From the way his mouth formed my name. Not my nickname. Not Itsy. The way it stretched and caressed out my *real* name. The name I was born with, the name my love called out that Christmas Eve as we conceived the child that would be born too soon.

"Let me see your palm," I asked as we lay naked side by side.

He smiled and held out his hand. The cool, smooth underside of his palm, the color of my skin after a long summer. "What are you looking for, baby? My love line belongs to you."

I was too busy staring at the truth I'd known my whole life. I pulled his hand and put it against my cheek. "Don't go back, Henry. Let's run away. Let's hide. One, two, three, you and me, right?"

He stroked my cheek. "You lookin' for a lifeline you can't find? You think I'm gonna die over there?"

I nodded.

"Well, I'm not. I'm not going to die over there, Itsy. I'm a good soldier."

And I smiled at him. I smiled because I didn't know what else to do. He *was* a good soldier . . . but he wouldn't die in battle. He'd die in his barracks. Friendly fire from a redneck racist. But my Henry was no coward. He wasn't going to run away from his duty to his country because of what I saw or didn't see in his palm. So I had to let him go. I had to make love to him and then let him walk away. He'd die overseas in a world of hate and genocide, far away from me and George. Far away from our beaches on Far Rockaway. In a place where I'd never be on one side and George on the other as we ran and yelled "One, two, three, you and me."

But he left me a gift. I placed my hands to my belly and knew. I knew she was in there. Her fate? Uncertain. But not defined. There was hope. Yes. For a little while I had hope.

17

Babygirl

She found the hiding place while playing sardines. It was a game Uncle George taught them. Well, he taught Babygirl and Anthony . . . Liz didn't like sardines, so she always went home when they wanted to play.

Babygirl was sure Anthony liked to play so he could place tiny kisses on her cheeks while they waited for George to find them. Uncle George was an old man but he sure knew some fun games. Sardines was a backward type of hide-and-seek. In sardines, one person hides and the rest have to find them. When you find the hider you stay in the hiding place and wait for the rest of the people to find you.

A game like sardines is scary, not so much for the hider but for the seekers. It's scary because you lose your companions and the whole world creeps up quiet and you slowly realize you're going to stumble upon a secret place where everyone will jump out at you. And then, when you are the very last seeker, you start to wonder if you're the only person in the world. If the hiding place somehow sucked up the players and the last one has to decide to run away or get sucked up, too.

And the hiders, it's kind of scary for them, too, because where they decide to hide needs to be very dark and they have to be very quiet. The world can disappear for them, too.

Babygirl was the best hider of all. Anthony always hid in obvious places and Uncle George was quite good at it but he was big. Bigger than his mind thought he ought to be, so parts of him always stuck out, making him easy to find.

The apartment building was a good place to play. It had hallways and closets and room after room. And then, by accident, while hiding under Uncle George's bed, Babygirl found the door. A small door, just her size.

She pulled it open by its little wooden knob, and there it was in front of her, a small incline and then another larger door. A clandestine entrance to the attic. The supersecret hiding place was behind that larger door. A little dormer made out of the rafters, big enough for a few child-sized people, or one grown-up person. Babygirl hid there when she was tired of the game, because no one ever found her. She'd hide there until she could sense the others had quit out of frustration and moved onto other things.

One day as she climbed out of her supersecret spot, Babygirl noticed a shaft of light illuminating one of the many steamer trunks that lined the back of the attic under the eaves. She went to it and tried lifting the top, but it was locked.

Ready for a treasure, she raced down the stairs to Aunty Fee and Itsy's apartment. Tiptoeing by Fee who was cooking in the kitchen, she could have stomped but she didn't (being extra quiet was making the sudden secret even *more* fun).

She went into Itsy's bedroom and took a hairpin off the porcelain jewelry tray on the bureau. She crept back past Fee and ran back up the stairs to the attic. She closed the door behind her. The sun was brighter and thicker now, the trunk practically glowed and throbbed in the light.

She placed the pin in the lock, felt for the catch and turned . . . click, it released. A trunk full of linens. The air that came out was at first stale, then lovely . . . earth and lavender. The smell of a well-tended garden in the springtime. Babygirl lifted the heavy sheet on top. As her hands touched the solid, cool cotton she felt a memory come. Babygirl knew this feeling. It was that dizzy wonderful feeling when she was going to see a story that didn't belong to her. Only this story wasn't a nice one. It was awful.

She saw a beautiful young woman cradling a small swollen belly with one hand as the other hand gathered the skirts between her legs. She was making her way through the halls of 170th Street, stopping to switch hands and leaving red, five-finger stars on the white walls.

✦

Itsy, who was in the garden, looked up into the cloudless summer sky. Her jaw opened as if God himself held the crowbar. A horrible sound began to come out, a groaning rasp. And then, it was gone. Someone had found her secret . . . and what? Closed it up again? How odd. Or maybe it was an old woman's head playing tricks on her in the hot sun.

✦

Babygirl shook her head clear of the disturbing scene. And went in for a deeper look, but then, Anthony was at the other doorway of the attic.

"Found you!" he said, and then ran away saying, "Betcha can't catch me."

Babygirl let the heavy trunk slam shut and dropped the hairpin onto the floor to run, squealing with delight, outside. Treasure forgotten.

18

Elly

"It must be that apartment. I swear, Mimi, I can't get her to leave it," said Anthony, eating an apple and leaning against the counter as Mimi cooked.

"There's nothing wrong with the apartment. Don't be foolish. She's finding herself. Piecing it all together. It's a good thing."

"But should I bother her? Or leave her alone?"

Mimi stopped stirring her pot and turned to face Anthony. "Do you love her?" she asked him.

"Always have," he said.

"Then why in the world would you leave her alone?" She turned back to the stove and stirred furiously, splashing bright red sauce over most of the stove. "I mean, what kind of a crazy person with mush for brains would look into the eyes of love and ignore it? Who could do such a thing? If you love her you must go to her, you must . . . ."

Anthony left Mimi there making a mess. It was obvious to him that she was in some other world entirely. He had the advice he needed, anyway.

He banged on the door of 2B. "Coming!" Elly yelled.

She was covered in all sorts of paint. Her hair, pulled back under a red bandana, had paint in it, too.

"I thought you'd never come!" she said, dragging him into the apartment. "Come see!"

"I thought you didn't want me."

"I've always wanted you. Remember? Don't be silly. Look. Look at what I've done! No one's seen. Well, Liz. Lizzy's been here almost every day! Such a love, really. Some of it was hard to remember, but some of it is wonderful! Oh Anthony . . . she loved me. Carmen. She really loved me. No wonder she was always so upset I didn't remember these things. They're fantastic."

Anthony looked at the woman he loved. In overalls stretched tight over her growing belly. Her eyes on fire, and then, he looked at the pictures hanging on the walls. They were hung in succession, beginning at what must have been Elly's earliest memories. She was so excited to show him she was practically jumping up and down behind him as he took a tour through her dreamlike childhood. All painted in Elly's style, bold colors and heavy sunset skies. Carmen depicted as a goddess with silver glitter instead of paint for her eyes.

"The paintings end where my memory of her ends. When the aunts and Mimi picked me up at the hospital in Fairview. Then snippets of other things from the time being here. So I have almost everything up until the end of that summer. Those are the memories I need back."

"You'll get them," he said.

"And there's something else. A secret," she said. "Want to see?" A childlike excitement washed over both of them. Elly took him by the hand and led him into the bedroom where they'd first made love. Now the nursery. Anthony looked around the room with wonder. A mural. The roots of a willow tree grew from the base boards as the trunk moved up the sturdy wall and the weeping branches seemed to fall down all over the room.

"It's amazing, Elly. I can't believe you did all this."

"Look up!"

The sky (ceiling) went from a night sky, deep blue with golden stars through a pink and orange sunrise all the way to the light blue sky of a perfect September day. Clouds and all.

"How did you do that?"

"On a ladder! I'm a fresco restorer, remember? I'm a trained professional."

"You could have fallen, I can't believe you didn't ask me to help."

"I can't believe you didn't just barge on in. This is something you are going to have to get used to about me, Mister Anthony Rivetta. You are going to need to realize that when I'm working, I'm consumed. Time stands still."

"Well, now I know . . . and this," he motioned around the sunny room with his arms, "is just fantastic."

"Well . . . thank you. *But* that isn't what I wanted to show you. Look at *this*."

Elly pushed aside the small bookcase and opened the little door. She led him up into the attic and showed him her secret hiding place.

"So this is where you used to hide when we couldn't find you? Excellent spot, Elly!"

"But there's more. It's about a treasure. Something of value is hidden up here. I know it. I just can't remember what it is." Elly squinted her eyes as if trying to force the memory. "I only know I have to find it."

Anthony looked around at the attic full of trunks, sewing forms, mobiles made of seashells from Far Rockaway clinking from the rafters. A corner with a large, old-fashioned bed that the older Amore boys used to sleep in when they were small.

"Something in a trunk maybe?" he suggested.

"Maybe—but Mimi and I looked through practically all of them to find maternity clothes. I just have to figure it out. I've remembered so much. I hate any dark corners," Elly reached down and picked up a large, leather-bound book at her feet. "And look at this. I've been reading it up here in the mornings. I'm afraid to bring it downstairs because it's so old, and it's used to the air up here. It was Margaret's."

Elly opened the pages of the large book to reveal large pictures of plants and flowers, some real ones even pressed between the pages. And there were pretty, cursive words scrawled in the margins.

"It's like a botanical book of shadows!" said Elly.

"It's incredible!" said Anthony taking a closer look.

"And at the back, just look," said Elly carefully turning the book to its back pages. "Recipes. All the ones Mimi and the aunts keep showing me. They know them by heart. But it's this one that I think is the most interesting . . . See here? "The Forgetting spell."

"Forgetting? Like . . . Oh yeah, with Cooper?"

"Yes. And me, too . . . maybe."

"You think they cast a spell on you?"

"That's what I'm trying to find out."

"You'll do it," he said.

"Maybe you can help. Tell me what you know, Anthony. Tell me what you know about The Day the Amores Died."

"Well, I only know what most people know. But maybe that's a little more than you. How about I tell you what I know while I show you what I love. You have to get *out* of this apartment!"

"Yes . . . I think you're right. The crying is worse up here, anyway."

"You still hear that crying?"

"Yes. First crying, then laughing, now crying again. It moves when I move. I have this crazy feeling like it wants me to chase it. Like when we used to play hide-and-seek or sardines. It's driving me a little nuts."

"Well, we can't have *that*! You're the only sane one around here. Let's get outta Dodge and into the day, okay? I'll take you on the ferry to Far Rockaway."

✦

It wasn't the first time they'd been on an adventure in the Bronx. From the first week she arrived, every Saturday morning—before Elly became consumed with her new apartment and heavenly art supplies—Anthony would come right into Mimi's apartment and call her. "Come on, E! Time for a walk, let's get that baby moving around!"

They walked all over the city, down by the river, and he showed her the secrets of her new home. The delicious smells and foodstuffs of Arthur Avenue. The butchers, bakeries, and dressmakers. The artists who lived in renovated factories and had studios and shows. The fishing community and the fresh lobsters sold right off the docks. The historic downtown that offered trolley rides to and from most anywhere.

But they hadn't visited Far Rockaway yet.

"How did my mother steal all this from me?" she asked him as they rode the ferry.

Anthony leaned against the rail. His black hair shining in the sun, his muscular frame. The back of his neck made her a little weak in the knees. *How I love him,* she thought.

"She didn't like it here. You can't make a person have an opinion. Likes and dislikes are subjective. It's a matter of aesthetics, you should know that, Miss Artist!" he said.

And then he kissed her. Elly was aware of her belly pushing against him, the belly that was making her more and more uncomfortable. Out here, away from her art, she felt unlovely and insecure.

"Why do you love me, Anthony?" she asked, holding her breath as she waited for the answer.

"Well, it is *my* opinion that you are the most beautiful thing I've ever seen. You're smart, you're exciting, and we were put here, right here on this earth to be together." He paused, kissed her again, and then said, "You know I've always loved you. Since we were little. Your misfortune seems to be my gain."

"How do I know you don't have some sort of hero complex?" she asked quickly. She'd been afraid to ask it for months. It had occurred to Elly all Anthony did was take care of people. His mother. Elly's own aunts, and Mimi, too.

Anthony looked down at the water for a moment and then back at Elly. He looked deep into her green eyes. "I see how you could think that—but look at this." Anthony took his black wallet out of his back pocket. He pulled out a folded piece of notebook paper. "Do you remember this? You wrote this to me when you were thirteen. I never forgot it, and I'm going to hold you to it."

She blushed. *"Dear Anthony, if we are not married by the time we are eighteen, you have to give me your sworn pledge that you will marry me."*

"I didn't even remember you then! Wow. I was bossy!"

"You were adorable."

And then he did the unexpected and rightest thing in the world. In the middle of the ferry ride he got down on one knee and looked up at Elly. He took out a black velvet box and opened it, revealing a stunning ruby ring in a simple princess set.

Just as she was about to cry and take the ring and scream, "*yes!*" into the universe, he snapped the box shut and put it back into the pocket of his heavy black leather jacket. Elly felt a different kind of tears prickle behind her eyes.

Anthony placed both hands on her stomach and pressed his ear there, too. "I'm sorry little one, I forgot to consult you first. Kick once if you give me permission to ask your mama to marry me."

He waited.

Elly waited.

"Oh for God's sake, Anthony! It's a nice gesture and everything but just ask me! *I* give you permission."

Anthony laughed and took the box out once again. "You *are* bossy!" He stood up and took the ring out of the box and slipped it onto her finger. A perfect fit, of course. "Will you?"

She took his face into her hands. "Forever and ever."

They kissed until the ferryman told them they'd arrived at the very destination where they'd married each other years ago.

As they made their way off the dock, Elly's excitement turned to disconcertment. This wasn't the Far Rockaway she remembered.

"Mimi told me it was gone—but I don't think my heart believed her."

"I know, it's really a cryin' shame. But the cottage is still there and the beaches, too. Let's walk while I tell you what I know."

As they strolled through empty parking lots and littered patches of green grass making their way to the cottage, Anthony told his version of the story.

"Well, the war was officially over in Europe, so I think your great-grandmother, the one who wasn't Italian?" Elly nodded. "Right, well, I think she thought she'd avoided the whole mess. But actually, it all happened on the very day the army people came to the door and told her the news. I don't know how everything happened from that moment on, but by the end of the day the parents, Margaret and Vincent, and the oldest daughter, Bunny, along with her own child Zelda Grace were all dead."

"I can't even imagine how horrible it must have been. Were Mimi, Itsy, and Fee all there when it happened?"

"I think Mimi was. I don't know about Fee. Itsy wasn't. Neither was George. I think they came to the building later on that day. Anyway, there's more. See, Vincent—your great-grandfather, he didn't believe in any sorts of magical ways. It was hard on them . . . hard on their love. A lot of stories come out of the walls of the buildings in the Bronx. So many people living so close together back then, it was hard to keep secrets. So, it was common knowledge that though they were in love, Margaret and Vincent had their problems. She was made of all things magic and chaotic, and he was made of straight lines and numbers. There are rumors that it was him, his plain ways, that blocked Margaret's abilities to save them all from that tragic day."

"People have so much influence over each other, don't they?" said Elly.

"Yeah, I guess, especially when it's all clouded with love."

"I wonder why she married him? I mean, they were so different."

Anthony simply winked at her. And in that instant she understood. Stability and constancy. It was part of the reason she was so in love with Anthony. But at least he understood the magic. Elly thought it would be maddening to be married to someone who couldn't see past the nose on his face.

Elly and Anthony were standing at the corner of a long, narrow street lined with broken-down beach cottages. Relics from another era.

"I know where to go," said Elly as if in a dream. She let go of his hand and walked down the middle of the deserted street. There was silence in the spring wind. The only sound was the soft "clink" coming from a sea glass mobile on the front porch. She walked up the creaking steps with Anthony behind and poked the mobile with her hands.

"We made this," she said.

"Yes. We did." Elly heard a hitch in his voice so she turned around. He was crying and trying to hide it. Craning his neck away from her.

"What's the matter?"

"You're back. You're really back."

Elly reached for him and held him tight. It occurred to her for the first time how lonesome it must have been. Waiting for her to come back. Waiting for her to remember. Always the one left waiting. "Let's go find out everything I need to know so we can start out this life without anything hidden, okay?" she whispered into his thick hair.

"You bet," he said roughly, regaining his composure.

Elly went to the door. "Crap! Anthony, we don't have the key."

Anthony went into his pocket and then dangled Georgie's rabbit foot key chain out in front of her again, like he'd done her second morning in the Bronx. "Got 'em!"

They opened the door and walked into the cottage. Margaret Green's summer home. The house on Far Rockaway that had once been filled with laughter and children dripping with magic summer honey sun.

It was perfect. Tidy. Not a thing out of place.

"She's been here," said Elly. "It's Itsy's cottage, isn't it? I can tell. It's hers and she's been here."

"Well, it's clear someone has."

"There's something sweet in that. But why do you think the old ladies haven't sold this cottage, Anthony?"

"Well, let me finish telling you what I know about your family. Rumor has it that Itsy had herself a man. And not just any man. A black kid. His name was Henry and he'd been George's best friend since they were kids. Both outcasts and all. So maybe she keeps it because she can't give it away?"

"Itsy in love. I can see it." Elly moved around the cottage touching things, absorbing their stories. "She lost much more than just her family that day, didn't she, Anthony? She lost her independence, her voice, her identity . . ."

Anthony nodded. "I know when we were kids and came back here, right after you got to the Bronx, Itsy and George were different."

"How so?"

"Well, when I was growing up they were just . . . well, old. But when we came back *here?* It was like they'd had a pint from the fountain of youth. The old ladies made magic again and George was playing with us—and soon I didn't even realize he was old anymore. And Itsy? Well, put it this way . . . she was running down the beach turning—"

"Cartwheels," whispered Elly.

19

Itsy

Mama always went a little crazy near summer solstice. It was to be expected. It's the most magical time of the year for us witches. The garden received her full attention and us, too. She'd make new summer dresses for all of us, and crisp white shirts for the boys. She'd make soda crackers to put in tins before the days got too hot to bake. She'd prune and plant and water. Cajoling, almost daring her garden to bloom louder than ever before.

She was a tidy woman, most times. But she had priorities, and cleaning was low on the list during the times when she felt her hands were full with other things. Piles of cotton and ribbon and spools of thread would pile up in the kitchen and living room. Mountains of flour covered the counters, muddy footprints to and from the back hallway marking her constant route.

Papa, though he knew she would be her old self soon, never seemed to have much patience for it. He'd yell and try to clean up after her. She'd yell back, telling him to leave her piles alone.

It was during this time of year that she told us the story of the "Mound Builders." I think she told us so that she could discount Papa's words without discounting Papa.

"The Mound Builders were people who lived here long before the earliest colonists arrived. They dug deep into the earth and created mounds to bury their dead. For them, the mounds were treasured. A way to remember, to memorialize. There isn't anything wrong with building piles to remind us of things."

But some years were worse than others. She'd whisper with Bunny and the boys would try to clean up after her as well. She'd swat at them with her dish towels and shoo them away.

✦

The year Mama took us on a day trip to Fairview was a year when their fighting was particularly bad. We took the train from Penn Station. The older boys stayed home, of course. Georgie and I were eleven or so, still able to be mesmerized by the station and the swarms of people and the elaborate red velvet seats.

Mama was quiet. We behaved. We knew there was something amiss. We got off the train in Boston and onto a smaller, fancier train. I felt like I was going deeper and deeper into a storybook the more miles we traveled. The stop in Fairview was in front of what looked like a fancy fortress. I thought it looked very romantic and wanted to explore it right away. Bunny whispered to Mimi that it was a lunatic asylum. Georgie heard it and pulled on Mama's skirt.

"What is it, love?" she asked, with an uncanny distance in her voice.

"Why are we at a lunatic asylum, Mama?"

Mama shot Bunny a look that could have been a poisoned dart.

"What? I'm sorry," she said.

We walked around the building and entered the center of a

bustling, pretty town. Mama guided us to a bench under a large willow tree.

"Listen close, my ducklings. Mama needs to go visit with your grandmother. One who you don't know. And she's ill. So you can't come with me. But Bunny's been here before, so she'll take good care of you. There are lots of fun things to do. *And* there's an ice-cream shop, and . . ."

"I have it under control, Mama. You go," said Bunny.

"Okay," said Mama, "But don't take them near the water. Promise me? No matter how hot it gets. They can jump in the fountain over here, just not the sea." Mama pointed at the fountain in the center of the town square.

"I promise, Mama," said Bunny.

"Swear a solemn vow," said Mama.

"I swear a solemn vow," said Bunny.

Mama kissed her cheek and disappeared into a crowd of people.

My sister was getting awfully grown up all of a sudden. I'd always known Bunny took after Mama more than the rest of us, but it was never so obvious.

The people in the town all looked the same, sort of. They all looked like Bunny and Mama. Lighter. Freckles. Light eyes. Yes, their appearance was similar. But it was other things as well. Posture and smiles and gait. They seemed to share an internal rhythm. Mimi, Fee, George, and me? It was as if we slunk behind like dark clouds in a sunny sky. I could tell we looked out of place, and Bunny knew.

"Oh Itsy! You're so sensitive. Get over it. Hey, do you guys want to see the house where Mama grew up?"

"Yes, yes!" we cried.

Bunny led us through winding backstreets down toward the beaches. There were beautiful houses lined up with massive trees in front. The cobblestone streets ached with history.

"There it is!" said Bunny and I almost lost my bloomers.

Mama's house. It was the largest house I'd ever seen, and certainly the fanciest. I'd learn later that it was a Victorian House. My eleven-year-old eyes only saw gingerbread and dolls. Lots of dolls.

"Does she still own it?" asked Fee.

"No, greedy," said Bunny. "But there's a private beach on the side. Do you want to see? I remember it looked like a mermaid cove."

"Mama said not to go near the water, Bunny," said Mimi, but Bunny was already running toward a small beach on the side of Mama's old house.

When we rounded the corner, I knew exactly what Bunny was saying about mermaids. There was a bit of beach, yes, but mostly rocks. Huge rocks creating a smaller pool of ocean. Natural walls and small openings made it seem as if the lost city of Atlantis was found, and Bunny—perched high atop a rock mountain—was its queen.

"Get down!" Mimi yelled from the beach. But beautiful Bunny just stared out at the ocean. I started to get scared. "She swore a solemn vow," I whispered.

George began to cry. *"You swore a solemn vow, Bunny!"* he yelled and his voice ricocheted off the rocks.

Bunny heard him. She shook her head and tapped at her ears as if someone or something was trying to convince her to dive in. To become a mermaid herself.

But, she quietly climbed down to join us and we walked

slowly back into town. I slipped my hand inside of hers. "I'm glad you didn't become a mermaid, Bunny."

Bunny stopped to pick me up and held me tight, "You are lovely, Itsy!" she said swinging me around.

"Who wants ice cream?" she asked.

George cried, "Me! Me!" And we raced through Mama's town with the wind at our backs and our feet knowing the way.

We waited for Mama, happy and sticky, eating dripping ice cream cones on the bench.

"Are you all ready for the journey back? Everyone fed? Anyone need to use the washroom?"

She rushed us onto a waiting train.

"Did you get what you came for, Mama?" asked Bunny.

"Yes I did, thank you," smiled Mama.

"What did you need?" asked George.

"I needed to be reminded."

"Reminded of what?" George persisted.

"I needed to be reminded of something so all the crooked angles in my mind could go straight again."

"What did she remind you about?"

"She reminded me about the sun and moon and sky. You see, Papa is the sun in my sky. And you are all my twinkling stars. The stars, they never go out. They twinkle brightly all the time. In the day, the ocean catches them and they dance under the surface. But the sun? It moves around—the clouds block its light. It's gone during the night. And the world gets so cold without its shine. I shiver. The shiver is the reason why I came back home."

"If Papa is your sun, and we are your stars, who is your moon, Mama?" asked George.

Mama didn't answer, she simply placed her hands on the window of the train car and looked back toward Fairview.

✦

I think about that trip often. I wonder about Mama's history. As much as we lost touch with the Amores, we never even had a grasp of the Green clan. And it rises, like the tide within us. Mama's magic ways. The strange and wonderful things we are capable of that we never even questioned. We all took to them naturally and believed in them like we took to, and believed in the wide, blue sky.

But Elly? She bubbles with a mighty dose of Mama. Even if she can't feel it or doesn't yet know what it means. And if I don't protect her, all that potential will be gone. Because as the days go by, her fate looms large. It casts shadows on everything I do.

20

Elly

They were quiet on their way back. The water and memories making both Elly and Anthony contemplative. Elly looked down at the water and then into the sky. She thought of Walt Whitman's "Crossing Brooklyn Ferry":

> *What is it then between us?*
>
> *What is the count of the scores or hundreds of years between us?*
>
> *Whatever it is, it avails not—distance avails not, and place avails not.*

"Oh, Itsy," Elly whispered. "You are so curious to me . . ."

"As you are to me," said Anthony jolting her out of her reverie.

"Oh yeah? What's so curious about me?" asked Elly.

Anthony turned around, placing his back against the railing. "What do you remember, now? How much?"

"I told you."

"Nope. You didn't."

"I showed you the paintings. And you know how much I remember about you."

"Fair enough—but can't you *tell* me?"

"What do you want me to say?"

"Tell me about your childhood. Before I met you. I want to know everything. I wish I could cut and paste myself right there with you, but I don't even know where to start." He pushed back a stray wave from her face and traced the side of her cheekbone with his finger.

"It was wonderful, and then it wasn't. But I can't really remember the bad parts. I can feel them, but I can't access them. It's like there's this curtain draped all around but I can see the actors' feet on the stage, you know?"

"Well then, tell me about the good. Tell me the wonderful parts."

"Well, it wasn't anything I'd like to replicate for this little bambina." Elly turned around to lean her back against the rails as well and cradled her belly with both hands. "But it was extraordinary, for sure."

"Tell me, Elly. Take me back there with you."

Elly turned to look at him, this man she was destined for, this man who she'd just pledged herself to for life. If there was anyone she could share this with, it was him. "She taught me how to dance," began Elly, "in this cottage she rented. A real English cottage. Roses climbed up the walls and everything. It was like a storybook. She played her favorite albums on a record player. Joni Mitchell. Mostly big band mixed in with a lot of sixties stuff. Her favorite was Procol Harem. She said she liked the tempo. Very dramatic and all that."

Anthony smiled, "Yep, sounds like Carmen. Tell me more."

"We'd go into town to some pub where they played jazz, and she'd sit around with the locals, mesmerizing them. She'd smoke and then they'd ask her to sing. She was famous there. I remember being so proud. I fell asleep in the booths and she'd pick me up and walk me all the way home. We'd snuggle in her bed and talk together for hours."

"Wow, I never figured Carmen to be the mothering type."

"See, that's just it. She wasn't. Not in my memories *after.* All the stuff I've remembered my whole life draws this cold, bitter picture. But in these new memories? In these she's amazing." Elly grew quiet.

"What is it?" asked Anthony.

"These new memories make me wonder if I could ever be as good to this baby as she was to me, initially speaking that is."

"That's some crazy powerful stuff," said Anthony.

"I know. But it's like she threw her whole self into the role of motherhood. She got it all right. It was the role of a lifetime. The best performance of her career. Right down to the cottage and the kitchen and the meals . . . until the drugs."

"Whoa! You aren't going to tell me Carmen cooked!"

"Yes! Wonderful meals. She had this big book. Compiled recipes from *The New York Times.* We had roasted chicken and homemade sweet potato gnocchi. She even made these amazing, elaborate breakfasts. I can still smell the brioche."

"Unbelievable," said Anthony.

"Tell me about it, I can't remember her cooking one meal later on. *Not one.*" Elly sighed. "But you want to know the most extraordinary thing?"

"Yes," he said pulling her to him, holding her as the ferry docked.

"All of that doesn't mean a damn thing. The best part of these memories is the absolute certainty that she loved me. I felt grounded in it. Like nothing bad could ever happen. She was everything to me." Elly pulled away, wiping the tears that stung her cheeks. "I feel her—not Carmen, that little girl. The one that was me. I feel her rising like a tide. She's coming back. She's slamming me with the fury of a thousand storms. She's so pissed off at me, Anthony. She'd like to wring my neck!"

"Why do you say that, babe? She's still you and you're still her. It's just a matter of jiving all the memories together. Finding the place where they meet, you know."

"Yes, that's it *exactly*. I have to find the exact moment when I pushed that little girl deep inside a trunk and locked her up. I have to find out how and why it happened so that I can add it all up. I already know the when."

"When? When you were here?"

"Yes. This is what I've been able to figure out. Not so much remember—because I don't remember it. But I've pieced it together. I was about to leave. Itsy found me. She clearly tells me something, something I can't remember, and something she obviously won't disclose. And then I'm out on the front stoop of the building surrounded by strangers."

"You know, I've wondered about that since the night when we were teenagers and you told me about all this forgetting business. What was that like? Having to go away from this place with no memory at all?"

"That's the thing. I didn't feel anything because there was nothing to feel. Carmen said she picked up a 'blank slate' that day. She calls it a *tabula rasa* for flash . . . but a blank slate is a blank slate. I started adding on layers of myself as they were given to me. The problem was, Carmen didn't have much to give me at all. As soon as she realized I wasn't fooling around, she never tried to retell me the story of my childhood. She just got mad, and stayed mad."

"But that seems weird. If the memories are as wonderful as you think they are, why wouldn't she tell you?"

"That's just it, everything hinges on the details I still can't remember. There has to be something, something *big* that I'm not remembering yet. And maybe when I put all this together some of it will make sense."

"Well, for the record I don't care if you remember or not. I'm happy with things just as they are."

Elly looked at him again. He seemed nervous. "Are you worried I'll remember myself right out of being in love with you?"

Anthony shrugged his shoulders.

"Well, that's not how it works," she said leaning forward and moving her lips against his cheek. "The more I let that little girl surface, the more she lets me love you. You see—she loved you first." Elly's mouth made its way to cover his.

He put his hands into her hair and opened his mouth to hers in the kind of kiss that Elly thought only lived inside of movies and romance novels.

As they got off the ferry Anthony pulled her aside once more.

"Do you ever think about him?"

"About who?"

"About Cooper?"

Just the name itself made Elly want to throw up. "Not if I can help it."

"So you didn't love him?" He searched Elly's eyes in desperation.

"No, I never loved him."

"But you *made love* to him?"

Elly could see Anthony was struggling. That he didn't want to pry but needed this information for his pride. For his sanity, even.

"Anthony. I'm going to say this once, but I don't want to talk about it again, okay?" Anthony nodded.

"The person I was, even a few months ago, was not a person I want to remember being. I was so damaged that I didn't know the difference between what I wanted and what Carmen—or anyone else for that matter—wanted for me. Carmen and I were at a show my freshman year at the Yale Repertory Theatre. Cooper's father recognized her from a production he'd seen in France. He approached her during intermission. Cooper was with him. I won't lie. He was amazing looking and he was also rich. When we left that night, Cooper asked for my phone number and Carmen gave it to him. She encouraged me to date him, so I did. I'd do anything to please her. Anything. She wanted me to be with him, so I did. But you want to know something?"

"What?" Anthony asked, relieved.

"The only thing that stopped me from falling completely under his control. The only thing that even warned me it wasn't a normal kind of relationship, was the time I spent with you. Those few moments we shared when we were just thirteen years old taught me more about myself, about what I wanted, than anything up until that point. It separated me from Carmen."

"How?"

"Because she didn't like you. And she didn't like it here. But I did. And that independence gave me a strength I didn't know I had."

"And now you're back," he said.

"Yes, now I'm back. And I'm not going anywhere."

"Elly?" asked Anthony as he led her to the taxi stand.

"Yes?"

"I've been waiting to hear you say those words for my entire life."

Elly laughed. "Well, thank God you're patient!"

"One of us has to be," he said and gave her hand a squeeze as he made a move to hail a taxi.

Pull him back from the curb . . . a voice—her voice—hollered through her mind. Instinctively she yanked him back just as a car swerved too close to the curb.

"Slow down, ya jerk!" he yelled. And then to Elly, "You knew?"

She nodded her head.

"So you have their magic?"

"I suppose. Does it bother you?"

"Not even a little," he said.

"Well, there's something that's bothering me," said Elly.

"What?"

"I've got some of their magic. It's amazing really. I can see things, and there's this glow around people I never noticed before. But the thing is . . . I've been able to get these glimpses, you know? Of the past and future. I can feel things. Almost like my senses are heightened. It's like I'm painting—only all the time . . ."

"That doesn't sound bad. What's the problem?"

"When I try to see the baby I can't. I can't see the baby, Anthony. Not even a little bit of her. When I touch my stomach all there is, is black."

"Have you told Mimi, or the aunts?"

"No."

"Why not?"

Elly began to shake. "I'm afraid they'll see the blackness, too."

Anthony put his arm around her shoulder and led her to a waiting taxicab.

21

Itsy

Mama took good care of us. Our bodies and souls, too. We were rarely sick. I can only remember being sick once, but that memory stays with me and fills my heart with a longing that only grows stronger as I grow older.

Mama never tried to force away our fevers. She said "The fever is your body fighting like mad trying to get rid of the illness, love." Instead, she'd lay us in her bed on white linens and wipe us down with rubbing alcohol infused with rosewater and lavender.

My turn under Mama's diligent care came when I was ten. We were getting ready to leave for Far Rockaway. I was in the garden taking clothes off the line when the warm June breeze turned suddenly cold against my clammy skin.

Papa carried me into their bedroom. I watched their projected shadows against the wall as they argued. My head was so heavy, I couldn't turn it around. I wanted to say "Don't fight . . ." but when my parents argued there was no turning back. They loved so fiercely.

"You need to go, Margaret!" said Papa. "I'll call my aunts and they can take care of her."

Papa was restless to be rid of us. He looked forward to the calm days when he had the building to himself.

"I would never leave one of my children, Vincent! It's as if you don't know me at all! And those women? Those stregas? I'd sooner leave Itsy with a pack of wild geese!"

Mama was always uncomfortable mixing Green magic with the Italian witchcraft. Though she struck a fine balance, it was new for her even while we were growing up. And pragmatic Papa never believed in the magic anyway, so he was always correcting her.

"It's a flock of geese, Margaret. A pack of wolves and a flock of geese."

"See! See how you are? Just assuming I've made a mistake? Maybe that's exactly what I meant to say. Those women are like a gaggle of wolves. A pack of geese. All nervous and ferocious—and silly at the same time!"

"That's not fair, Margaret. They love these girls as much as you do. And their ways aren't so different from yours. It's not their fault you dominate our children's minds! They can't see past you. It's not good, that fierce loyalty. You need to cut some of these apron strings you hold so tightly to."

It wasn't that Mama didn't get along with Papa's family; it was the other way around, actually. No matter how long they were married or how many of his children Mama bore, she was forever referred to as MargaretGreen. One word. They'd come to visit us, run their gloved fingers over the tops of picture frames inspecting for dust, and then they'd say, "Well, hello MargaretGreen, my how pretty you always look!" They were masters at the backhanded compliment.

Mama didn't keep us away from them, but she didn't encourage us to have relationships with them either. So in a way, I suppose Papa was right. And it was true. Most of the women on Papa's side of the family were midwives, so they understood a bit of herbal healing.

I wonder whatever happened to them all, all those other Amores. After the funerals we never saw them again. Or maybe we did and I simply don't remember. There were some lost years, lost in a fog. Like being inside of a fever.

I must have fallen asleep as they argued, because when I woke up it was evening already. Mama's dim bedside lamp bathed the room in golden lowlight. She was humming and rubbing me down with her magic water. "I see the moon and the moon sees me . . ." she sang. I tried to sing with her "and the moon sees someone—"

"Hush, my Itsy. Let me get the fever down."

Tears burned my eyes and my head began to throb. My throat was sore. "We can't go to the cottage tomorrow because of me, Mama?"

"Oh Itsy!" Mama climbed on the bed next to me and fit my body into hers like a puzzle piece. My head rested on her chest and she looped her fingers over my forehead and into my hair and back again. "Bunny is old enough to open the cottage now, and she's excited to do it, too. She's in a hurry to be a lady and wear her hair up. I'll stay here until you are well and then we'll take the train together. Footloose and fancy free. And you want to know the best part?"

"What?" I whispered through a closed throat.

"When we get there it'll all be done and we can relax, won't that be nice?"

I nodded and fell asleep again. I was sick for days. In and out of a dreamlike state.

Mama must have been worried, because I think the Amore women were summoned. I recall a thick paste layered on my chest that didn't smell like Mama's cures. Mama's cures always had an earthy smell. This one was sour and hot.

Mama sat on the end of the bed and held sparkling jewelry up to the light, trying to tempt me to sit up and grab for it, as if I were still a baby. She sat me up and brushed my hair. One hundred strokes. All of this melted together in my mind. Mama trying to feed me oranges. Making me suck on ice. Laying close to me and feeling the bottoms of my feet, making sure the fever didn't grow out of control.

The fever broke in the late afternoon, light filtered through the windows, thick like honey. I started coughing and Mama rushed in saying, "Cough it out, that's right, the germ wants to come out now, Itsy, you can do it, cough it out . . . ." And I did. The glob that came out in my mother's handkerchief was a dark gray and looked unearthly. As soon as it was out, I felt immediate relief.

"My! What a week this has been. You frightened me, my Itsy!"

"I'm sorry, Mama," I said.

"Sorry for what? Getting sick. Psh. Don't be silly. Come, let me bathe you."

I remember the apartment feeling unfamiliar. My eyes and legs were wobbly.

"Tell me what you saw in your fever dreams, Itsy," said Mama as I sat in the bath.

"I don't know. You mostly."

"Me? Well, that's a special gift."

"Why?"

"What we see in our feverdream is what our heart desires most."

"Really?"

"Yes."

"I do love you, Mama," I said, trying to stay a big girl, trying not to let her know that she was absolutely right, that she was my heart's desire.

Mama wrapped me in a fluffy white towel and picked me up like a baby.

"And I love you, my Itsy. I love you so, so much."

When we got to the cottage Mama started up the front steps but I held back. I let her hand slip out of mine as my siblings flooded the porch and swarmed around her. George locked his arms around her middle and hugged her, moving as she moved. Bunny looked annoyed and was going on and on about how much work she did and how nobody was helping her and how there *was so much more* to do. Mimi and Fee were telling her about the hundreds of June strawberries that they'd just picked from the garden. They were holding up their red stained hands.

I knew my moment with Mama was lost. Everyone else was taking over. But then—then she turned and caught my eye, smiled and winked. A warmth, better than the summer sun, seeped into my bloodstream. She wasn't forgetting me.

"Itsy!" yelled Bunny. "Stop daydreaming and take George to the beach. He's terribly in the way and I need Mama to help me. How can she help me with him wrapped around her like a sea star?"

"No, Bunny," said Mama, "why don't *you* take George down to the beach and relax. Sit on the sand, watch the waves. Itsy can help me, can't you, Itsy?"

"But, but . . . what about dinner, Mama? I figured *I'd* finish cleaning up with Fee and Mimi and *you* could make dinner . . ."

Mama took a stern note, "Bunny, I said take George down to the beach. I know you have your hair piled up on your head now, and you think you have the whole world figured out, so go complain to the ocean. Fee and Mimi can make the beds and Itsy will make dinner while I take a look around."

"But, Mama," I said, finding my voice lost on a wave of love, "what can I make?"

"How about strawberries? We can have strawberries and toast for dinner. I think it sounds lovely. Can you wash and cut the strawberries? Can you put the toast in the oven and then butter it? Fee can go to the market for butter."

"Yes! I can do that!" I said.

"Mama! Strawberries for dinner? What in the world would Papa say?" exclaimed Mimi.

"Papa? I don't see Papa," said Mama, looking around in a silly fashion and teasing us. We all laughed. Even Bunny, who took George to the beach.

Those were the sweetest strawberries I ever ate.

I'm so glad I got sick that summer. I'm glad I got to spend that time with Mama. It turns out, that was the only time I'd ever get to be alone with her. Just me and Mama. Even though she didn't die until 1945, the world always conspired against us. The busy, busy world.

In the time that followed that fateful day, I often revisited my sick days with Mama. The otherworldliness of them. When I woke in the morning, I tried to force myself to linger in the place between asleep and awake. To open all the channels of time and will myself back into her all-knowing arms.

And now? Now it's clear to me. I'll be with her soon. Oh yes. Soon enough I'll feel her arms around me once again.

22

The Sisters Amore (Past)

When all was said and done, the arrangements made and the bodies in the ground, the three remaining Amore sisters sat at Mama's kitchen table to think things through.

Mimi's belly was getting bigger by the second even as her arms and legs got thin. Fee couldn't stop eating and still couldn't hear anything. Itsy wasn't talking but took to writing things down on a notebook, and when that got too cumbersome she got little spiral notebooks from the dollar store and pinned them to her sweaters along with a pen.

"What are we going to do about George?" yelled Fee.

"You really have to stop yelling, honey. We can hear you. If it sounds like a whisper to you it's normal for the rest of the world. Try it," said Mimi.

"Okay!" yelled Fee. Mimi shook her head, put her hands together as if in prayer and looked up at the ceiling. "What did I ever do to deserve this?"

Itsy was writing. *Let George be. Let him live like he's a grown-up. He'll come around.*

"Okay, so we let George be. Do we rent out Bunny's apartment?" Fee asked.

Itsy wrote feverishly on her notebook. *Rent it out to Nancy Rivetta. She needs a place. Okay, Mimi?*

"Sure, we can do that." Mimi was wringing her hands.

It was Fee who finally stated the obvious. "Mimi, what are *you* going to do?"

"What do you mean?"

"Are you blind?" asked Fee.

"I'm sorry, I don't know what you're talking about." Mimi got up and started to pace, her hands placed at her lower back, supporting her heavy belly.

Where is Alfred, Mimi? wrote Itsy.

"Alfred?"

"Your husband, where is he? He hasn't been home since the funerals," said Fee.

"Alfred's gone. I sent him away. And I'm changing my name back, too. I'm an Amore again."

"But Mimi, why?" asked Fee.

"Why? Why?" Her pacing became frantic as she banged on the walls and pulled at her hair. Her sisters felt the electricity in the air. "Because it's all gone to *shit*! Didn't you notice? How can I go forward with any sort of life? It's all about us now. You two and me and George. This building. What's left? He had to leave. I made him leave so I wouldn't lose him, too."

"Okay, even if we thought that made sense . . . what about the baby?" asked Fee.

"What about her? Put your hands on my belly. You tell me what you see."

Fee and Itsy placed their hands against Mimi's belly. They

looked at one another and nodded. It was sad . . . the loss, the pain. One more person who would leave them.

"See?" said Mimi sitting back, satisfied.

Itsy sat back and wrote furiously. *But Mimi, it can be changed. You can change that kind of future. It all stems from you.*

"Oh yeah? And Mama could change what she knew was going to happen? I just don't believe it. It is what it is. I'll have this baby, and I'll care for it, but I won't lose myself. No. As soon as it's ready . . . we'll send it on its way."

"But that's so *sad,*" cried Fee.

"It is what it is," said Mimi.

What about George? wrote Itsy.

"What about him? He's gone, too. All alone up there. Something in him died, and it's more than just . . . you know. There's more. I can feel it," said Mimi.

Itsy started to shake.

"What is it Itsy?" asked Fee.

Itsy started to cry silent tears.

"Do you know something, Itsy? Do you know what happened to George? Did he say something to you? Did he do something you need to tell us about? Itsy, please! You are blocking me, I can't see . . ." begged Mimi, crying, too.

Itsy shook her head. She mouthed the word "No!" up at the ceiling. And then they were all crying, all three sisters, holding onto one another in the heart of the building. And then the skies cracked open and the rain poured down, commiserating.

23

Itsy

When the child was born Mimi didn't want to look at her. She was beautiful, extraordinarily so, but we'd seen that coming. I tried to reason with her, to explain that Mama didn't have any control over the war. That Mimi's own actions were the catalyst for what would be with her own child. So she could change it. But Mimi was beyond reason. We all were. We didn't even give the baby a nickname.

"What will you call her, Mimi?" asked Fee.

"Carmen, after Alfred's mother, of course."

No, what will you call *her?* I scribbled.

She turned her head from us. I could feel her body trying to arch away from the nursing infant. "She doesn't need a nickname. She's not one of us."

And that was that.

You see . . . we'd found we were more powerful when we were together. Mama always told us about the natural numbers of things. How the numbers had power. Five leaves on a rosebush. Three women pruning those roses. The holy trinity. We'd always been different, but now the difference was palpably stronger.

It happened slowly. First we talked over coffee and realized we'd dreamed the same things. Then we noticed that those dreams came true. Mr. or Mrs. so-and-so had divorced. Little Bobby down the block went missing. (We knew where he was; he was dead in a drainpipe. Mimi slipped a note under the door of the police station and then we asked Mr. Lender, the boy's murderer over for lunch.)

We'd always been able to sense things, see things the way Mama did, but never at the heightened level when it was the three of us. Carmen was born at the wrong time.

Mimi couldn't love her. She couldn't love anyone. Love was dead to us. And me and Fee, we ignored her because . . . well . . . I don't know. Because we knew she'd leave us? Because we wanted to circle in close and keep it just us three? We were ignoring George and he was busy ignoring us. After all that happened, George spent more than a few years not leaving his apartment. We left him food three times a day, and the priest came every now and again, but I didn't care. I was glad he shut himself up. It was wicked of me, but all I wanted were Fee and Mimi. Just us three. When we held each other's hands we were whole again. It didn't matter that my voice was gone or that Fee had some sort of trauma-induced hearing loss. It didn't matter that Mimi was turning a blind eye on her child and any sort of emotion that would remind her of that day. Nothing mattered but the fact that when we touched each other's hands one thing was certain. We weren't going anywhere. We'd be old and alone together on 170th Street. Bleak future or not, it was a future. It was a solid thing. We three were a solid thing. And we held tight.

There was a drunken sort of wonder those first years. We were giddy with the power. On Sunday after church the front bell wouldn't stop ringing. Everyone wanted a tea or a tincture or a talk.

Carmen danced in and then out of our lives. Her childhood was a safe one, and like it or not, there was truth in what we all saw that day with our hands on Mimi's belly. Carmen was a cold soul. Still, she tried to win Mimi's affections, but children learn early how to survive and Carmen knew soon after she was born that though she was physically safe at home with us, she had no emotional support. And she knew Mimi didn't see her.

It makes me sad to think about it now. How we shut her out. She could have been a loving child. I can remember her doing chores and talking to herself, making up friends and scenarios. She had a flair for the drama from the git-go, that girl. How she cried in the night for Mimi. We all heard her, even Fee. And Mimi would go to her. But when she went, she took her time, and when she sat by Carmen's bed, there wasn't as much love and comfort as there was impatience.

Carmen left home when she was only sixteen. She left not knowing anything about us. She won a scholarship to an acting school in Manhattan and rarely came back. Mimi watched her go with a look on her face that said, *See, I told you she would go.*

I'll never forget that day. The wild fight they had. I don't really think either of them thought it would escalate the way it did, but so much can get lost so quickly.

It started with a dress. Carmen had her suitcase open on the bed and she kept putting dresses into it and Mimi kept taking them out and explaining why she couldn't take this one or that one.

"Fee made that one for you," she said of one.

"I don't have that pattern anymore," she said of another one.

"Fine!" yelled Carmen, emptying out the suitcase. "I'll just bring the things I paid for myself." She grabbed some long Indian skirts she bought from the Persian ladies down on 187th Street, a few t-shirts and *The Bell Jar* by Sylvia Plath. "It'll be lighter anyway! Thanks for the favor!"

I was standing in the doorway and she pushed past me. She turned around to look at Mimi who was carefully hanging up the unpacked dressed when I noticed her eyes move to the rocking chair by the window. Mama's rocking chair she'd brought with her from Fairview. Mimi saw the look, too.

"Oh no, you don't," she said.

Carmen took in a deep breath and dropped the suitcase. She swept back into the room and picked up the rocking chair over her head.

"Oh yeah?" she said. "Just you try to stop me, old woman."

I backed out of the doorway because I knew she'd plow through me. She carried that rocking chair all the way out of the building. Once at the stoop she put the chair down and tried to hail a cab. None were coming down 170th Street. With Mimi and the rest of us on her heels she picked up the chair over her head again and ran for the corner. Really, I'll never forget it. Her long hair in the wind. Her cheeks flushed with anger.

A Checker Cab stopped for her and I watched as she tried to shove it in the backseat. It wouldn't go, of course. I watched her talk and yell and cry . . . her hands moving all around her. The cabbie was won over, of course, and he put it in the trunk but it wouldn't fit there, either. He got some rope and tied the trunk together somehow.

And that's how Carmen Amore left 170th Street. She left with nothing but Mama's rocking chair hanging out of the back of a Checker Cab and a copy of *The Bell Jar* she must have dug out and then shoved in the back of the waistline of her long purple skirt.

Mimi watched with me. Fee and George were long gone, back in the house for lunch. Mimi didn't cry. I did, a little.

"She's gone now, it's over," she said.

I nodded.

"She's going to have a really hard life. Maybe it's good . . . maybe she should have Mama's chair. Something solid to cling to when everything goes to hell."

And Mimi was right. Carmen's early life unraveled itself just as it had under our hands when she was inside Mimi's stomach. But was it fate? Or was it our doing? I don't know. All I know is that when Babygirl came to us as a little girl herself, I tried to make it right again. We all did. We threw ourselves at the child because we all felt guilty about Carmen. We didn't talk about it. We just knew it.

And it worked. For a summer. Everything seemed okay again. When Babygirl was with us she reminded us of the days before. She didn't hinder us or our power the way we assumed another little girl a lifetime ago would have. She made us even stronger. And I know how.

It was George. George who'd become a hoarder, a recluse. She fixed him. She brought our Georgie back. One hundred seventieth Street shimmered with laughter that summer. With Babygirl and Anthony, with my sisters, George . . . and Babygirl's very best secret friend, Liz. The channels were open between the Bronx and Far Rockaway, between the Amore clan and the Greens. Mama and Papa were resurrected inside all of us.

It was brilliant. And then she found my secret, I made a promise, and we all went back to square one.

24

Elly

Elly didn't go to her graduation from Yale. There were many reasons why. It was hot. She didn't feel like explaining her belly (that had "popped" since her last visit) to those that might ask, and she didn't want to risk seeing Cooper. She'd successfully avoided him all semester by going directly to and from the art studio. And Cooper had no reason to go there, especially since he didn't realize she existed anymore. Mimi explained the spell they'd woven around him, the one that made him forget her, would be broken if he saw her. So she decided to stay on the safe side. She painted and she left. She was never happier she'd gotten all of her course work done early, ceremony or not, she was *done.* And it felt good to be free.

She celebrated by painting a little and then gardening with Fee.

"My class is graduating today," she said as she found the cluster of five leaves on the rose bush and used the sharp garden shears to cut just above them.

"Oh yes," said Fee. "This should be a big day for you! Do you want us to have a party? It would be fun! Mimi could have a houseful of people here in an hour if it pleased you. What do you say?"

Mimi, who was hard at work on her hands and knees scrubbing the floor of the back hall couldn't help but overhear Fee's loud voice. She sat back on her heels and poked her head outside. "Would you like that? A party?"

"*No,*" said Elly. "I feel as if I've already graduated. Moved on from that life. Even commuting was surreal. Go to the studio, leave. I felt invisible."

Fee laughed.

"What?" asked Elly, a smile growing inside of her, Fee's laughter was so contagious.

"You *were* invisible," said Fee.

"You witches and your spells! How did you manage that? Slip me an invisibility cloak or something?"

Mimi walked out into the sunshine and placing her hands against her round sides, stretched her back. "No. Nothing like that. It was *you* Elly. You did it."

"What? What did I do?"

"You wished yourself invisible and so became invisible. The world sees what we want it to see. It's the same for everyone, really. It's just we . . . Mama's children . . . and you, too . . . we notice the magical nuances of life."

Elly stood up. "Okay. Then here is my wish to the universe. I wish Aunt Itsy would tell me her secret. And I wish that Liz would come over so we could sit around and be lazy. And I *really* wish that kid in our walls would stop crying! Those are my graduation wishes."

Mimi went to her and hugged her close. Elly was growing so fond of Mimi's smells. Garlic and perfume and bleach.

"Well, I guarantee you a visit from Liz. But Itsy? She won't spill her beans. Not even for you," said Mimi.

"Okay, then what about the crying kid?"

"That's your problem," said Fee. "We can't hear it."

"You can't hear anything," said Elly quietly so Fee couldn't hear her.

Mimi laughed. "You're so bad!"

"I'm learning," said Elly.

With the gardening done, and Mimi and the aunts out shopping, Elly walked around the side of the building lazily, letting her fingers dance across the brick and mortar. She looked at her hands, fingernails blackened with garden soil. Stepping over a few low bushes growing in the narrow space between 170th Street and its neighbor, she walked out into the light. Liz was sitting on the front stoop.

"That was fast," said Elly.

"Come again?" asked Liz.

Elly lowered herself slowly down on the stoop. She was getting bigger by the day and it was hard to keep her balance. Liz put out a hand for support.

"Well, a little while ago I was pruning roses and getting a lesson on things we wish into the universe. And I was wishing you'd come by and we could spend the rest of the day just lazing around. And here you are!"

"The sun is strong for this time of year. It's going to be a hot summer," said Liz.

Elly looked at her friend. She seemed pale and tired. Her

energy so different from the rambunctious girl she'd met in the snowy garden.

"You okay?" she asked.

"Yes. I'm fine. Just a little world-weary. Let's go inside and be lazy, like you wished. Okay?"

"Yes! Let's!" said Elly.

They headed to Elly's bedroom where she changed into light pajamas—a deliciously indolent thing to do in the afternoon—and the two sat on her bed and painted their toenails red while listening to Carmen's old records.

"This is so much fun," said Elly.

"What?"

"Laying around and listening to records. I never had a girlfriend growing up."

"You always had me," said Liz.

"I didn't remember you."

"That doesn't mean I wasn't with you. Sometimes heads and hearts don't communicate so good, you know?"

"I *do* know. Like today . . . I knew Carmen wouldn't call. But I wanted her to. I tried wishing her to. But even if my head thought she might, my heart felt she wouldn't. Is it better to listen to your heart?"

"*Always!* The only problem is the heart is quiet. It takes a very special kind of person to hear what the heart says. Most can't hear it at all and they have to guess. There are a lot of people walking around just guessing."

They moved side by side, stretching their legs out so the box fan in the window could blow their toes dry. Elly turned her head on the cool cotton pillow to face Liz, whose eyes were closed.

"I'm afraid," said Elly.

Liz's eyes fluttered open. "About what?" She reached out her hand to tuck some of Elly's stray hair, loose from her messy bun, behind her ears.

Elly reached up and held Liz's hand to her face. She closed her eyes and tried to think of a way to put her fear into words that would make sense. The emotions ran high now that most of her memories were coming back. It was easier *not* to remember. Before the memories there'd been a wall, tall and high all around her. It kept Elly from herself and her feelings. It kept her safe, in its way. And as that wall crumbled she was afraid to see what lay beyond. It could be a magical garden like the one blooming in the back of the building. Or it could be blackness—the blackness she saw every time she placed her hands on her belly and tried to dream of a moment in the future with her child.

"I'm afraid my baby is going to die," she said, picking the deepest, realest fear.

"Why on earth are you afraid of that? Your baby is just fine." reassured Liz. But Elly noticed right away Liz didn't seem shocked, or even surprised.

"See . . . you can feel it, too. Some kind of 'wrong' I just can't put my finger on," said Elly.

They drew closer as their words came out quieter, the unspoken things now out in the open. *This is what it feels like to have a friend,* thought Elly. She looked back upon the months she'd been here. Getting to know Liz. Remembering her as a little girl. She thought about painting the mural with her, laughing about Anthony's goofy and spectacular love. Telling Liz about her engagement as they walked together to church and her screaming in delight. Reminiscing about the days at Playland. And it was true, Liz had changed, grown serious, older, and pale.

"Are you sure you're okay?"

"Well, I might be getting sick or something," said Liz. "It's you I'm worried about. Here, turn over and lie down on your left side."

"Why? I'm spoken for, you know!" joked Elly.

"Just do it!" laughed Liz.

Elly smiled, glad to see Liz spunky again. She turned over as Liz scooched in close, putting her hands on Elly's stomach.

The baby started kicking furiously.

"How did you do that?" Elly squealed in delight.

"Your heart is on the left side. When you place your body on the side of your heart the blood shifts. It wakes up the baby."

"Thank you, Liz," said Elly.

"You are welcome."

A quiet fell between them, the soft whir of the fan lulling them into comfortable silence.

"Liz?"

"Ummmhmmm?" answered a sleepy Liz.

"I know you and I were friends here . . . when I was ten. And I have most of those memories back now, thank God. Drips. They came like Chinese water torture . . . And I remember you from the time before. The time when it was just Carmen and me. And I don't know how that can be, because I didn't know you yet. Did I?"

Liz paused a moment. "I think I met you when you got here . . . and you probably had an imaginary friend before that. Maybe you just made her into me, or vice versa. No matter, really. And when you came back, when you were thirteen? For that short visit? I got to see you then too."

Elly rolled over, bouncing the bed like Aunt Fee . . . and

faced her friend. "Ha! I got you! I *didn't* see you when my mom brought me back here that Christmas! I remember everything about that night. Carmen got drunk. She didn't want to come back. But she'd made a trip to India and the yogis told her to make *peace with her past.* I swear she *never* forgave the whole damn country of India for that fiasco. And I fell in love with Anthony . . . and I fell in love with this whole place, really. But not you. I don't remember you."

Liz turned even paler and looked at the ceiling. She covered her hands with her face, sighing. "Oh yeah," she said. "I watched through the window . . ."

"Why didn't you come in?"

"You weren't there long enough. By the time I got up the nerve to knock on the door you were gone."

"Yeah, Carmen wanted out of that situation so badly," said Elly. "I wish I'd seen you then. You at thirteen would have been fun . . ."

"Me at thirteen? Lord. I was nothing but an open wound."

"Me, too."

"Maybe all girls are," said Liz.

"Maybe," Elly said, yawning.

"How about we take an afternoon nap? It doesn't get any lazier than that," suggested Liz.

"Yes. Let's. How about you sing me a song. Like I remember from when we were little?"

"Sure, glad to . . . *Don't sit under the apple tree, with anybody else but me, anybody else but me, anybody else but me . . .*"

And in the moment between sleep and awake, when one realizes *great* things and believes they'll be remembered forever but never are, Elly Amore realized Liz never sang her that song when they were ten and playing on the beaches of Far Rockaway. She sang it to her when Elly was very small, in Europe, with Carmen.

✦

Later when Elly woke, the memory was gone and so was Liz. She went to the dressing table and opened her diploma. They'd sent it to her early when she filled out the papers saying she wouldn't "walk." A hard blue case and a beautiful piece of paper. A real accomplishment. She held it down and lifted up her pajama top just above her belly button. Elly was convinced her baby could see out from that one spot, like a periscope. "See this, baby? Mommy did a good thing!" And the baby kicked.

Elly tried not to think about how Carmen hadn't called. But she knew Carmen was just being Carmen. And that Elly wasn't on the top of her list of priorities right now. A heavy feeling, the blanket of sad that always accompanied Elly remembering that she had a mother who she missed and loved began to descend. A note came flying under the closed door and across the shiny wood floor stopping at the fringe of the Persian rug.

She loves you even if she doesn't know it. Be strong. Give your baby the love you feel you never got. You'll heal that way. Don't make the same mistakes, make different ones. We all make mistakes . . . no need to compound them!

"Thanks, Aunt Itsy!" Elly yelled at the door.

"She can hear you, she's not deaf you know!" yelled Fee through the door.

"You birds sure can hover," said Elly.

✦

The next day Elly moved into apartment 2B with Anthony. Mimi and Fee gave their approval even as Itsy growled in the background.

Anthony knelt down and put his head against Elly's stomach. "And so we begin our lives, little one."

Elly knotted her fingers in his thick black hair and threw her head back in happiness, laughing. A sound that bubbled up like champagne. A new sound. An old sound. The laugh of the Amores.

✦

Itsy watched them bring things up and down from the trunks in the attic. Cooper was coming, she could feel it. She'd have to move the trunk soon. It was all happening. Unfolding like a Venus flytrap in the sun. Time was running out.

Summer

25

Itzy

The forgetting spell is tricky, but popular. When we were little and the winter set in, there'd be a stream of people who'd come to the 170th Street apartment so Mama could cast their bad memories away. There are a few ways to do it. Some more powerful than the others.

If you want someone to forget something without them knowing, you need pine syrup and Valerian root powder mixed with something else. A conduit. Some flavor powerful enough to mask the strong flavors of the botanicals. Garlic works well. Tomato, too. And then you have to concentrate on what you want them to forget, and you have to be specific. If you aren't specific you could wipe out a whole chunk of thoughts never intended to be lost. And this only works until the person is reminded of whatever it is they forgot. Then it's all over. Whoosh! The memory returns.

If you want to forget something yourself, you can wish it away and drink a cup of Mama's special tea. She labeled it "*Loss*" in a tin in the kitchen. (Mimi still has that tin with Mama's writing on it.) Again, this spell is only as strong as your resolve. It's weak with heartache because no matter how much someone *thinks* they want to forget a lost love, they don't. I know this for a fact. I know it because I tried.

The most binding forgetting spell is one where you are *desperate* to forget something. It's the simplest one of all. No teas or tinctures or sauces required. Just a witch and a wish. Those spells are the hardest to break, even when you want them broken.

Mama taught us her magic like she taught us to walk. As if it were the most normal thing in the world. She couched it in sayings like, "Everyone has different talents," and "Strange things happen everyday, we're no exception." And through it all, through the removal of curses on midnight on New Year's Eve; through the endless recipes for herbal remedies and gardens full of magical ingredients; nothing about what we learned scared us. It all seemed as right as rain. Except the Forgetting spell. That incantation went against everything Mama ever taught us. And in that respect, we feared it.

It was a base art. Something only uneducated people (meaning those who didn't understand the concept of loss) would do.

Mama understood loss. She knew we needed it in order to feel fully alive. She pitied the people who came to her for the forgetting spell.

And we never used it. Not even when we could have to ease our own sorrows.

And when I finally *had* to use it, I had no idea how powerful it was.

Each day, I learn. And each day, I wonder.

But sometimes the Forgetting spell needs to be used for protection. Sometimes not remembering can keep us safe.

Of course, Mama would disagree. But I'm only half Green, and she always seemed to forget that about her children. There's an obstinate Italian side, too. Magic angry people. What a mixture!

26

Elly

"I need some Valerian root for the "Loss" tin. Elly, can you go to the Chinese market and buy some?" called Mimi from the kitchen. She was rummaging—half annoyed—and clanging about as she took inventory.

Elly loved to walk through the streets of the Bronx. The odd, old-fashioned pragmatism of New York's ways fascinated her. People who didn't live in the city always thought about it on two ends of the spectrum, magnificent and forward thinking, or dark and violent. But Elly was learning the truth. New York was the keeper of all things good. Old ways and new ways gathered together in a perfect hum of logic. She promised herself when she was no longer pregnant, and could string two thoughts together properly, that she'd create a series of street paintings.

"I'd *love* to, Mimi," she said. "Is there anything else you need?"

"I could use some cat's eye marbles. But I don't know where you'd find them. George had boxes of them but Anthony got rid of all that. That boy. I swear. He's so good about most things until he thinks of *you,* and then his sense jumps out the window."

"There's a flea market today on Fordham Road. I can go look around if you want."

"Don't tire yourself, love. You're getting on in this pregnancy now."

"Join the twenty-first century, Mimi. Some mothers-to-be are running marathons."

Mimi turned around and shooed away Elly with her hand.

Elly chose to walk out into the back garden and leave through the gate. The garden was in full bloom now. It brought delight to every single sense that Elly had—especially the sixth one that she was quickly developing.

Studying Margaret Green's book gave her a constant litany of facts about the plants.

Geranium for knowledge
Echinacea for health
Lavender for luck
Chamomile for calm
Pine for forgetting

She chanted slowly in her head as she walked by each plant. She moved quickly, though, because there was always the lingering fear that if she stood too long in one place in Margaret's garden that her feet would take root and she'd be a rosebush in no time.

The gate squeaked open and Elly stepped out onto the back streets of the Bronx.

"Hey there!" said Liz, suddenly right in front of her. She seemed to step out of the sun.

"Hey! I've got some errands to do, want to join me?"

"Gladly. I'm bored, hot, and tired," said Liz.

"And invisible. I didn't even see you when I opened the gate."

"You had sun caught in your eyes."

"I guess, or else it's just this crazy pregnancy. I need to keep my mind occupied on other things."

The two young women headed toward Fordham Road.

"What kinds of things are you thinking about?" asked Liz as they walked.

"Well, I've decided that if I figure out Itsy's secret, I'll be able to see my baby. It's the one thing still blocking my view."

"Okay, so how do you want to figure it all out?"

"I don't know. I can't think straight."

"Have you ever thought about going to Fairview?" asked Liz.

"Fairview?" Elly asked, confused. Then she remembered Mimi's story and the information Anthony gave her about Margaret Green. "You're right! Fairview," she said. "Let's go!"

"Right now?" asked Liz.

"Yes. I'll go back and tell Mimi I have something else to do and we'll take Georgie's car."

"*Ooohhh,* sounds like an adventure!"

"Hey, Liz?" asked Elly as they walked back through the garden gate.

"Yes?"

"I hope . . ." Elly stumbled on the words.

"What?"

"I hope that there isn't one memory with you in it that gets left behind. I want to have our whole history."

Liz winked at her and walked ahead, up the back porch, opening Mimi's apartment door. "Well, then! Right this way, m'lady! Let's get to rememberin'."

And as Elly, suddenly graceful, moved through the doorway, Liz gave her a hug. "I . . ."

Elly hugged back. "Oh, Liz. I know . . . I love you, too."

✦

"You drive, okay?" asked Liz as they slid into Georgie's car. "I never learned. But I'll be co-pilot. I know the way. Get on I-95. Take I-91 North to Route 84. Then get on Route 128. Fairview is just a few exits down after that. There's a big sign. You be the Lone Ranger. I'm Tonto."

"The Lone Ranger, huh? Wow. Didn't you even have basic cable growing up? And how do you know how to get to Fairview? Do you have some sort of internal GPS I don't know about?" asked Elly already driving, the windows down, happy to be on a grand adventure.

Liz looked serious for a moment. "I used to go there when I was little."

"What is this odd connection between the Bronx and Fairview Mass?!" Elly exclaimed. "It's so freaking strange."

Liz opened the passenger side window and put her hand out to catch the breeze. "Maybe not so strange."

"How do you mean?"

"Haha!" laughed Liz. "You're starting to talk like Mimi!"

"Whatever. Just go on, explain thyself, woman!"

"Well . . . If you look really close, you can find a lot of Fairview in the Bronx. Or anywhere in New York City and her boroughs . . . really. Probably mostly in Far Rockaway."

"Nice . . ." said Elly, a little distracted by the I-95 ramp. "You know what I'm really interested to find out? What their *names* are! Their *real* names. I mean, *no one* will tell me. Do *you* know?"

No answer came from the passenger seat. Liz was fast asleep.

"Some crappy Tonto you make, Liz."

The drive was boring, but Uncle Georgie's car made good time. Elly was comfortable, if squished. The air got cooler the farther north they went, and she was pumped full of adrenaline. The view though . . . felt faded. Stretch after stretch of East Coast summer foliage, wide swaths of uniform color. The artist in Elly tried to at least see the contrast of different shades of green, but in the end it was all a big mass of marginal, dull, deciduous green. Until she drove onto the smaller, Route 128, that is. Then the trees gave way to sweeping ocean vistas. A Yankee landscape for sure. Not unlike New Haven, but wilder. More magical.

The exit was clearly marked and the drive into town lovely—Rockwellian with a touch of Poe. Right after the ENTERING FAIRVIEW EST. 1672 sign there was a rotary at the center of which rose the hospital. You actually had to drive *around* the hospital to enter the town. It obscured Fairview completely. A Gothic structure with gaping orifices pretending to be doors and windows. A modern sign FAIRVIEW MENTAL HEALTH FACILITY, stood on the grass median of the rotary but did nothing to obscure the massive stone archway of the entrance to the hospital itself in which the older, less politically correct name SAINT SEBASTIAN LUNATIC ASYLUM was carved.

"Nice," mumbled Elly as she entered the parking lot. "You think they could have positioned the place differently. I mean, it must *kill* the tourist trade."

"I think that's precisely why they did it," answered Liz.

"Well . . . Heeeeeellllllo! What an amazing help you've been so far! Thank God we're here, Liz, because I've got to pee. Something fierce."

"I'm sorry, I've just been so tired lately. I feel like something's catching up with me. I could sleep away my life."

Elly parked the car and made a break for the entrance. "Well, we can talk about your problems on the ride back. Right now I have to find the ladies room and then figure out my whole existence. Okay?"

"You're the boss," answered Liz. "But why don't you go ahead and I'll catch up. I'm not feeling so well, Elly."

Elly looked at her friend who did look quite pale and then ahead to the hospital. "Okay, but I don't want to lose you. So why don't you just wait in the car?"

"Sounds like an excellent plan. These old cars have exceptionally comfortable back seats." Liz winked.

"You're a naughty one," laughed Elly as she made her way as fast as her belly would let her, up the steps into the hospital in a mad rush to find a restroom.

✦

Elly stopped short in the massive lobby.

"I don't want to stay here, Mama. Please. I can take care of you."

Carmen was crying. Saying good-bye. Two nurses at the side and a doctor with a clipboard standing behind her, nodding his head and smiling. Little girl Eleanor wanted to bite him. Hard.

"You don't have to stay here, Eleanor. I've sent for your Grandmother."

"The one you hate? I won't go." Babygirl stomped a patent leather heel and the echo went on and on and on.

Carmen's face twisted up into deeper grief. "Have I told you that? Have I burdened you with that as well? My God." She looked at the ceiling.

✦

Elly looked up at the domed painted ceiling, a crazy reproduction of the Sistine Chapel, only there were mermaids instead of saints.

"Can I help you?" A young, pretty nurse in an old-fashioned white uniform stood in front of her.

"Oh, yes. I need some information about my family," and then blushing, realized how she must look. Pregnant, staring up at the ceiling and about to ask for a bathroom. "But first, do you have a public restroom? I've been driving for a while."

The nurse smiled. Her teeth matched her uniform. "Of course, dear. Right this way."

The marble bathroom was a blinding white. While Elly washed her hands in the sink she thought about Carmen. She looked in the mirror. "You were addicted, weren't you?" Elly washed her face and looked into the mirror again. She saw Carmen staring back at her.

"Yes. It went from wonderful days of wine and roses to lost days full of heroin. I hurt you. I never meant to hurt you," said the image of Carmen through the looking glass.

Elly touched the mirror. "I know, Mommy."

There was a knock on the bathroom door. "Are you okay in there dear?" asked the nurse.

Great, thought Elly, *now she hears me talking to myself.*

✦

Elly took a moment to let all the memories, bad and good sink in. She knew this couldn't stop her. She had to absorb it all like a sponge, from one end of her to the other in even measure. She'd lost her mother a long time ago, and this was not an excursion to find Carmen anyway. It was a very different errand all together. Composing herself, Elly returned to the main lobby. At the desk she introduced herself and asked the nurse about her family.

"I can't share any of their records with you, I'm so sorry."

"No," said Elly. "I don't think you understand. I don't need to see my mother's records—wait, did you say '*their* records?' "

"Yes. I can't open the records of Carmen Amore or those of Faith Green."

"Faith Green?"

"Why yes—don't you know?"

"She must have been my great-great grandmother," said Elly.

"Well," continued the efficient nurse, "I can't show you their records, they're sealed."

"Do you know where I can go to find out more about the Greens?"

The nurse smiled again. "The library, of course!"

Elly wondered if there was such a thing as Stepford nurses.

"How do I get to the library from here?" she asked.

"The best way is to just walk through the hospital. The back entrance opens up to downtown Fairview and the library will be right ahead of you. You can leave your car where it is."

The car. Liz. I can't just leave Liz, thought Elly.

"I have a friend waiting for me, I'm just going to check on her, let her know where I'm going, okay?"

Elly went back to Georgie's car. Liz was gone. "Where'd you go, Tonto?" she asked the breeze. Elly looked around. There was an eerie quiet to the whole place. The empty parking lot, the sound of crashing waves.

"She must have taken a walk or something." Elly told the nurse when she reentered the hospital.

"No worries, dear, if she wanders in looking for you, I'll tell her where you've gone."

"Thank you," said Elly. "You've been very helpful."

✦

Elly found herself in a long hallway lined with stained glass windows. The glass was covered with the same pagan, mythical designs as the ceiling of the hospital lobby. She tried to peek through the colored glass to see the town, but only saw the ocean in distorted jewel tones. Fairview is a peninsula . . . she remembered George telling her when she was little.

"Do you know how to spell peninsula? p e n i n s u l a. That's a big word."

And they'd jumped around the little cottage, Itsy, Anthony, George, and Liz spelling out peninsula.

The memories were flooding her now; she'd known they would. "This was a very good decision, Elly," she said to herself.

The back entrance was just as grand as the front and the doors *did* open up to downtown Fairview. It was like opening the gates to a fairytale land. The gleaming afternoon sun shone down on architectural perfection. Cobblestone roads and a massive fountain in the middle of the plaza stood between Elly and the building that had to be the library.

Greco-Roman with Doric columns and lions on either side of the wooden doors, the building excited both Elly's artistic mind and her treasure hunting spirit. She'd find answers in that building. It just *looked* like a place where all the answers in the world might be found. And next to it was a large willow tree, an exact match to the one she'd painted in her baby's nursery. And next to that tree, a bench, not unlike the one in the garden in the Bronx.

More and more curious, thought Elly as she entered the dim, cool library. The information kiosk was in the middle of the first floor. The librarian looked to be about Elly's age. She was disappointed. She'd assumed there'd be an old woman there with a raspy voice that would simply tell her everything she needed to know.

"Can I help you?" asked the bouncy, un-old, un-interesting librarian.

"I hope so. You see, I'm here to find out more about a member of my family."

"Oh! Is your family from Fairview?"

"Yes, well, half of them. Anyway, do you have any information about a woman named Faith Green?"

The librarian's eyes lit up. "Grandma Faith? Dear Lord, Yes! She's famous around here. A local heroine of sorts."

"She's a relative of yours?" asked Elly.

"No, everyone used to call her that. She was like family to the people in our little town—until she went crazy, that is." The librarian made the twirling loony motion with her hand next to her head.

"So she's a local hero who was crazy?" *This place gets stranger by the second,* thought Elly.

The librarian just laughed. "Oh, you'll understand. Come with me. A reporter did a whole story about her. You see, she lost her son, Ephraim, at sea and she lost her ability to speak. I'll load the whole thing for you on the microfiche downstairs."

Lost her voice? Like Itsy? thought Elly . . . and then wondered, *What the hell is a microfiche?*

✦

The basement of the library was not dark and depressing like most. It was full of natural light from a garden room attached to the back and it smelled like good, loamy earth. The microfiche turned out to be a satisfying device that loaded old text documents onto film. It was like reading and watching a movie at the same time. She was scrolling through newspapers from 1920–1925—and then there it was:

Admired Local Woman Loses Voice

When her son Ephraim set out to win the Fairview Regatta last Saturday, his mother did not expect she'd never see her boy again. After an extensive search between the waters of Fairview and the Island of Fortunes Cove, Massachusetts, Ephraim was pronounced dead, or as the natives of the area say, "Lost at Sea." A tragedy in its own right, Ephraim's death was not the only blow to this community. Mrs. Faith Green, an admired pillar of Fairview, Massachusetts, was stricken with paralyzing arthritis, which curled her hands upon themselves and somehow closed her vocal chords as well. The affliction appeared on the very day her son went missing.

This is a devastating loss to the community as Mrs. Green runs the local gardens, supports the cultural programs in the town, and is also an avid art enthusiast.

Possibly the most interesting part of the whole event is what the locals themselves have to say. After interviewing many people from the town of Fairview there is a consensus that Faith Green is also looked at as a local Witch or Shaman. She's a woman who descends from a long line of women who can foretell the future as well as heal the sick. Most of the interviews conducted during the course of this bizarre case mentioned that Faith Green helped almost all the people she knew in one way or another.

It is interesting to note, that in this odd, little village of Fairview the people readily accept the notion of magic. Magic for good and/or evil is not something to be feared or even tolerated. It seems to be a way of life.

There is a local consensus that Faith Green's inability to speak or move her hands will end her days as the local "Healer." This makes the town a sad and nervous place today.

Her one surviving child, Margaret Green, stated that she believes the only way her mother will be able to regain her voice, and thus regain her position in the community, is if the body of her brother is found.

"You find my brother Ephraim," said Margaret Green. "When you find Ephraim my Mother will find her voice. Then you can ask her all you want about what we do here and why we do it," said Margaret when interviewed.

To date, his body remains undiscovered and lies somewhere at the bottom of the sea. Faith Green no longer lives in her stately Victorian home, but has committed herself to Saint Sebastian's Lunatic Asylum. Margaret Green has moved and is reportedly set to wed one Vincent Amore of the Bronx, NY, next June.

Engrossed, Elly hadn't heard anyone come up behind her. The tap on her shoulder shot her up in the air, almost knocking over the microfiche.

"Excuse me, dear! I didn't mean to startle you," said the librarian. "Did you find what you were looking for?"

"Yes, I think I did. Thank you very much," said Elly.

"You know," said the librarian, whose eyes suddenly seemed deeper and oddly shimmery, "the Green family home is at the end of Main Street. Where the ocean meets the land. If you'd like to visit."

All of a sudden there wasn't anything Elly wanted to do more. No secret was more important than seeing that house.

"Thank you," she whispered and the librarian raised her arm and pointed to the stairs that would lead Elly up and out of the library so she could find her way—home.

The sunlight sifted down on her as the streets grew quiet. All she could hear was the pounding of her heart keeping time with crashing waves. Her vision tunneled down Main Street toward the large Queen Anne at the end of the block, toward the garden gate—that led—to a beach all its own. Quietly, one step in front of the other, she walked as if she were on a balance beam. One block. Almost there, the porch within arms reach, the water waiting for her. She'd be a mermaid soon.

"Elly!" someone yelled from far, far away. She turned around and was face-to-face with Liz.

Liz whispered in Elly's ear. "It's time to go. This isn't your place. Not yet. Let's go, Elly."

Elly looked around, stunned. She couldn't remember leaving the library. She cleared her throat and focused on her friend. "You betcha, Tonto," she said.

They made their way back up Main Street and through the hospital. They hurried past the nice Stepford nurse who tried to beckon them back. Once in the car they sped away so fast the tires screeched and Elly accidentally drove over a portion of the median, spitting dirt into the air. Elly felt like she escaped something she couldn't understand.

"God, what *is* that place?" asked Elly.

"Part of you," said Liz. "Anyway, did it work? Are you remembering everything that's left to remember?" Liz seemed edgy.

Elly laughed. "Yes, I sure am! It's coming in these waves now."

Liz shifted in her seat.

Elly's brows furrowed with worry. "Liz, is there something I'm forgetting? You seem nervous. Is there something I'm supposed to remember about you?"

"Nope. Nothing. I'm just sleepy. Like a dormouse. Maybe I'm sick," said Liz.

"Just rest, Liz. I'm running on adrenaline. I can't wait to get back home."

✦

"Where's Elly?" asked Mimi.

"She took Georgie's car and went to Fairview," said Anthony.

"Alone?" yelled Fee. "Or did Itsy go with her? I haven't seen her all day."

"No, she went with Liz," said Anthony.

"She's gone with Liz? I sure hope Liz isn't driving!" said Mimi.

27

✦ ✦ ✦

Itsy

Mama loved animals, though we weren't allowed pets. It never bothered me. I've never been much of an animal person myself. But Georgie? Georgie was. He'd bring home strays on a regular basis, and Mama would have heated, hushed conversations with him in the back hall.

"George! You know Papa won't allow it!" she'd say.

"But Mama, look at it! So sad and all alone. Please?"

It was hard on Mama. Animals were drawn to her like babies to breasts. I remember watching her once, alone in the garden with a sparrow right on her shoulder.

So sometimes, more often than not, the answer was "no," but *sometimes* she conceded. In Mama fashion. With conditions.

No animals were to live inside. And if George wanted to keep one, he'd have to keep it out in the yard at the cottage. Papa wouldn't notice it there.

George listened, of course . . . and most of those animals that Mama saw fit to allow ran away in the stretch of weeks (sometimes months) that elapsed between our infrequent visits to the cottage in the fall and winter seasons.

All of them except for one. A ginger kitten that George named Cat.

Perhaps she stayed because George found her there during the summer so she got used to us, or perhaps (and this is what Mama believed) she was *supposed* to find us. It didn't really matter, because that cat didn't end up belonging to George. She belonged to Mama. And for a good five years she stayed put. She didn't run away during our absence. Instead she grew prettier every year, and greeted us on the front porch weaving her orange striped fur through the railings.

"But can't you think of a better name than *Cat*?" Bunny asked.

"Oh Bunny, I think it's a grand name. Now we won't ever get confused!"

How Mama loved George. Her love showed *me* how to love him. And now that I think on it, perhaps that was the whole point. She showed me, through everything she did, how to act that way myself. Bunny was always too critical anyway.

The summer Cat turned six a terrible thing happened. She died.

But she didn't die in a normal way. She didn't get killed by the cars that were moving faster and thicker through the narrow streets of Far Rockaway. She didn't get eaten up by a big, old dog. She contracted the rabies.

I was playing sardines with George. It was his favorite game and my least favorite. And I was mad, because I didn't want to play. We were too old, twelve at the time, and we were playing alone. It always took George an *age* to find me. I was standing between two bedspreads Mama had hanging on the line. I'd tried to find a spot so obvious that the game would be over quickly. My feet were clearly visible. But George didn't notice and was already hunting around in the neighbor's yard. I could hear him.

The thing I noticed first was a low, grinding noise.

Like labored breathing, asthma even, but not from a person. I looked toward the sound, peering down the narrow makeshift space created by the bedspreads. And there was Cat. At first I was relieved. Our orange beauty had been missing for a few days and Mama was beside herself. She'd grown so fond of that cat. And I knew I would be the one to bring her good news. The thought warmed my heart. The idea of Mama smiling still warms my heart to this day.

Cat started to walk toward me but fell. Then she tried to get up but couldn't. Suddenly, I knew it wouldn't be good news I'd be bringing Mama, and that a smile was the last thing I should expect. Cat was sick. And my instincts told me not to try to scoop her up. My stomach urged me to run away, grab Georgie, and get Mama.

And that's exactly what I did.

Over George's whining about not finishing the game, I explained what happened to Mama who was at the sink washing dishes.

"What do you mean Cat's sick?" asked George.

Mama grabbed us both by our wrists and took us into her bedroom. She closed both windows and told us to stay put. "I'm going to find the girls," she said before shutting the door. I remember it got hot quick. So hot in such a short stretch of time.

Mama was back quickly with Mimi and Fee.

"But Mama," Mimi complained. "I can help you, too! Why only Bunny?"

"You just stay here and take care of your sisters and George. I have to do something no one needs to see. You hear me? If I could do it alone, I would."

Mama was shaking and there were tears in her eyes. That scared me more than seeing Cat all wobbly and foamy. It scared George, too. He started to cry. Mimi and Fee joined us and cuddled him. I felt sick to my stomach.

Mama and Bunny were gone a long time. When the door opened Bunny came in alone. She opened the windows. We watched her for a moment or two, no one speaking. It was George who asked the question we didn't want answered.

"What happened, Bunny? Is Cat okay?"

Bunny didn't face us. She leaned against the windowsill and looked out, down the street toward the beach.

"No," she said. "Cat was sick and Mama had to . . ." Bunny's voice changed and got thick. She cleared her throat. "Mama had to send Cat to heaven."

Even though I knew the moment I saw Cat that this was the likely outcome, a sadness rose in me and I began to cry. We were all crying.

Mama called to us from the yard. "Come here, my darlings!"

We went outside and found her standing over a small mound of newly turned earth. "Let's hold hands and say good-bye to our beautiful Cat."

We made a circle around the small grave. I noticed one of the bedspreads was gone, and taking Mama's hand . . . The Sight showed me what happened. *Mama and Bunny folding the bedspread and then Mama telling Bunny to stay back, inserting her arms into the folds and picking up Cat. Wrapping it up tight and pressing out the air.*

"How could you?" I whispered.

Mama knelt in front of me. She put her hands on my shoulders and began to gently stroke my arms. Shoulder to wrist.

"Itsy, you must understand. I did what had to be done."

"But you loved her!" I said.

"Yes, but she was sick. And if I let her, she could have hurt one of you. And I couldn't let that happen. You hear me, Itsy girl? When we are given the gift of *a way* to stop harm before harm is done, we must try as best we can to save those we love. One bite from Cat and I could have lost you!"

"But why you? Why not Papa or one of the boys? Or a neighbor?"

Mama's patience was wearing thin. She stood up and grabbed my hand again and Fee's on her other side.

"Do any of you see Papa here? Or the boys? Hmmmm?"

"No, Mama," we said.

"That's right. They're not here. They're still in the city . . . what a stunning surprise. And do you suppose I wanted to burden a neighbor with what was surely my own problem? Is that what we do? Do we let others take care of things?"

"No, Mama," we said.

"Alright then. Now let's go around in a circle and say something nice we remember about our lovely Cat. You start, George."

Mama listened patiently to all of us. But through all the eulogies she was squeezing my hand. I knew I hadn't heard the last from her on that particular subject.

✦

She woke me in the middle of the night. I knew she would.

"Let's sit on the porch and listen to the waves, Itsy," she said.

I followed her onto the porch, being sure not to let the screen door slam and wake the others. We sat, side by side, on the stairs.

"I'm sorry if I disappointed you," she said.

I stared at the ground.

"You must remember today. How you *knew* the animal was sick. You may find a sick animal again one day, and you'll need to know what to do."

"I couldn't, Mama. I could never!" I said.

Mama turned my chin and made me look into her eyes. "Yes, you can, Itsy. You can and you will. When something is sick and dangerous you do what you have to do. Don't leave it up to chance. I didn't raise you to be squeamish or weak. You are strong. You are the strongest of them all, Itsy."

✦

I didn't believe you, Mama. I went back to bed full of pride and forgiveness . . . my heart overflowing with love. But I didn't believe you. And now that I'm standing here, caught in a never ending game of sardines . . . waiting for everyone to find me and unable to make a sound . . . I see the rabid cat in front of me again. And you were right. I know what I have to do, and I'll do it.

28

Elly

It was hot and Elly was huge. The summer stretched out into one long agonizing day after another. Each day she was sure the sun would never set. Uncle George's apartment was now fully inhabited by Elly and Anthony. There was already a nursery set up, but even with the fans set on high, the apartment stifled her. She spent most of her time on the first floor in Mimi's apartment drinking fresh lemonade poured over crushed ice. Mimi enjoyed spoiling Elly and Elly enjoyed being spoiled.

It wasn't just the heat that kept Elly on Mimi's flowered sofa. It was the crying child. She knew it wanted to play. She'd tested it. As soon as Elly made chase, the giggling started. But it was getting harder to keep up with, and Elly was expecting a baby of her own. It was like a mewling kitten you couldn't kick out of the house. Elly would just be falling asleep when the crying—it was mostly crying again—started. And because she didn't know the source, she couldn't quiet the damn thing. It seemed to Elly that if she could only remember everything, fill in all the black spaces, that perhaps she'd be able to rid the building of its wailing, invisible tenant.

It was that thought, more than anything else, that drove her to make the decision to find out all the secrets once and for all. She needed to find out what Itsy said to her all those years ago. So she'd asked Itsy. Again and again. A thousand different ways. But Itsy wouldn't tell her anything. She'd gone all the way to Fairview and back, assaulting her aunts and grandmother with information about Faith and Ephraim to receive no answers, only some comments like "What a lovely trip!" and "Interesting, we never knew about that."

A likely story.

Elly'd even tried the "Truth Tea," a mixture of bluebells and sage from the garden that Mimi showed her how to make, on Itsy, but she was a sharp old hag. One taste and she fled into her own apartment and locked the doors.

"How did you think she'd fall for that one? I thought you were smarter than that," teased Mimi.

"Oh shut your face," said Elly, fat, hot, and frustrated.

"Just go lay down and I'll bring you a glass of lemonade. There's a breeze coming in. A storm's on the way. Rest your mind, Elly."

Instead Elly opened the freezer and leaned her head inside.

"Close that freezer, missy. You want all the food to defrost?"

"Why did you let her go?" asked Elly, not closing the door. The cold was too delicious.

"Who?" asked Mimi, not turning her head from squeezing lemons in an old-fashioned glass juicer. Elly closed the freezer door and turned around to face her grandmother's back. She knew Mimi was playing dumb because the lemons were getting an extra twist and turn.

"You know who I'm talking about. Don't play dumb with me, Mimi. *My mother.* Why did you let her go?"

Mimi wiped her hands on her apron and turned around. Her eyes warned of an emotional line not to cross. "I didn't let her do anything. She just went."

"But you didn't try? You never called. Didn't you miss her? *I* miss her. I could never let this baby leave me," she caressed her belly.

Mimi pointed a finger in Elly's face. She was shaking. "Now you keep your judging to yourself. I had my reasons. Good ones. You don't understand anything. That girl . . . your mother . . . she was predisposed to running. I knew she'd leave me. I *saw* it. And why should I try to stop her? It was already decided by the fates. What would you have me do? Throw some more love at a person who was going to leave?"

"But you didn't know that for sure, Mimi. I think these things, these visions, are more like chances than anything else. Warnings of things to come . . . not fact." Elly was thinking about the blackness that washed over her when she tried to visualize a future with her baby. A chill went down her spine.

Mimi turned back to the lemons. "Now you sound like Itsy. That's the way she thinks. Go into the living room, okay? It's too hot to dredge all this up. I'll bring the lemonade to you like I said."

"Thanks, Mimi. Can you bring two glasses? I think Liz is coming over."

"Liz?"

"Yes. My *friend*. Liz. Why do you always seem to forget about her, Mimi? You didn't even set a place for her at my birthday!"

"Don't get worked up, Elly. She's a quiet one is all. It will be nice to see her."

✦

Lying on the flowered couch—the soft, late August morning breeze Mimi promised disturbing the sheer curtains and teasing the house plants in front of the window—Elly felt sleepy and comfortable for the first time in days. The baby inside her, taking up most of her small frame, was sleeping, too. How quiet and lovely everything was all of a sudden. And then there it was. The crying.

"Oh for the *love of God*! Please!"

Mimi ran out of the kitchen with lemonade sloshing from two glasses. "What is it?"

Elly was rocking back and forth with her hands over her ears. "The *crying* ghost baby!"

Mimi sat down. "Interesting. I still don't hear it."

"I know you don't. No one does."

"Maybe it's some sort of message just for you?"

"You think?" Elly asked sarcastically.

"Oh just drink your lemonade . . . a sour drink for a sour girl." Mimi left, swatting Elly with a dish towel. Elly groaned.

"What's all this?" asked Liz from the doorway. Elly jumped.

"You scared me!"

"I didn't mean to."

The fan blew back Liz's curls exposing her thin neck.

"I swear, you're going to disappear if you don't start eating something. You make me feel fatter than necessary," said Elly.

"Whatever, hey. I have an idea. Let's go to the feast."

"But the feast doesn't start until tonight, right?"

"Not necessarily. They're setting up now, and I think it's almost time for them to bring the statue out of the church."

Elly closed her eyes and heard the loud sound of a low trombone, almost out of tune and then joined by somber drums.

✦

"Look, Babygirl, here she comes!" said Uncle George, hoisting up her little girl body onto his old man shoulders.

"You'll kill yourself, Georgie!" yelled Fee.

"Oh shut your fat face and mind your own beeswax, Fee." George and Babygirl laughed so hard. Babygirl could feel his giggles all the way up her spine.

The saint came down the stairs, the handsome boys held her on long wooden rods. The small parade, led by the serious looking priest reading from the Bible and the band right behind.

"Where are they taking her?"

"To the stage at the end of the street. Then later tonight we can pin money on her for luck!"

Mimi and Itsy pulled Babygirl down from George's shoulders, tsking about the weight and his back.

Babygirl linked her pinky with his and pulled on his sleeve. She whispered in his ear when he leaned down, "Pay no attention to them, Georgie, I know you are strong enough to carry me. You're strong enough to do anything."

George smiled and kissed her cheek. "Let's go see if the fried dough stand is open, I want some zeppoli!"

"What's a zeppoli?"

"Oh you poor deprived child!" exclaimed Aunt Fee. "A fried ball of goodness with some powdered sugar on top. . . ."

✦

"Let's," said Elly to Liz. "Maybe the fried dough stand has some zeppoli ready. Fatten you up."

"You sure are part of this now, aren't you?"

"What?"

"You seem so comfortable."

"Well, I'm not. I'm fat and hot and uncomfortable all the time."

"No . . . comfortable in here," Liz patted Elly on the forehead.

"I guess I am," Elly smiled. She felt like a moving part of the neighborhood, of her aunts, of her foundling memories. So sure of herself here. As the realization surfaced the whimpering started from the walls. "*Dear sweet Jesus* get me out of here!"

"The crying again?"

"Yes, my own personal bit of insanity. Call me an Amore for sure."

"Let's hit the feast."

"You sure I look okay like this?" Elly was wearing a sundress stretched tight against her stomach and short.

"You look cute. And a little sexy, too! For anyone who might be attracted to pregnant girls."

Liz helped Elly off the couch, the two laughing at her awkward belly. Elly slipped on a pair of flip-flops, the only pair of shoes that would fit her swollen feet, and they left the building. The same flip-flops that would be floating off the beaches of Far Rockaway when the moon rose high in the sky that very same night.

✦

The hot summer air drifted slowly through the streets, heavy with the perfume of a city at play. The smell of loamy, green earth near the giant trees whose roots lifted up the cement sidewalks into kaleidoscope cracks. The burning dough and bubbling garlicky sauces of baking pizza. The oils and incenses of the street vendors. The scent of the people crowding the streets early, seeking a refuge from the heat just like Elly and Liz.

The two girls found a bench near the church and watched the procession of the saint.

"I watched this from Uncle Georgie's shoulders when I was little. Do you know how much I like saying things like that?"

"Yeah, it's nice to have a history. A point of reference for everything else."

"I want an ice. I think that stand is open," said Elly, pointing to a white truck set up with an aluminum awning. "Want one?"

Liz looked positively translucent. "No thanks, I'm going to have to go home soon anyway to . . ." her voice trailed off to a whisper.

"What? I didn't hear you?"

"Have to take a rest or something. Just so tired, you know?"

"Wait until I get back, okay?"

"Sure."

Elly stood in the line for an Italian ice. She thought she'd get lemon, but the vanilla looked too good walking away with other customers. It had nuts in it. Once, Elly looked back at Liz and waved. But she didn't wave back. When Elly turned around—happily licking the vanilla ice—to walk toward the bench, it was empty. Liz was gone.

A sick feeling washed over Elly. A sadness she didn't understand that got caught in her chest.

"Hey, you okay?"

Anthony came up behind her. "You look lost," he laughed.

Elly looked around. It was evening all of a sudden and her ice was a sticky pool in the paper cup, some dripping down her hands.

"Here, let me help you, babe," said Anthony, walking her over to a hot dog vender.

"Leo, lemme have some of your napkins, huh?"

A young man about Anthony's age dipped a huge handful of napkins into the tub of ice water cooling the sodas. "Want a soda or a dog, you guys? On the house? She okay, Tony? She looks sick."

"She's okay, I think. You okay, honey?"

Elly let Anthony wash her hands like a little kid. "Yeah, I think so. Did it get dark *really* quickly?"

"I don't know what you mean, babe. You're worrying me."

"What's worrying you?" asked Mimi coming up from behind, Fee in tow.

"Our girl here, she seems off."

Mimi put her arm around Elly's waist. "Of course she's off. It's almost her time. Men. You can't even imagine what we go through."

"*Men, you can't even imagine* . . ." Fee yelled, nodding along with her sister.

"Here, love. Let's pick up this hair. So hot against your neck, no?" Fee began to pull Elly's hair into a ponytail. Elly wriggled free of all of them.

"*Wait!* Look. It was *just* daylight and I *just* got an ice and Liz was *just* here and now . . . now? Where's Itsy? I'm done with all of this! I need to know what she's keeping from me. Is she coming?"

"We left her pinning money on the saint," said Mimi. "Maybe she's still there?"

The saint. Money. Zeppoli. Reality.

"Where do you buy the zeppoli? Is it on the way to the saint?" asked Elly.

"It's just down there, past the peaches and wine," said Anthony, blowing some hair out of his own eyes. "Do you want me to go get some for all of us?"

Mimi and Fee nodded.

"Elly?"

Elly nodded along with the old ladies. Anthony smiled at his women. "Okay, well go sit down and I'll bring 'em back to us, okay?"

"And then we find Itsy? And you all agree we make her tell me her secret once and for all. Like an intervention or something? Okay?"

"Yes, yes, sure, sure . . ." said Mimi and Fee clucking around her.

The three women worked their way through the now crowded street back toward the bench where Elly and Liz first saw the ice truck.

Fee and Mimi flanked Elly, each woman interlocking with one of Elly's arms. Elly knew she was safe and protected. She relaxed into the moment, leaning her head against Mimi's shoulder and letting them direct her body. She almost let her eyes close when the sisters came to an abrupt stop. "What's going on?" asked Elly.

"Well would you look at this!" exclaimed Fee.

"It's just the same isn't it, Fee?" asked Mimi.

"Looks the same, could it be?" asked Fee.

The two stopped in front of a multicolored tent nestled between the hot dog stand and a beer garden, with a sign that read TAROT AND PALMISTRY: 5 AND 10 $ READINGS.

Elly laughed a little. "Like we'd ever need anything like this! What a waste of cash, no?"

The sisters looked fidgety and their eyes wouldn't meet hers.

"What, what is it?" asked Elly, her laughter fading.

A set of knobby, wrinkled hands parted the red and purple curtains of the tent. The small, ancient woman dressed in scarves dripping with coins on the fringes jingled toward Elly.

"Is it you, Willow?" asked Mimi in a hushed voice.

Elly wanted to run back into the crowds and find Anthony. She wanted to throw herself into the arms of the neighborhood surrounding her. She didn't want to know this Willow person. She didn't want to figure anything out. She was tired of the mystery.

A wrinkled hand clamped down on Elly's sweaty wrist. "Come with me, Eleanor. I've been waiting for you."

Elly watched as Mimi and Fee stood still, frozen. No one would rescue her. She went inside the tent with Willow Bliss.

✦

The inside of the tent was deceptively large with a table covered in the mandatory black velvet, tarot cards, a crystal ball.

"I don't want my fortune told," said Elly.

A wide, strange grin spread throughout the wrinkles of the ancient woman's face. Elly hoped it wouldn't crack.

The woman wrapped a heavy, deep red, crocheted shawl around her small frame. "Well, Elly. I've been waiting a very long time for you. I thought you'd never be born. And then I thought you'd never come. I have something for you."

"Who are you?" asked Elly.

The woman laughed, a sprinkling of gold teeth winking at Elly. She thought they were beautiful. "I'm the fortune-teller who broke your great-grandmother's heart. I'm Willow Bliss. We grew up together in Fairview, Massachusetts. She was my best friend, Margaret was."

Elly did the math in her head. "But that would make you over one hundred years old . . ."

The woman shrugged. "Who's counting?"

Willow reached inside a large blue sack embroidered in stars that sat at her feet. Finding what she sought, she brought it out as if it were so precious it might break. Her overly satisfied smile triggered Elly's curiosity tenfold. Her hands itched to hold what Willow was holding.

She turned to Elly and slowly opened up her hands exposing the treasure. "This—is for you."

Elly looked down, hesitantly, almost fearfully, expecting the Holy Grail. But instead it was a small, plain, replica of a steamer trunk. She felt a twinge of disappointment.

Nevertheless, it was hers, and Willow was expecting her to take it, so Elly plucked the tiny trunk from Willow's cupped hands.

"Go ahead," urged Willow, her eyes glowing brighter. "I've been waiting a long time to give this to you. Open it up!"

"It opens?" asked Elly, her curiosity growing again.

"Of course it opens, silly girl! It's a trunk!"

"Well," said Elly, "Technically it's a box that's designed to look like a trunk. I mean, it could be a model of a trun . . ."

Willow cut her off. "Dear Great Goddess! Elly Amore of the Bronx, *open it*!"

Elly felt around the sides and found a small latch. She lifted it with a fingernail and opened the box. It wasn't just any box. It was a music box with a mirror on the inside.

"Wind it up!" said Willow. She was leaning in, looming almost over Elly. *How many times over the years must she have wondered about this gift?* thought Elly as she wound the metal crank. It played "Let Me Call You Sweetheart." Carmen's song. Elly marveled, once again at the genetic connection between Carmen and the world she was falling in love with. It didn't seem possible Carmen was rooted in any sort of magic. But she was. Here was a song to prove it. The song that lulled a baby Eleanor to sleep. A song Mimi must have crooned to Carmen. A song that carried love through the generations.

A tiny ballerina popped up and began to twirl . . . only . . . *was she holding something in her arms?* She peered in closer. The ballerina was holding a miniature swaddled baby. *But, why?* "What does this mean, Willow?" asked Elly.

"Look deeper, Eleanor," said Willow, her voice mesmerizing Elly.

She tilted the box in the dim light and realized that a piece of the box flooring wanted to come up. She gently lifted the small, red velvet base.

"There's something in here!" she exclaimed to a satisfied Willow Bliss.

"So there is," Willow responded.

Tucked into the mechanism was a perfectly preserved piece of folded paper. It looked like a Victorian calling card. The name, Margaret Green, was engraved on it and bordered by vines and tiny violets. In smooth script it read:

Dear Elly,

Would you be a darling and fix this whole mess for me? It's all gone to hell in a handbasket, hasn't it? I'd appreciate it. And, tell them I love them. Tell them Mama loves them so, so much.

Love,

Great-Grandma Margaret

A wave of dizzying dark washed over Elly. She tried to lean against the fabric of the tent but it gave way under her hand. Willow helped her to a folding chair. They sat together as Elly looked at the letter and then back at the music box.

"Think, Elly," said Willow. "You have all the pieces now."

Trunks.

Elly searched her mind.

Searching for maternity clothes with Mimi . . . The secret hiding place in the attic. The trunks. She'd found something once, a treasure. When she was ten. And Anthony interrupted her. But then, on the day she was supposed to leave the Bronx. The very day she lost her memories, she found it again. What was inside? A secret big enough to allow Itsy to break her silence. *Something of Itsy's was hidden in a trunk?* A light went on in Elly's mind. She knew what she had to do next. And it had an urgency about it that Elly sensed was more real than anything else.

She looked frantically at the woman standing in front of her.

"I can fix it! I can fix it all!"

"Yes, yes! Go!" said Willow shooing her out with her hands, her bracelets singing out a jingle-jangle song. "You've gotten what you've come for."

Elly went to leave, and then turned, hugging Willow. "Tell me my fortune, Willow," she whispered in the old woman's ear. "Tell me?" Elly pulled Willow's hand to her belly.

Willow withdrew her hand quickly, as if she'd been burned.

"Dearheart, all this can be changed. You have the answers now. Maybe not all that you want, but all that you need."

✦

Elly threw open the fabric of the tent with a fierce determination burning inside of her. Elly saw Anthony pushing through the crowd balancing bags of zeppoli and sodas. She ran to him without considering her enormous shape and knocked into a couple right in front of her. The man spilled something and turned around.

"I'm so, so sorry . . ." started Elly and then she recognized the face even if the face didn't recognize her.

"No problemo," said Cooper Bakersmith. Elly knew that voice. He was trying to keep his cool. He didn't like strangers to see his inner, seething self.

Anthony came up next to her, almost dropping the bags of fried dough when he saw Cooper. Elly elbowed him.

She was starting to hyperventilate but knew she needed to remain calm.

Cooper looked at them, a confused expression furrowing his brow, but the girl at his side urged him to get going. He turned to walk away.

Elly and Anthony walked in the other direction, fast.

"Did he recognize you?" Anthony asked under his breath.

"No, I don't think so," answered Elly.

"Well, whatever you do, don't look back."

Elly couldn't help herself. Like Lot's wife she went directly against Anthony's suggestion and—looked over her shoulder.

Cooper, with the spell slowly breaking down, had started to remember.

When Elly looked back, he was standing stock still in a pool of fluorescent light, staring at her. His blond wisp of a new girlfriend asking (from what seemed a very long way away), "What is it? Who is that girl, Cooper? Who is she?"

"I can't believe it," he said and dropped his soda on the ground.

"Run," said Anthony.

"It's too late," she said. And she was right.

"Eleanor!" Cooper yelled and ran the space between them with inhuman speed. He grabbed her arm, yanking her away from Anthony.

His eyes searched hers, scanned her and she tried to look away. "Eleanor? What the fuck? What are you *doing* here? Where have you been?"

"I've been here, with my grandmother, like I told you," said Eleanor, trying to keep her voice steady.

"Leave her be, Cooper. She doesn't belong to you," said Anthony.

"Shut up," said Cooper through his teeth. "Just shut up! I'm trying. I'm *trying* to figure all this out! Why haven't I been able to remember you?"

"Cooper, take a deep breath. Everything is okay. Just let me go. Your girl is waiting for you." Elly thought it was like handling a rabid dog. Calm, careful, and controlled. No quick movements.

Cooper looked back over his shoulder at the blond girl, then back at Elly. He looked at Elly's hand. The gem on her left ring finger glistened.

Crap, thought Elly, her heart sinking.

"What's this?"

Elly felt Anthony stiffen next to her. She shot him a look, warning him to keep his cool.

"You're marrying him? And pregnant? I always knew you were a whore," said Cooper.

"Yes. That's right, Cooper. I'm no good. So just let me walk away, okay?" Elly's hopes that Cooper wouldn't remember the baby she was carrying was his were dashed as she watched the full swell of recognition wash over him. The spell was broken. Cooper remembered everything.

He let go of her arm just long enough to grab her by her long hair, yanking her head back so she had to stare up into the light. *Hadn't Fee wanted to put it up?* Why hadn't she listened? Anthony dropped the fried dough and sodas on the ground. The soda fizzed over Elly's exposed toes. Anthony rushed at Cooper, but Cooper pulled harder. "Stay back, you fucking wop, or I'll pull all the hair out of her head." Anthony stood still. He knew Cooper was just crazy enough to do it.

"I don't know what the hell is going on." Cooper was in a sweaty panic, tugging at her hair. "Why are you walking around half clothed? All proud of your fat stomach, you pathetic pig!" His foot came up and Elly tried to reach forward to cover her belly, knowing that would be right where he'd kick her. It was just the move Anthony was waiting for. He grabbed Cooper's foot midair, toppling him over.

Cooper scrambled to his feet. The two men exchanged swings.

Elly searched for Mimi and Fee in the crowd, but they weren't there. Someone yelled that the police were coming and Anthony took a quick look around before he hammered Cooper with one enraged punch that clipped the side of his head and tipped him off balance, giving him the time to grab Elly. He picked her up as if she weighed nothing and the crowd parted for him as he ran with her, trying to get her to safety. And it closed against Cooper who battled to no avail. By the time he broke free, Elly and Anthony were already down the block and in the hallway of 170th Street.

"We can't stay here. Do you have Georgie's keys?" asked Elly.

"Sure. Always. But where are we going, Elly?" asked Anthony.

"Far Rockaway. Itsy's cottage. I have to find the trunk. There's something hidden in the trunk."

"But this building has like, a thousand trunks in the attic. Why not start here." Anthony was looking over his shoulders. It was clear to Elly that he wanted to lock her up, keep her safe. But her quest was more important.

"Anthony, me and Mimi looked through almost all of them when we were digging for these *fine* maternity clothes," Elly said as she pulled at her dress. "And we found nothing. Then, when I was decorating the apartment, I tore through what was left. There are no secrets there. Not anymore."

"So why Far Rockaway?"

"It's the only other place I can think of. Where else would Itsy hide a secret?"

"It's Itsy's secret?" asked Anthony as they got in the car and began to drive away.

"Yes. It's always been hers. But I'm about to figure it all out."

You hear me, old woman? I'm going to figure it all out . . .

✦

Itsy stood alone in the center of the attic, listening through the air vents waiting for Elly and Anthony to leave the building so she could put her plan in place. Those damn air vents. *They* were the cause of all the issues, really. If no one had heard her talk that day, maybe no one would have piqued Elly's curiosity. Too late, too late. And now Cooper would come and she'd have to do something unspeakable. If she was lucky. Itsy let out a papery rasp, a swallowed chuckle, at the thought. Imagine. She was hoping for something horrible to happen. Because the irony of life is too simple, sometimes. In order for Itsy to save Elly, she'd have to destroy Cooper Bakersmith. Tearing apart a human life was no small task, and it would put her soul in jeopardy. Or at least that's what Mama would say. *But if I don't,* thought Itsy, *then I'll never be able to prove that these things, these awful things we see can be changed! And don't forget, I have to save her. I swore a solemn vow.*

She'd need her voice. She tested it. Tried to cough but no sound came out. *No, not yet . . .* she thought. *Not yet, but soon.*

29

✦ ✦ ✦

Itsy

There isn't a magical "Take Me Home" spell. No ruby slippers. Once you're grown, you can't go home again.

In my cottage by the sea, the one so filled up with Mama and my sisters and George when I was young, I rocked myself to sleep and cried. Even before all hell broke loose over, upon, and inside my family on that day in May 1945, I was a broken girl. Abandoned by the rest of them, left to fend for myself, and with Henry only able to be with me in secret . . . the lonesome was so hard to bear sometimes.

I started getting homesick the second Mama took out my braids and piled my hair on top of my head. I was breathless to grow up, to be like my older sisters. Breathless at thirteen, to be with Henry. I was sick of being Georgie's caretaker and the last in line for Mama's attention. But when she sat me down in front of her dressing mirror stroking my braids with her chin resting on the top of my head so we were looking square at one another and asked, "Are you ready?" . . . I wasn't. A queasy feeling opened up in the pit of my stomach. I wanted to cry out, "No! No,

Mama, I'm not ready!" But there was no going back. Henry's lips had touched mine already. The spell of adulthood was cast.

I think she understood, because as she undid my braids and pinned up my hair she said, in the way Mama said things, no holds barred, "You can't go home again, Itsy. I'd like to say you can but you can't. I'd like to tell you that you can stay little forever, but I'd be lying and I don't lie. The truth is, time marches on and you have two choices: You move forward, come what may, and you experience all the sour and sweet things that fly at you from around the corners, *or* you sit still. Don't sit still."

George never grew up, not in his mind. He was forced to sit still. And it was hard for him. Watching me and Henry fall in love. Watching us laugh over jokes he didn't understand. He felt left out. I remember him, his strong adult body trying to squish up in my lap, crying about it all on the porch of my cottage.

"But it's not *fair,*" he whined. "You and Henry all alone, keeping me outta things. I wish, I wish . . ."

"What, my Georgie, what do you wish?" I asked, trying to soothe him.

"I wish things were the way they used to be. You know? One, two, three, you and me? And I wish you didn't live here. I wish you'd come back home and we could save this place for the summers. I hate coming all the way out here to see you guys. Why'dja have to move anyways? I just want you to come home. Come home, Itsy? Please come home?"

And then, just like a real grown-up, I had to say the words that grown-up people say but never believe. "I am home, George. This is my home, now."

He sat up and made fists. His face surged with red anger. He pounded on the columns of the porch. "Well, I don't like it!" he yelled. "I don't like it one little bitty, bit!" He ran away from me then, down the street and toward the beaches yelling, "I'm telling Mama you won't come home! I'm telling her you play kissing with Henry here at the cottage!"

Mama knows, George, I thought. Mama knows. *She put me here. Mama knows everything.*

It took a long time for me to figure out my own home. The internal one, the one that's made of memories and pain. But you still can't go there, and stay. The best you can do is dip a toe in now and then. Cry your eyes out.

For me, home was in Mama's words, her stories. In the herbs she used for cooking and weaving magic . . . and in the tangible things she made for us.

I put my baby inside the trunk with my mother's linens and lavender. I always hoped, that even though I couldn't find my way back home, that somehow my tiny baby could.

30

Elly

"It has to be here somewhere. Isn't there an attic?" They'd searched the small cottage and found no trace of a steamer trunk.

Anthony looked up. "Wait, look, it's right here." He stood on tiptoe and pushed a piece of ceiling out and over. He grabbed the edges of the exposed hole and hoisted himself up. "Here's the ladder, babe, be careful."

Once she was up they let their eyes adjust to the light. It was a very small space that held only one object.

"Here it is, Anthony! I knew it would be here." Elly threw open the trunk. The scent of old linen and lavender came out like wind.

"More sheets?" asked Anthony.

Elly picked up the first layer of sheets and took in a deep breath. Lavender layered with an earthy, human smell. Elly had refocused her eyes so the tears that rose wouldn't blur her vision. She had to get a very good look. She had to make sure what she was seeing was actually there. Not a memory, not a flash of premonition. She squeezed her eyes shut and then opened them again.

There it was. The secret. The tiny, skeletal remains of a prematurely born infant. Bones clad in a beautiful lace christening gown. The tears fell freely from Elly's eyes, her throat closed against them and Elly panicked for a moment, thinking she, too, would lose her words now that she found the treasure. *No, you won't,* she thought . . . *I've found something, not lost something . . .*

"Oh God! It's too much. It's just too much. What is this? Why would someone do this?" She cradled her belly in her arms, wishing she could take the child out now and smell its head and cuddle its warm, alive body.

"Dear Sweet Jesus," said Anthony, who did the sign of the cross and kissed his crucifix. "Are you remembering, Elly? Is it working?"

Elly reached into the trunk and placed her hands behind layers of fabric to ensure that she wouldn't harm the remains. She carefully lifted up the child's bones nestled against Amore lace. "No. I'm not remembering anything. I'm sensing things, but I can't remember." She covered the front of the child with a soft, white blanket.

"Maybe we have to bring it to Itsy, ask her what it's all about?" suggested Anthony.

"Yes. It's hers," said Elly sniffing and regaining her composure. "It's why she lost her voice. Loss is magical. You can't lose something without something to show for it. It's a balance. I have to get this baby back to Itsy, then she'll get her voice back and tell me what she said to me that day."

"Sounds like a plan," Anthony said, helping her down from the cramped attic space.

Shortly after, on the drive back to the Bronx, Elly suddenly felt heady with nausea. "Stop the car, Anthony, I'm going to be sick."

Anthony pulled over by the boardwalk and ran around to the passenger side of the car. Elly threw up by the curb. "Something's happening, Anthony!"

"Is it the baby? Dear God, Elly, is there something wrong with our baby?"

"No . . . I need . . ." Elly heard the water, the waves surging onto the shore. "I want to go swimming before we go back."

"But Elly, honey, it's nighttime!"

"Anthony! Please, just listen to me!"

He walked her down the beach and watched as she disappeared into the night waves off Far Rockaway. She went in wearing her flip-flops, kicking them into the sea as she felt her feet become buoyant. She swam until the truth came. And then she floated on her back, her short dress floating up past her belly button so the baby could look up at the stars, too. Her long hair free and swirling all around. Mermaid hair. The sky was wider, somehow, than it'd ever been before.

Her hands moved to her stomach. She took a deep breath and bravely commanded The Sight.

"Show me."

A bright light danced behind her eyes. She was gliding through the inside of herself, tumbling into a vision of a sunny kitchen and a bowl of baby cereal on the table. "Mommy's coming!" she yelled with a little impatience. And then the light went out.

Elly smiled and opened her eyes. "Mommy's coming," she said. "And you know what? I was supposed to die. Ten seconds ago. You, too, my baby. And now? Now I have an unforeseen life. What shall we do with it, little one?"

She turned around to see Anthony pacing on the shore, in the moonlight. Behind him she saw the ghost lights of Playland and heard echoes of laughter, long gone.

Elly swam back to her future.

31

Itsy

"I knew you were going to come back for her. Saw it years and years ago. Sour souls can't give up. They aren't strong enough to say good-bye. We were strong enough to keep you away but here you are again. Evil doesn't learn. It's thick-headed. Even so, I kept praying it wouldn't come to this."

Cooper turned around to face Itsy. She'd been hiding right out in the open. The doors to the building were unlocked and he'd barged right in, as she'd know he would. The only inside door that was unlocked was 1A, the same place he'd been the day they poisoned him. Itsy's scratchy voice came from behind and made him jump.

Itsy was even more surprised by her resurrected voice. She ran her hands up and down her neck. "She must have opened the trunk." She laughed, her throat raspy but strong. "Sit down, boy, sit down and hear my story."

Itsy had planned this moment for six months. And so far, it was all working out the way she'd hoped. Well, not the way she'd *hoped.* She'd spent a long time hoping it wouldn't have to end like this. That the Fates would figure out another way. Or even Elly herself. That she'd just *leave.* But just like Itsy always told Mimi, don't underestimate The Sight. It was true. All of it unfolding like it had in her mind the second she'd held baby Elly in her arms.

Cooper was staring at her. Disbelief in his eyes. She knew the cause. He could feel it, too. Most ordinary people can tell when their fate is being affected. And his whole future was about to be cut short. Itsy watched Cooper taking in the whole scene, adjusting his own plan. She saw his eyes settle on the candles burning in the center of the room.

"That's a Henbane Candle Ring. A bit of black magic. We don't practice it as a rule, but sometimes certain situations call for action. Mama was fluent in those arts, but hid them from us most of the time. We are only supposed to use them in the most serious of times. And this counts, doesn't it, Mama?" Itsy looked toward the ceiling and then back at Cooper. "By the time you . . ."

She watched as Cooper sniffed the air.

"Oh my," she said, "you've already inhaled their perfume. Now you'll feel your limbs get heavy and numb. I'm sorry about all this. But family is family, Cooper. And family always comes first."

"You can't think you're going to get away with this," said Cooper sounding hollow and unsure.

"With what?" asked Itsy, a hint of uncharacteristic sarcasm in her voice. *Power is a funny thing,* she thought.

"With whatever it is you are planning to do," said Cooper, shifting from one foot to the other.

"I can try. Soon your voice won't be there either so speak your piece before I speak mine. Your feet are already tingling, aren't they?"

"You're crazy," Cooper said as he tried to lunge for her. But he couldn't and fell in a great heap onto the Oriental carpet and tried to wriggle his body into a corner, squirming like a worm. He didn't get far.

"Yes, yes . . . we'll get to that *crazy* part, but not yet. Now is the time for you to listen. This is *my* confession, not yours." Itsy picked up a teacup. Her hands shook with adrenaline and age, and the cup clattered against the saucer for a moment. Itsy smiled. It reminded her of Mimi, and she knew she wouldn't set living eyes on her sister again. How she loved her sisters. Everything in her life had always been built around her siblings. All the choices. All the pain. All the joy.

"Are you ready for my story, Cooper? Because I'm ready to tell it, and you're not the perfect person to tell, but you're all I've got right now. And besides, somehow I think you might understand better than most would. And I'd like that. Someone to finally understand."

"What makes you think I'd understand your crazy confession?" asked Cooper, still struggling to move his legs, not understanding his invisible binding. There was sweat on his brow and panic in his voice.

"Because only someone with a dark soul will be able to fully recognize what I have to say. Not that it matters, really, as neither of us are leaving here intact."

Cooper tried to talk, but the toxins were already in his lungs.

Itsy took a sip from her cup and began to spin her tale.

✦

"On Victory over Europe Day, May 8th, 1945, I was teaching seventh grade at Bayside Public School. It was almost time for my afternoon break, and I was starving. I can remember hearing my stomach growl, and the children giggling as they completed their quiet study. The classroom phone rang. I remember *knowing.* Staring at the phone on the wall until everything around it was dark gray and fuzzy. I walked to it with my hand stretched out. The children were murmuring. I supposed I did look odd. My sensible heels clicked on the floor. That smartass kid—I still remember his name—Bobby Horrowitz. He said 'Are you gonna answer that or not, Ms. Amore? It might be my Ma callin' me home!' And the kids laughed. The kids were laughing while Mimi gave me the news. I left the phone dangling, I think, and walked out of the room.

"I must have taken the train. I can't remember. It would have been smarter to take a taxi. But the A to the 145th Street station and then to the D train was a shorter ride. About an hour and a half all in all. An hour and a half I can't remember. I remember flashes, I guess . . . and then—poof—I was standing in front of my family's building. 1313 East 170th Street. Home. I opened the iron gate, walked up the cement steps, and faced Mama's fortune-teller's prophecy.

"In the events that followed the coroner leaving with half of my family, I went into the garden to try and breathe. It was too much. So much I couldn't feel anything at all. It scared me—that numb. It reminded me of a story I read in *National Geographic* where a man almost froze to death but lived to tell about the experience. He described it as a peaceful feeling. How he was suddenly warm and sleepy. Comfortable, even, as everything inside of him was shutting down. Even though he knew he was about to die. The lie of death. The invisible tragic comedy of it all.

"The baby inside me wiggled. It was the first movement I'd felt. My heart soared. I put my hands on my stomach and proceeded to make a very bad mistake.

" 'Shhhh, little one,' I crooned. 'It's over now. You're safe. You'll be born with Mimi's baby who's supposed to live.'

" 'Who are you talking to, Itsy?'

"It was George. His face was swollen and purple with grief. Why did I leave him alone? He was so frightened. Why hadn't I gone to him right away? I knew his hiding places. It was really *all my own fault,* what happened next. My fault in so many ways.

"He took me by the shoulders. The roses, Mama's roses blurred together in great swatches of pink as he shook me back and forth.

" 'Is there a baby inside of you?'

" 'George, stop shaking me.' My voice sounded like the A train.

"My brother slapped me across the face. I looked at him, my tall handsome twin. What a man he could have made if he'd been whole. He pointed a shaking finger at me, even as the rest of his body arched away repulsed.

" 'You're . . . you're not married. You can't have a baby unless you are married. Sinner! Sinner . . . Sinner!'

"He came at me then, my brother, and began to beat me. I don't remember much after the first blow: It was aimed at my head and tossed me into the garden wall. I tried to protect my stomach, but George couldn't stop himself. He kicked and hit. Everything was pouring out of him and raining down on me. And all I really remember is trying to figure out how to save him from hurting me, because I knew he'd never forgive himself. I've heard that nowadays people who have children born like George put them in institutions. A shame. Really. Because George was not a violent person. He simply couldn't process all the pain. And I knew, no matter what came next, I'd never remind him of how he hurt me. I'd never speak of it again.

"Nancy, a young girl my age who lived next door, found me and helped me inside. The halls seemed endless. She put me in Mama's bed and delivered the baby. Dead. I woke to see her standing by the window holding a tiny bundle in bloodstained blankets. There was a sickening moment of hope where I thought it might still be alive. Where I forgot to remember that they were all dead.

"Nancy turned to look at me. The blanket dropped and I saw the top of a blue-tinged head, bruised and still tempting. Fuzzy hair.

"'What do you want to do with her, Itsy?'

"With her? *Her.* I opened my mouth to speak, but nothing came out. I had to show her, instead. I had to show Nancy what we would do with my daughter.

"Later, when Nancy needed a place to live, I wrote Mimi a note. *Give Nancy Bunny's apartment.* Mimi looked at me, inside of me, and didn't ask any questions. Nancy had the apartment and I moved back home, too."

Itsy stopped to take a breath.

"Nancy is Anthony's grandma. They've lived here for a long time, the Rivettas. That boy is part of us. But not you. You're an empty one, aren't you, Cooper?"

Cooper tried to answer her and couldn't.

Itsy kneeled next to him on the floor and placed her cup on the coffee table. She moved his hair back from his sweaty brow. "That's right. You can't talk. I am so sorry about that. *I* know how difficult that can be."

Cooper tensed as much as he could under her touch. She could sense his fear.

"Don't be afraid. You'll be a better person when this is all over. And there are plenty of people who live their lives an empty shell. And it isn't pretty. Like George. Not George when he was little, George when he was joyless. I don't think anyone should live like that. But George was different in that he was special, you know . . . innocent. There's not *one bit* of innocent in you, is there, Cooper?

"And I know you think I'm crazy. Perhaps I am. The truth is everyone is crazy, haven't you realized that yet?"

✦

"You see I was *just trying* to fix what was *so, so* broken. Trying to prove we could change what we see. It was the day when Carmen came back to get Babygirl. George ran down to find me. He came for me yelling all the way. The whole block could hear him.

"'Itsy!' he was yelling. 'They're trying to take her!'

"When he found me in the garden (Babygirl must have just opened the trunk in the attic), I'm sure I looked a sight sitting there with my hands on my neck trying to hold back all the coarse words that wanted to spill out.

"He skidded to a stop. 'Are you okay, my Itsy?' George always reverted to his smaller self when he was nervous. He let the fake grown-up slip away. I nodded. I began to ask, 'Where is she?' but closed my throat against them. I didn't trust the deluge that might come. I scribbled:

"*Where is she?*

"'In the attic.'

"Of course she was.

"That's where the trunk was. Where she found it the first time.

"I moved it, you know. When she moved back here last Christmas. I moved it over to Far Rockaway so she wouldn't be here when you came. She's out there right now with her real true love uncovering my secrets while I'm taking care of hers.

"Anyway, when I got up there that day long ago and I found her so small, so frightened. She asked me for help and help her I did. I fixed everything. She asked me if I would help her to forget. A child's silly, selfish request. If I hadn't seen the future, if I didn't already know that I needed to protect her from this building, from all of us, from you, I'd have soothed the girl a different way. But don't you see? She figured out a solution to my problem without even knowing it, that little witch. If I granted her wish, and she forgot all about us, then why would she ever come back? I thought I was fixing things for the better, but I only made it worse. You know what they say about *pride goeth before the fall* and all that nonsense. Anyway . . . I wove my magic right there in the attic, fingers crossed it would work. Boy, did it ever.

"We came out of Georgie's apartment holding hands. Carmen was already there, the door to the front of the building wide open to the sunny, late summer day. The girl cocked her head to one side as she watched Carmen fall to her knees and hold her arms out with grasping hands. 'Eleanor! Come to Mommy! Mommy's home, baby!'

"Her little hand left mine in slow motion, and she walked down the stairs, taking tentative, princess steps. George ran in. He looked around at all of us wildly. He met her halfway on the staircase.

"'Babygirl?' George called to her, quietly.

"'Stay away from her, Uncle George! She's coming with me!' screamed Carmen.

"Mimi put her hand on Carmen's shoulders. 'Give them time.'

"George looked at his best pal. 'Babygirl?' The girl hesitated and George . . . my sweet brother George, plopped right down on the stairs and turned her around to look into his eyes.

"'You're gonna stay with us, okay?' he was sniffling. 'You don't have to go if you don't want to.'

"'Who are you?' asked Babygirl.

"'What?' George was choking back his tears. 'Please don't leave me. Please? I need you. I love you. Please?' An old man begging a young child. It was heartbreaking.

"The girl put her hand on his cheek ever so gently, like cupping an orchid.

"And that's when the enormity of my mistake occurred to me. She didn't remember anything. There she was, alone on the stairs, surrounded by strangers. How brave she was.

"'I'm supposed to go with you? Are you my mother?' she asked Carmen.

"Carmen, confused and flustered, pushed off Mimi's hands. She ran to Babygirl and picked her up. Babygirl was too big to be carried. Her skinny legs dangled by her mother's side. It reminded me of the rocking chair. Carmen was always running away with things much too heavy for her to handle.

"Anyway, she carried her daughter out of the building screaming all kinds of things out of her mean mouth. Things like, 'What did you do to her?' 'Fuck you people,' and 'crazy.'

"Again, we are all crazy. Every human being has the capacity for crazy. I suppose Carmen knew that best of all.

"The taxicab was gone in a smudge of yellow and we were all left there alone, each in our own way. Little Anthony, who watched the whole thing through the banister bars, Fee from the doorway of 1B. Me at the top of the staircase . . . Mimi on the front stoop watching her little family get away—again.

"But none of us was left more alone than George, who began to weep.

"I tried to comfort him. There was so much to make right. I thought maybe my deal was one way. Perhaps I could use my words, forgive him. I opened my mouth but all there was, was that ever so familiar dryness. 'Get off me!' he shouted shrugging my touch and standing up . . . shorter somehow.

"He went to the top of the staircase. He looked down over all of us. For a moment he began to shimmer, I thought he might just disappear, but it wasn't that at all. It was the light coming out of him.

" 'I am not Georgie anymore. I am only George. Old man George. I will no longer play,' he stated before he went into his apartment and slammed the door. 'Leave me alone,' we heard.

"And that was the day Georgie died for the second time. Killed The Day the Amores Died. Resurrected that sweet summer by Babygirl, and killed one more time by yours truly. Grumbly George of 170th Street became a mean old man. Smelly, too. Was it worth it? I don't know. Now that she's back, I don't know anything anymore. And you don't know anything either, do you, Cooper? Don't know who you are or what you want. Not even a full person. 'New to the planet,' Mama would say. And if I don't kill part of you, you'll kill her. It's clear as day to me. And Cooper, I can't let that happen. I have to protect her the right way this time. Mimi was wrong. So was Mama. We *can* change what we see. There's more power inside of us than we'll ever know."

Itsy stopped talking and took a long look at Cooper.

She sat down on the floor. "So it's my job . . ." Itsy felt the pain at the back of her neck pulse through to her chest. "My goodness? Is it time already?"

And then Itsy, with one frail hand, covered Cooper's mouth. "Don't be scared, Cooper. You won't die. I'm no killer. But I can't let you leave here remembering anything. So I have to try the Forgetting spell one more time. Only this time, I have to make sure it's completely binding and can never be undone. So I'm taking your memories with me, Cooper. It's the only way."

She applied pressure to his mouth while letting the constriction in her own chest pull at his soul. It didn't take long.

Itsy laid her head in Cooper's lap waiting for her death, waiting to see the blankness of the spell envelop his eyes. Her soft silver curls fell gently across his legs. Then, there it was, the look. A wave of anguish, a kind of empty sorrow she'd never felt. It was Cooper's soul. Free and yet not free. "Forgive me?" she asked. "Please forgive me, Mama? Henry? George? I did it for Elly!"

The pain came again. And passed again. Cooper was looking down at her with a curiosity that assured her she'd wiped him clean. He was a tabula rasa. A blank slate. No past. No violence, no memory of Elly.

Itsy waited for the final, suffocating pain, but it didn't come. Instead, she saw Henry in his uniform open the wall in front of her, the wall covered in dogwood flowers had become a dogwood forest.

He called her by her real name, and she ran to him shedding

her old lady self on the floor with Cooper. One dead, one newly born. One young, one old. Both traveling in different directions through light and time.

✦

The boy looked down at the old woman, dead in his lap, and began to cry. He didn't know where he was, or who he was. But he knew the woman had something of his that he could never get back. The tingling in his limbs began to fade and soon he was able to get up, making sure to lay the woman's head gently on the ground. And then sat on the couch. The boy waited for something to happen, because there was nothing else to do.

32

The Amore Sisters

Fee and Mimi came home from the feast late. After Elly had gone with Willow the two decided to go to the saint alone and pin money on her. Mimi felt a tugging in her soul that told her they needed some luck. When they reached the building they were welcomed by flashing lights and sirens. They looked at one another exchanging a knowing glance. Itsy'd warned them, but they'd hoped—there was always hope.

The two sisters reached out for each other's hands. Together they pushed past the emergency people. Together they watched Elly and Anthony speaking to police officers. Elly's hands waving in the air importantly. Elly saw them and she tried to lunge past the blue uniforms, but they held her back.

Mimi said "I live here" to a younger officer who was guarding the front door. She placed her old, shaking hand on top of his. He started to stop her, but a look of warm recognition washed over his face. "Mrs. Amore! What an honor. My Ma came to you a few years back. Terrible headaches she was having. That tea. It cured her! Thank you!"

"It's what we do," said Mimi. "Tell your Ma to come see us anytime."

The officer let them into hallway. "He's been here," said Fee trying to whisper.

"I know. I can smell him. She's orchestrated this whole thing, our sister. She did a wonderful job," said Mimi.

"Are you ready?" asked Fee.

"Are we ever ready?" asked Mimi as she opened the door to her apartment.

Mimi and Fee found Itsy's body on the gurney in the middle of Mimi's living room. Her face was zipped over with black plastic.

Mimi unzipped the body bag and touched her sister Itsy's cold face. "My, how things change, love. That other day, the day the rest of them went, there was white cotton against them. Look at this," Mimi flipped the cold, hard plastic. "Time cheapens everything, doesn't it?"

Fee started crying. The sisters took hands for one last time. Two alive and one dead, they made a circle. "Godspeed Itsy," cried Fee.

Back on the front stoop Mimi spoke to the police officer.

"What happened to the boy?"

"Are you related to him? We took him downtown. He doesn't remember anything. Said he woke up and Itsy was dead. If you know him you can collect him."

"And if we don't?" yelled Fee.

"Then the state will take care of him."

The two old women nodded. "As it should be," said Mimi.

✦

Later that night Elly went in search of her grandmother and remaining aunt. They were in the garden sitting on the bench. Both had their hands, palm up in their laps.

"Mimi?" asked Elly, softly. "Fee?"

The women tilted their heads toward her in unison.

"May I sit with you?"

"No," said Mimi.

Elly was startled by the cold response, "Why?"

The women did not answer her.

Elly realized that she was witnessing a quiet grief she'd never seen before. She left them alone, but was more determined than ever to be one of them. She would claim her spot as an Amore woman. She'd never sensed so much strength, so much wisdom. So many treasures. Elly knew she had to earn a spot on that bench, and this new Elly wasn't one to step away from a challenge.

✦

There was a line outside the funeral parlor that stretched down the block. The wake started at three. Mimi, Fee, and the new third Amore, Elly, were seated at the right hand of the casket in pink velvet chairs. Anthony sat with them, and there was an extra chair for Carmen, in case she showed up.

"I wonder where Liz is? I wonder if she even knows. I haven't heard from her in days," said Elly.

"I'm sure she's here somewhere, there's so many people," said Anthony.

The flowers were lovely, the sentiments were real. Elly could tell when the mourners kissed her on the cheek—each touch a spark of a nice memory. Itsy would be missed.

The next morning they all arrived again. Another testament to Itsy and her quiet yet appreciated life. It was time for a final goodbye. Elly knelt on the prayer bench and placed a square, white, crocheted blanket she'd made with Itsy. The blanket had Itsy's baby inside. Then she put her hands on her aunt's cold hands. A shock of light went through her mind, and this time she knew the memory would burn itself there. This was the real thing. A solid thing. The true answer.

✦ Babygirl ✦

Babygirl heard Mimi on the phone. Carmen was coming back, coming to take her away. Babygirl turned around in circles not knowing what to do. She ran to the front windows, it was so hot and her hands, nervous already and sweaty moved back and forth over the twisted metal bars that decoratively kept them all safe while they slept. What will keep me safe now? *she wondered.*

She looked for the yellow taxicab to come and take her away. No! She had to find George. She ran out into the hall but Mimi had her by the neck of her dress. "You have to go home, honey. She's better now and she's your mother. You belong with her."

"No I don't!" cried Babygirl, kicking and screaming. She turned around to bite Mimi's wrist. Mimi let her go.

"Georgie!" She ran up the stairs. Uncle George would keep her safe. He always could. She ran into his apartment.

"What, Babygirl, what's goin' on?"

Babygirl told him her news. She could tell he was mad. "Oh. We'll just see about this. I'll go get Itsy. You go hide."

"Hide where?" Babygirl was quiet. Her eyes were wide. Frightened.

"Hide in that place where we can't never find you. Duh!"

Babygirl smiled and went on tiptoe to kiss her Uncle. "You are the smartest uncle in the world, Georgie! I love you so much!"

George kissed her back, blushing and left the apartment. Babygirl could hear him running down the stairs calling, "Itsy!"

Babygirl knew just where to go. She ran through the apartment and went through the secret door. She hid in her special spot and waited. It didn't take long before she noticed the trunk, the one she'd forgotten all about . . . and now was as good a time as any to do some serious treasure hunting.

The hairpin. Was it still on the floor? Yes! She opened the trunk and . . . *Everything. Most all of Elly's memories came through in that very moment.*

✦

Elly was hunched, crying, and didn't notice Carmen make her appearance. She felt a presence next to her and heard the creaking of the bench as Carmen knelt next to her. Elly didn't want to look up. Didn't want to hope it was her mother.

Carmen cleared her throat, "They sure made the old girl look good."

Elly looked up. It *was* her mother.

"Mom? Mommy!" Elly threw herself into Carmen's arms. Carmen, unused to this sort of affection from her usually distant daughter, timidly patted Elly on the back. "What is it, Eleanor? It isn't *so* sad, you know. She *was* old."

Elly lifted up her head. "No, not that," she sniffled. "Well, it is, but it isn't. It's so much more than that!" she stood up. "Oh, Mom! I remember! I remember everything now!" Elly, overcome with all that she now remembered and understood tried to hug Carmen, who pulled roughly away.

"Why didn't you take my calls? Why won't you hug me? I need to talk to you." Elly begged.

"Please stop, you're embarrassing me!" said Carmen through clenched teeth.

Elly searched her mother's eyes for any sort of compassion. She searched Carmen looking for the mother she remembered. The mother from "before." All she saw was confusion and rage. Elly ran from the room.

"Well?" asked Mimi. "What are you waiting for, Carmen? Better go after her. You only get but a few chances in this life to make things right."

Carmen looked at her mother and started to say a million things. They poured out with stuttered starts and frustrated pointer finger accusations. In the end, she gave out a small yell, threw her hands in the air and stomped out of the room after her daughter.

"What a scene!" yelled Fee.

Mimi just shook her head.

"Don't worry," said Anthony, putting his arms around both women. "They'll be fine."

"You're a good boy," said Mimi, who rested her head against his strong shoulder for support.

✦

Carmen left the wake room with everyone's eyes on her. A state she usually lived for and thrived in, but right now it seemed everyone wanted her to be someone she wasn't. There was a part of Carmen that didn't want to chase after her daughter and make amends. A part of her that felt it was too late.

But being a mother is just like playing a role, and Carmen wasn't about to be the dysfunctional one. Mimi's understudy? Carmen thought *not*. "Where did you go, preggers?" she whispered under her breath in the lavish funeral parlor hallway. A cool breeze danced in from the direction of the back hall. Carmen took the cue. At the back door there was a restroom. She investigated. No Eleanor.

"May I help you?" an overly tall man asked, surprising Carmen.

"Have you seen an *enormous* young woman try to run this way?"

The man shook his head and walked back to a door that read "Office." Carmen noticed an unmarked door next to that one.

"What's in there?" she asked the man's back.

"Our showroom. Have a look around. Then he turned to her and smiled. He was missing some of his teeth. "Let me know if you see anything you like."

A chill spread across Carmen's skin, even under her black, silk crepe sundress. She opened the door to the showroom and saw rows and rows of coffins. She walked in and closed the door behind her. "Yeah . . . right. Something I like, my *ass*!"

Carmen identified the classification of coffins immediately. The cheapest were pushed off to the side. The more expensive caskets lined the ends of the row. The whole room reminded her of a church, only there were caskets instead of people lined up in pew formation. At the "altar" end of the room was a row of what seemed to be the priciest. And one coffin, silver with gold trim, was not on a stand, it was on a small platform and it was slightly ajar. Carmen smiled. "Found you," she said.

Carmen walked down the row and then lifted the lid of the coffin revealing Elly, her pregnant belly too large to close the lid all the way. Her arms crossed over her chest. The scene, both hilarious and surreal, gave Carmen a moment of pause. This was *her* child. And estranged or not, it was overwhelming to see her in a coffin.

"Get up, Eleanor." Carmen was done with the funny part of the situation.

No answer from the coffin, just the rise and fall of her swollen belly.

"Get up!" demanded Carmen.

"Call me by my name," the pretend corpse said.

"Oh for Christ sake! Get up, *Elly,* please?"

Elly sat up, her hair and eyes wild. "Will you talk to me now?"

"I came to find you, didn't I?" Carmen rummaged in her large, soft leather purse for her cigarettes. She found them and took one out, tapped it on the case and lit it up.

"I don't think you are allowed to smoke in here," said Elly.

Carmen laughed. "This from the pregnant girl in the coffin? Nice job, by the way. Very dramatic. There's a little of me inside of you, don't deny it."

"It wasn't very well thought out. I couldn't close the damn thing," said Elly.

"Language!" Carmen teased. They both laughed. Tension melted away.

Elly tried to get up. "Can you help me? It was easier getting into this thing."

"Sure, love."

Love, she said love . . . thought Elly.

Carmen rested her cigarette on the coffin beside the one Elly was in and helped her daughter, gracelessly, out of the box.

Elly held on to Carmen even after she was free of the coffin. "Mom, I missed you so much. And I miss *her.* I miss Aunt Itsy so much and it's all my fault. Cooper was coming for me, not Itsy. And she felt she had to protect me. And if I'd remembered everything sooner I'd have known. I'm good at knowing things. Or I was. When I was little, right? I had good instincts about people."

"Well, you did have good instincts about the schmuck who sold me that bad junk that made me crazy. You kicked him in the shin before we left the pub that night."

"And I tried to stay away from you because I knew you didn't mean to hurt me," said Elly.

"I don't want to talk about that. It wasn't *me* who did that to you. It was the drugs."

"I know, Mom. I know. I forgave you a long time ago . . . I just didn't remember."

"Well now, isn't this charming? I always figured you just forgot about everything because you hated me for hurting you. That's why I never pressed the issue. So if it wasn't that, then what was it? What made you forget it all? I always thought you just wiped out the good with the bad," said Carmen.

"It was that summer, Mom. I was so *sad* to leave them. I wanted so much to be with them."

"With those old, crusty, damaged people?"

"My people, Mom. *Our* people."

"Whatever." Carmen pushed Elly away and sniffed. "I guess we should get back to *them* then. I assume this means you'll stay? Here? With them?"

Elly realized that she hadn't considered anything different. "Yes. I'm home."

She saw the hurt pass across her mother's eyes.

"You could stay, too, Mom. There's a vacant apartment."

The two women looked at each other and then both laughed so hard they lost their breath and tears rolled down their cheeks. That would *never* happen. They laughed so hard Mimi found them.

"Well," she said, her voice echoing down and bouncing off the rows of caskets. "Now that the two of you have reacquainted yourselves, do you think you might join me at the cemetery so I can bury my sister?"

Silence fell heavy between the three women. Carmen grabbed her bag and headed for the door. Elly followed.

✦

Because God has chosen to call our sister from this life to Himself,
we commit his body to the earth,
for we are dust and unto dust we shall return.
But the Lord Jesus will change our mortal bodies to be like His in glory,
for He is risen, the firstborn of the dead.
So let us commend our brother to the Lord,
that the Lord may embrace him in peace and raise up his body on the last day.

The priest stood at the open mouth of the hole in the ground. Elly, Mimi, Fee, and Carmen sat on chairs facing him. Anthony stood behind Elly, a protective hand on her shoulder.

Fee cried loudly. Mimi stared. The casket was lowered into

the earth, an orifice. It creaked like a ship in the wind on a wide ocean. Elly felt seasick. She couldn't breathe. There didn't seem to be any way out of the situation. There were no gray areas, no teas or tinctures to undo the deadness. She felt awash with panic, a panic she'd never felt. And that's when she realized she wasn't alone, that she was feeling the fears of everyone sitting around them in the crowd. It wasn't just her own grief and terror of the unknown—it belonged to everyone there. Elly felt it all.

The mourners washed up in waves of black and fed the mouth handfuls of earth and flowers.

Before Elly knew it, the whole ceremony was over. Relief washed over her with the heaviness of their feelings gone, but she knew she'd feel it again when she went back to the building. She needed a break.

"We have to get back to the house. People will come," said Mimi, standing up and tugging on Fee.

"I'm not coming, Ma," said Carmen.

"I'm *so* surprised," shot back Mimi.

"Please! Can't we try? Just for today?" begged Elly.

"*Fine,*" said Mimi and Carmen in unison.

Mimi, Fee, and Anthony returned to the waiting limousine.

"I need a sec, okay?" Elly said to Anthony as he walked away looking handsome yet stiff in his black suit.

"Take all the time you need, babe."

"Babe, huh? Very imaginative," said Carmen.

"Oh please, Mom. Give it a rest, could you?"

"He's just *such a meathead,* you could do so much better than—"

Elly put her hand up to her mother and shook her head as if to say "no more."

They sat in silence. The leaves on the trees were huge, like a great man's palm. They spread out, a green canopy covering the gravesite and most of the folding chairs. But the sun shifted, and Elly found herself warming in its summer shine. It was peaceful. Elly didn't want to leave. She wanted to stay with Itsy and with Carmen. To sit and listen to the faroff drone of lawn mowers and the silent whispers of the breeze in the branches of the tree. They had so many stories, those branches.

"You really *do* belong here, don't you?" said Carmen, examining the contented look on her daughter's face.

"I suppose," said Elly, squinting at Carmen.

"You have their magic?"

"Yes, I guess I do. Or at least I'm trying to learn."

Carmen looked as if she wanted to say something, something real. Something *like I wanted to learn too,* or, *Why didn't they take care of me the way they take care of you?* But she didn't. She looked away. "I grieve for her so, you know. Ache for her," she said.

"For Itsy?" asked Elly.

"No. For you. The you who you were supposed to be."

The statement hit Elly's gut like a sucker punch. Here she was feeling almost sorry for Carmen, and now *this.* "You did *not* just say that." The mower in the distance grew louder. The tree's branches crunched together. The sky faded gray for Elly.

"Yes. I did. We're being all *honest,* right? Well, memory loss or not, my issues and mistakes aside, you didn't turn out the way I'd hoped. Far from it, actually." Carmen lit a cigarette and took a long drag inside the pregnant pause.

Elly stayed calm, "And what or who were you hoping for, Mom?" she asked, trying to keep her voice even.

Carmen exhaled and the smoke flew across the sweet summer breeze. It chilled Elly, sending shivers down her spine. It was a kind of smoke eclipse—Elly knew a moment was coming she didn't want to face, a moment she'd been running from for a very long time.

Carmen tilted her head back and closed her eyes, trying for a suntan even in a graveyard. She let the cigarette drop and smolder in the grass.

"Let's see. I suppose I always thought you'd speak fluent French. That you'd play the piano and tell sarcastic jokes. I supposed you'd be funny looking until you were sixteen and then you'd find my clothes and surprise me by your exceptional beauty. That I'd take you to all the best clubs and restaurants for your debut. That you'd laugh and tell stories of when you were little. Of the crazy capers we had. Of our grand adventures. But you couldn't do or be any of those things, because you were a *tabula rasa* when I picked you up from these people. They'd wiped you *clean*." She looked back at Elly. "Do you understand? You were lost to me."

"Yes, I understand that part," said Elly trying not to cry. "You've always made that *very* clear." Stinging tears ran down Elly's cheeks. Her head throbbed. She took in a deep breath, "What I don't understand is *why*?"

"Why what?" asked Carmen seemingly nonplused.

"Why didn't you fix it back then?" asked Elly, gaining courage and wiping her tears back with the heels of her palms. She grabbed Carmen's hands, holding them, feeling their softness, "Why didn't you march me right back to the Bronx and demand that they tell you what happened? Why didn't you take me to one of those fancy places in Europe to get my head shrinked? What kept you from helping me? All you did was blame me. You never tried to help me remember."

Carmen twisted away from Elly, yanking her hands free.

A sob hitched from the inside of Carmen who fell to her knees and spread her black dress out on the ground. She cried as she fanned it out around her. Fingering the hem of her skirt like a nervous child. Elly thought she looked like a Degas—like a black swan.

The baby kicked. Elly put her hands on her stomach, and pushed in, answering her baby's kick. "The baby, Mom, do you want to feel?"

Carmen didn't answer. She continued pulling at her skirt.

She doesn't want to feel my baby kick . . . thought Elly.

Elly got up and walked to the headstone. She moved her fingers over the names she knew. Names that comforted her. Margaret, Vincent, George.

Carmen looked up and cleared her throat. "Well, I'm glad you have your memories all back again. But if you'd remembered sooner, you wouldn't be like *them*. I know it."

An unexpected anger surged through Elly. "What kind of play are we in right now, Mom? Is it a drama? A comedy? A tragedy? Clue me in, okay?"

"And still you say you love me?" asked Carmen.

"Yes. I love you." Tears burned against Elly's eyes. She wanted to open her arms up to her mother but her hands felt stuck at her sides.

"You can't love me and say such things."

"I can and I do."

A warmth spread up through Elly's fingers and into her arm and heart, "But that's what you want, isn't it? You want me to tell you I don't love you. That's it, right? Of *course* I love you. And you love me. You can say all the lines you want, but I know you love me. And I know you love Mimi and Fee. You can't run away from it, Mom. You don't get a clean exit line here. You just *don't.*"

"What do you want from me, Eleanor?" shrieked Carmen with her hands stretched out to the sky. Elly was reminded of when her mother played Blanche Dubois in *A Streetcar Named Desire.* She remembered the handsome actor at the bottom of the stairs on his knees screaming, *"Stella!!!!!!!!!!"*

"What do I want? What do *I* want?" her words came tumbling out unguarded. "I want . . . I want to dance on your feet again. I want to eat ripe peaches off the trees in Greece with you. I want to sit at a table and sip champagne while watching you sing—to me! I want you to sing to me, Mom. To me." Elly pounded her finger into her own chest. *"To Elly."* She whispered out the last words through sobs that wouldn't stop.

Carmen stood up. She shook her hair that bounced back into place. "Are you done?"

The icy pause helped Elly turn a corner she'd meant to turn years ago. Liz's words rang in her ears. *"Listen to your heart . . ."* Elly's heart knew her mother loved her. And no matter how hard she tried, she wasn't going to get the mother she wanted just like Carmen wouldn't get the daughter she craved. It was lose, lose. The only difference? Elly was ready to bend. Carmen wasn't built for bending.

"Yes. How about you? What do you want, Mom? Besides a different daughter?" The words came out without anger, without tears. They came out with a truth that Elly finally accepted.

"What do *I* want? Hmmm. What. Do. I. Want?" asked Carmen, rocking back on her heels and speaking clearly through clenched teeth. "I want . . ." She got up, smoothed her skirt and then her hair, "To go to France. Yes. It's time to pack up the

London flat and move back to Paris. I see you've lost your hat, by the way. At least *now* I can say I have a daughter who doesn't wear a knit hat in the summertime."

The wall was back up. The intense air between them deflated. Carmen deliberately took her energy out of the conversation and it left Elly flat. Elly knew the discussion was over and that somehow, in her own mind Carmen had written the scene with the ending she wanted anyway. It's hard to go to war with someone so skilled at pretending. They can pretend anything away.

Elly watched as Carmen turned and walked away from her. She got about ten feet and one of her heels stuck into the soft, green earth. She wobbled and then paused, regaining her balance. Elly thought Carmen might turn around. But she didn't. She just swept up one of her arms, ever so gracefully, and turned her palm around to face Elly, and then made it wave good-bye. Elly looked away and leaned her heavy body against the Amore grave and cried for a thousand years.

"I think we should go now," said Anthony, surprising her.

"Where'd you come from?" sniffled Elly.

"George's car. I sent Mimi and Fee home in the limo, but I think you need to leave now. This is no place for you."

"She left," cried Elly.

"That's what she does."

"Let me pay my respects first, okay. Let me let her leave completely."

"Okay," said Anthony, giving her a supportive arm to lean on as she turned to see the gravestone next to her.

"So, here lies Margaret Green. The one that gave us all our fancy ESP, right?"

"So they say," said Anthony, his voice resonating with a supportive patience that made Elly want to cry again.

"And Vincent," continued Elly. "Who stole her heart."

"You women with Green blood can do that to a man," said Anthony.

"The more I learn, the more I wonder why she married him."

"From what they told me it was a real case of true love. Also, Margaret needed to escape her own life," said Anthony. "But it seems a little like 'frying pan into fire.' "

"Right?" laughed Elly. Anthony was bringing Elly back to herself. The unfinished tears were drying up from the inside out of Elly Amore. No more tears for Carmen.

Under Margaret and Vincent's names were three plaques in memoriam for the three boys lost at war and buried in Arlington. ENZO, DANTE, AND FRANCO AMORE: WAR HEROES.

"They had some kind of courage, those boys," said Elly and Anthony together.

"Are we done?" asked Anthony. Elly nodded and leaned on Anthony and he turned her toward the car. She tripped over a little rise in the earth at the base of the Amore plot. "What's this?" she asked

"More headstones . . . or footstones. That's the way they sold these plots long ago. They'd sell them and then fit bodies on top of each other, on either side. Itsy's name is on the other side, waiting for Mimi and Fee, too. I think there's even room for you and Carmen here," said Anthony.

"Nice."

"Yeah, well—when someone tells you your whole family is going to die, you take precautions, I guess."

Elly leaned down and tore at the earth encroaching over the stones.

"Oh, look! I've found Zelda Grace, and who's Bonita?" asked Elly, confused.

"What do you mean?" asked Anthony.

"Who's buried next to Zelda?"

"Her mother." said Anthony.

"But I thought Zelda's mother was Bunny."

"What do *you* mean?" asked Anthony.

"Here, who is buried here? Another aunt I don't know about?"

"No. They nickname everyone. You know that. Everyone but the boys. Bonita was Bunny."

All of a sudden Elly turned pale. She shook herself free of Anthony and slowly walked around to the back of the gravestone.

"What's the matter, Elly?" asked Anthony, concerned.

Elly shook her head, tying to push away the truth that was unfolding in her mind. *It couldn't be* . . . She had to see it with her own eyes. She couldn't simply trust her instinct. *Trust then verify . . . trust then verify* . . . she told herself as she rounded the stone and read its chiseled verification.

George Amore: Always a Child at Heart

And the newly carved name:

Elizabeth Amore: Beloved Sister

"Liz?"

"Liz?" echoed Anthony.

A pain went through Elly. A pain she'd never felt. She doubled over. All Elly wanted was to run. To run away and find Liz. But of course, she wouldn't be there. The closer Elly'd been to putting all the pieces together, the more distant Liz had become. Liz . . . Itsy . . .

"She's in the ground? Oh no! She's in the ground now?" Elly fell to her knees, another pain ramming through her abdomen.

Anthony ran to her in two bold, magnificent strides. He scooped her up and held her close to him like a baby as he ran for Georgie's car.

✦

Elly Amore was in labor. As she writhed in the hospital bed, Mimi told Elly the story of the nicknames. She spoke in a soft voice that helped Elly through her contractions. "They called Bonita, Bunny and Fiona, Fee. Filomena, well that one belongs to me, and Itsy? Itsy's name was Elizabeth."

Deep in the throes of childbirth Elly found herself doing cartwheels with Liz and Itsy on the beach of Far Rockaway. Slowly, as she began to push, Itsy and Liz cartwheeled into one person. Elly Amore's lifelong best friend. Elizabeth Amore of the Bronx.

✦

"She's running a fever."

Elly heard someone say a million miles away.

She was sleeping and couldn't wake up, tired of fighting. There were murmurings from the real world, snippets of language that acted like horrible anchors yanking her back to the surface of the heavy topside. She wanted to laze about in her dream, it was lovely there. She was in a flowering meadow surrounded by high pines. Elly knew the ocean wasn't far, she could feel the tide in her blood and her pulse was the waves—or was it the other way around? She was watching a little girl dance. A little girl with a mop of curly red hair.

"Come dance with me, Mama! Come dance," she laughed.

Elly could smell her. Cotton and milk and sweet, wild, meadow sage.

"But if I dance with you now, we won't be able to dance later, love."

The child stopped turning and Elly drank in her features. Soft nose, lovely cheekbones, a dimpled chin—Elly's own green eyes. "You are right, Mama," said the child who began to spin in circles once again. The skirt of her white dress flying up into the air, "What are you waiting for? Go back already!"

"—Elly! Wake up! Do it for me. It's time!" Anthony was shouting at her. His dark eyes focused with concern. His hands pushed on the bed, bouncing Elly's whole self back to the world of the living.

"Time for what?" she asked.

Anthony started laughing and crying at the same time. "You're back!" And then over his shoulder, "Mimi! She's back!"

"What's going on?" asked Elly.

"You've been sick, Elly, don't worry. It happens sometimes during labor. Infections. You're okay now and you must concentrate because the doctors say it's time for the baby to come out," said Mimi, coming to her side.

A sharp, undeniable pain shot through Elly's pelvic bones. "Oh God!"

"Do you think you can push?" asked a nurse.

Elly thought of the child in the field. Her feverdream. The thing she wanted most in the world.

"Did my mother come?" Elly asked.

"No, Elly, I'm sorry, babe," said Anthony.

She channeled her hurt and anger into the next phase of her life. "You bet your ass I can push," she said through clenched teeth.

"Do you want to listen to some music?" asked the nurse.

"Do you have any Procol Harem?" asked Anthony.

"Ah, you've lucked out! I'm an old hippie," said the doctor, a man with kind eyes and a close beard. "What song?"

" 'Whiter Shade of Pale'? " asked Anthony.

"Hey, that's one of my favorites, too. How do you know that one? It was before your time."

Anthony shot a thumb at Elly "She taught it to me."

"I did?" said Elly, propped up and ready for the next contraction.

"Yes, a long time ago. When we were little. It was our wedding song."

"She's got good taste in music," said the doctor, who positioned Elly's legs so wide she thought she could touch the walls with her toes.

"Will you help me, Anthony?" asked Elly.

"All the time, every day, forever," he said and then sat her up so he could sit behind her. As she pushed he leaned up with her and whispered the lyrics in her ear:

That her face at first just ghostly,
Turned a whiter shade of pale.

The baby was born with a shock of red hair. She came into the world quietly, dancing on her mother's dreams.

Mimi put her head next to her granddaughter's and asked, "What should we name her, Elly? Should we name her Babygirl like we named you all those years ago?"

"No, Mimi, she's still in here," Elly placed her hand softly on her own chest. "She doesn't need a redo. Itsy does. Let's call her Elizabeth."

"Okay, but what will her nickname be?" asked Mimi. "It seems we've used them all up. Mama was so good at this. You are like her, my Elly. You come up with something."

"Bitsy?" suggested Elly.

"Too much like Itsy," said Mimi.

"Lili?"

"Sounds like a baby name," said Mimi.

"Oh and Babygirl wasn't?" teased Elly.

"How about Elizabeth the Second?" suggested Mimi.

"Oh, it's very regal. I like it. But a little long, no? And QEII is a ship."

Elly thought for a second and then her eyes lit up, "Mimi, you're a genius! Let's call her your majesty. Maj for short. How do you like it, Maj? Oh Majestic Magical Maj."

"I once knew a woman in Holland with that name," said Mimi with a wicked grin.

"Mimi? You've been to Holland?"

"Oh yes! Itsy and Fee, too. We went to Amsterdam . . . you know . . . some herbal research."

Elly laughed quietly, "You are full of surprises, aren't you, Mimi?" And then to Maj, "Hello little Maj, hello redo," said Elly to her baby. She took Mimi's hand and placed it on the swaddled bundle. "Tell me, Mimi, what do you see? Do you see anything I should know about?"

"No," said Mimi, who took baby Maj from Elly and cradled her. "I don't see anything but happiness."

Elly sat back in the hospital bed and pouted a little. "You wouldn't tell me anyway, would you?"

Mimi took her hand and placed it on the swaddled bundle. "What do *you* see, my Elly?"

A shot of memory not her own ran from Mimi's hand into Elly's mind. "I see you, Mimi. You going softly into Carmen's room after she fell asleep. Carefully picking her up out of her crib so's not to wake her and rocking her in the rocking chair. Holding her close to you, until her heartbeat and yours were one. Only you didn't know, Mimi—one time you *did* wake her, but she pretended to stay asleep just to feel the love come out of you."

Mimi was wiping away tears with her index finger, shifting the weight of the new baby and holding her close while Elly remembered. "It's why she wanted the chair," said Mimi. And Elly, crying with her grandmother now, nodded in agreement.

"We should call her, Mimi. We should tell her we love her no matter how she feels about us. Shouldn't we?"

Mimi's face drew tight. Elly knew the look. It belonged to Carmen, too. Mimi was pulling back. She was afraid she'd revealed too much. She was closing the door. Elly wanted to say *"Mimi! Don't close the door!"* but it was too late.

"Here," Mimi said, pushing an envelope at Elly. "She wrote you a letter."

"Who?" *Carmen? Was it Carmen?*

"My sister, Itsy. I guess she had more to say to you. More things I don't know." Mimi's tone was raw and gruff.

Elly tried not to look disappointed that it wasn't from Carmen.

"How about I read it out loud, Mimi? And then we can both listen to what she had to say."

Mimi was already at the door to the hospital room. "No, if she meant it for me it would have *Mimi* scrawled across it with her chicken scratch. It clearly says *Babygirl*."

And then she was gone, and Elly was left alone with her new baby cradled in one arm, a letter from her dead Aunt in the palm of her hand, and her fiancé snoring on the blue, vinyl couch.

"What do you say, Maj? Let's read Itsy's letter."

Maj looked at her mother and made an "O" with her rosebud lips.

"I'll take that as a yes, then."

Elly opened the envelope.

33

Itsy

In many ways it *was* a letter from Carmen, only Itsy delivered it using The Sight.

Dear Babygirl, (I know you're grown and have a grown-up nickname, but you'll always be Babygirl to me)

I'm dead now. As you read this letter, I'm dead. I don't think it feels the way it sounds. At least I hope not. The words in Italian, morto *or even* inanimato, *seem a better fit. They end in vowels. Vowels are open letters that allow for sound and air. Mama always said death would be like that. Open. The whole universe cracked right open and there on a silver platter for all of us. Part of me can't wait.*

I need to talk to you about Carmen. I had a dream a few nights ago, and it was the kind of dream that wasn't a dream at all. The Sight comes through strong while we dream. Make sure you can tell the difference. Those dreams that are related to the real world, the ones that help us figure out things we simply can't grasp in our waking hours, those are the best kind.

So I was dreaming about being dead, and I was flying. Flying around everywhere, and I knew *I was dead. So I began looking for Mama. But who do I find? Carmen. Carmen in all of her multicolored dissatisfaction. Carmen with a gray plume of smoke rising out of her head. She's bitter, yes. And selfish, too. But in my dream I could see it all, I know we made her that way.*

She had potential, and we ripped it from her because we were afraid.

I travel alongside her. She's on a plane back to Europe. I can watch her through the window as I fly right beside.

Carmen is crying on the plane. She's sick about leaving you behind. She has the mother knot that wants to be with her own child as she bears a child of her own. But Carmen runs from pain. She runs from love. She runs from the knot.

It was such a betrayal, that day on our stoop when you didn't know her. Carmen took it on herself to trust you. To pour all of Carmen, the good and bad, into you, Babygirl, no matter how small you were. And then, when I did what I did, I took Carmen away as much as I took you away from yourself. You'd think I'd have known better. Every spell has a ramification outside of what you intend. Many are bad. It's the way the world works, Mama told us so. Remember that, okay?

Flying next to her I can see Carmen as who she really is. She's not so bad. I know she cries more for herself than for you, Elly. Or Mimi. Or even me, though she never really knew me well. I follow her off the plane. She wants to call New York. Wants to see if you're okay . . . what sex the baby is. But she can't.

I hear her mantra. "I'm alone and okay. I'm alone and okay."

"No, you're not, Carmen." I place an invisible hand over hers as she grabs her luggage from the conveyor belt. She stops and catches her breath. Looks around. She shrugs her shoulders. Shrugs

off The Sight. Only then do I realize she's always had it, too. Just never opened herself up to it.

We walk into her flat in London. It's a beautiful place. I think it's a shame Mimi won't see it. Mimi and Carmen both like fine, sparkling things. It's a similarity they don't even know they share.

In an alternate reality I can see them, giggling over china in a catalogue. Shopping for clothes together at Bergdorf Goodman. There's only one thing in Carmen's flat that doesn't seem to fit, and she has it center stage. Right in front of a bank of windows. My own dear Mama's rocking chair.

In my dream I try to think into her mind. Even though I know I'm seeing the future, I'm hoping my energy can stay with her. I send a silent hope. Please hear me, Carmen. Please hear me. For once in your life, forgive us. Forgive us, forgive yourself, and remember who you really are. Elly needs you.

I fly back on air that feels like oceans and leaves and cotton, too. I'm in the hospital room with you. Anthony is asleep. But not the baby. Not Maj. You and Maj (it's a wonderful nickname, you're good at it, like Mama was) are reading my letter.

Stop crying, Elly. Please. Happy and sad walk hand in hand.

I touch Maj's upper lip with my finger.

Mama always said that babies chose where they were to go. That they all lived together in the guff and that when they were born the birthing angels placed their fingers on ghostling lips and said "Shhhhh, don't tell."

"That's what makes the dimple there," she'd said.

"But why would babies want to come somewhere to die?" We'd ask her.

"Babies are wise souls in the guff, full of sight. They can see the whole picture of the lives they touch. Sometimes a baby needs

to come all the way from the guff and into a woman's womb even when they know they won't be born. But no matter—the soul did its job and it goes into the guff to wait again.

"Perhaps that's what happened to all my people. We didn't listen very well, and we remember echoes of the future from our time in the guff."

Mama was the wisest person ever to be born. In my opinion. But you run a close second, Babygirl, even if you don't know it, yet.

I used to place my finger against my brother Georgie's mouth while he slept. Just like I'm doing right now with your baby.

And one more thing my Elly, my Babygirl . . . I'm not gone from you. I've seen us in the garden. Mama's garden. Perhaps you'll find me there.

Love,
Lizzy

Elly put her finger over the dimple in Maj's perfect upper lip. And a flutter of joy began to ease the steady stream of tears that had been pouring, from the very start of Itsy's letter, until the very end.

34

The Day the Amores Died

The day they brought the baby home Elly noticed a gray hush had fallen over the building on 170th Street. Halfway up the stairs to their apartment, the doorbell rang.

"I'll get it, babe. You go take your shower."

Elly watched how Anthony held little Maj, so comfortable, so adept. And she *did* want an actual shower. The shower at the hospital seemed a joke at best. "Thank you," she said.

"Anything for my girls," he said more to the baby than to Elly.

When she turned off the water Anthony called to her from the living room. "Elly, come see. You really need to see this."

She wrapped herself in soft white towels and looked at her reflection in the mirror. She remembered the night at college when she'd lost her virginity—violently—to Cooper. She'd tried to find a difference in her appearance, something that others would notice. She'd only felt sad, sick, and red-faced. Younger and more vulnerable, if anything.

But not this time. Elly looked in the mirror and loved what she saw. Not a washed-out version of Carmen anymore. Elly was seeing herself for the first time. Strong, wild, and powerful. An Amore. A Green.

She walked out into the living room. And there he was. Anthony, rocking little Maj in Margaret Green's rocking chair.

"Oh God! The chair. It's so beautiful. Way more beautiful than I remembered it," Elly said as she sat down next to it and watched the arched rockers creak across the floor.

"You should'a seen the delivery guy try to get it up the stairs! It came with a note. Here."

He handed her a handwritten letter touching her softly as she took it from him. His eyes brimmed with support.

Dear Elly,

Don't let go of her. Not for one second. Hold her tight. Rock her when her eyes are open. Tell her how much we all love her.

Bien à toi,

Mommy

"She must be in France now. This chair's been all around the world," said Elly, carefully folding the note into an origami crane.

"Are you okay? Do you miss her very much?" he asked

"I'm okay. I'm home. I have you and Maj. The truth is, I'll miss her forever, I have to get used to it. It's more a case of me missing Itsy. And Liz."

"Ah yes, the incredible disappearing Liz," said Anthony.

"Do you really expect me to believe you never saw her but always thought she was real?" asked Elly.

"What do I know? I'm just a guy. She was real to you, so she was real to me. And besides, I grew up in a family where strange things I didn't understand happened on a regular basis, you know?"

Elly sighed. "She *was* real to me. Too real. I don't know what to do without her."

"Why don't you go get Mimi and tell her to come see the chair. I bet it'll make her happy to know it's back home where it belongs," said Anthony.

"That's a good idea," said Elly, getting up and kissing them both on their cheeks. She threw on a nightgown and went to get Mimi.

She knocked on Mimi's apartment door. It took Mimi a long time to answer, but Elly knew she was in there.

"Do you need me?" asked Mimi, who looked exhausted and older than usual.

"Mimi, you have to come see. Carmen sent back the rocking chair!"

"How nice for you. Is that all?" Mimi closed the door in her face. Elly stood alone in the hallway. Fee, always curious, hadn't even emerged from her apartment. It was odd how the 170th Street building was so quiet with Itsy gone. There'd been no sound from her in years and yet the air was still with her absence.

Elly closed her eyes and could see Mimi and Fee sitting motionless on their respective easy chairs each one alone in their respective apartments. Each cried silently. And though they moved slowly anyway, the building seemed to be stuck on pause.

"This will *not* do." Elly said into the air.

✦

"You'll figure it out, you're so resourceful," said Anthony, in bed after she told him how strange things were all of a sudden.

"I thought I had it all figured out already. All the secrets are out in the open. It's all supposed to be fixed, like great-grandma Margaret asked. But suddenly it seems more broken than ever."

"Well, are you sure you know *everything*?" asked Anthony.

Elly sat up and turned on the bedside lamp. "It's that day! The day they all died. I still don't know how it all happened."

"Mimi would know," said Anthony.

"Yes, she would. And she *has* to tell me," said Elly.

"How are you going to get her to talk?"

"I have leverage," said Elly rubbing her hands together.

"Oh yeah, what kind?"

"I know what Itsy said to me the day she broke her silence."

"How'd you find that out? Was it hidden in one of the memories?"

"Yes, and no. I did what you told me to do when I first came here last winter."

"And what kind of wisdom did I give you way back then?" asked Anthony with a smile.

"You said, 'Ask Itsy,' so—I asked her. And finally, when she found her voice, she answered me."

✦

The next day, with baby Maj on a walk with Anthony for her very first tour of the Bronx, Elly sat with her grandmother and held her hand.

"You can't live like this, Mimi. You've overcome much worse. It's not good for little Maj."

Mimi yanked her hand away. "What do you know of overcoming? What do you know about anything?" She sounded petulant, like a child.

Elly'd had enough. She flew to the window and opened it, letting out the oppressive heat. She was in charge now. It felt so good. She crossed her arms in front of her, her posture demanding attention from Mimi. "Do you still want to know what she said to me?"

"What?"

"Aunt Itsy. Do you still want to know what she said to me all those years ago?"

Elly watched Mimi's face brighten a little. Watched her shoulders relax. Mimi and Elly were alike in so many ways. Like Itsy, too. Treasure hunters. Secret keepers. Magic makers. Elly sat back down and took her Mimi's hand once again.

"You wanted to know what she said. Now I know." Elly took a deep breath. "But I'm not telling until you tell me what you saw. Now I know it all. I have all the pieces. But I need to know what you saw. What did you see, Mimi?"

"Why do you want to know such things? Horrible things?"

"Because we owe it to Itsy and to everyone else. We owe *ourselves* the whole truth. Mimi, I love you and I love this life you've given me. Don't leave me now. I need you and Aunt Fee. I need this place to breathe again. Maybe if you tell me what you know, and I tell you what I know, the broken pieces can come together and start to heal. What do you say, Mimi? Give it a try, won't you?"

Elly saw her reflection in Mimi's eyes. She was changed. Grown up . . . but grown up in an Amore way. A glimmer in her eye, a secret in her soul. There could be years of laughter ahead of all of them.

"Well, I suppose I saw everything," said Mimi giving in to the temptation. "And paid the price. When it was all over I was crying blood. Doctor Ryan said I almost cried my eyes out. Literally. They bandaged me for weeks. I was blind to everything but my sisters. They took care of me. The deaf and mute taking care of the blind. Prophetic, cliché, and crazy."

"Oh Mimi, I can't even imagine it. Won't you please tell me about that day? I feel like I need to own a piece of it, especially now with Itsy gone. I've lost my connection."

"You will never lose your connection, love. You can't. It's inside of you. Okay, you want the dirty details? I'll give them to you." Mimi got up and went to the window. She needed to say the words into the building itself. To tell it its own story.

"The day was lovely. I remember that, and the trees were moving the way they do on a midspring day. God's breath making wishes on the leaves. Mama and I were baking. And then—the doorbell rang.

"Our hands were gooey. 'Fee?' asked Mama pushing her hair back with her forearm.

" 'No, she's at the church decorating for the festival,' I said.

" 'Bunny?'

" 'Shopping.'

"Mama sighed. 'Call Papa.'

" '*Papa*!' I yelled. She hit the back of my head with her hand,

" 'Ma! You got flour in my hair.'

" 'And so what? I have to do everything myself.' She wiped her hands on her apron and walked to the front door. That was the beginning and the end. I never saw her alive again. Later that night Fee wanted to wash my hair. But I put up such a fight she gave up because she didn't want me to bleed from my eyes anymore. I wanted to keep Mama's flour in my hair. I never wanted to wash it out.

"'Can I help you?' I heard Mama say.

"There were mumbled, masculine voices and then a thud. I heard Papa come down the stairs and yell out Mama's name.

"I ran into the front hall. There were two soldiers at the door and Mama on the floor, ashen, eyes opened. Dead.

"'What happened?' I cried out. Papa was cradling her and crying. 'No, no, no!'

"The men at the door told me about the boys.

"I can remember asking something silly like, 'All three? All three at the same time? Aren't there some kind of rules against that?'

"They asked what they could do.

"I told them to get help.

"As they left, I saw Fee coming home. She was running down the sidewalk. Holding up her skirts. 'What's happened?' She was yelling too loud. People were coming out of their buildings like bugs.

"Papa walked away staring out of dull eyes with a pale face, letting Mama's head thunk against the floor. He walked back into the apartment. It didn't take long.

"Fee and I were standing, crying over Mama, waiting for help. Fee kept putting her fingers in her ears and saying, 'What?'

"The shot was loud. It came from Mama and Papa's room. I got up. 'Fee, did you hear?'

"She looked puzzled. 'What?'

"I ran into their bedroom and Papa was across the bed. Shot himself in the head. I remember thinking, *No . . . this can't be happening. Too much. How did it all fall apart in five minutes?*

"Bunny came home, I heard her scream and shoo Zelda Grace up the stairs to their apartment, to shield her from the tragic chaos.

"I ran to her, my big sister. My new mother.

" 'Papa! He's dead, too. Shot himself. And the boys! That's how it started, Bunny . . . that's how it started. All three.'

" 'Isn't there some rule about that?' she asked, echoing my own thoughts.

"The discussion was surreal. We didn't know what else to do. Fee wouldn't stop fussing with her ears. 'I can't hear right,' she said, rocking back and forth on her heels.

"Policemen were everywhere by then. Like buzzing bees. But they didn't pay much attention to us. Most of them were gathering at the back of the house around Papa. I'm sure it was one of them who called the ambulance.

"Bunny sat on the bottom step and stared out the doorway. I sat next to her.

" 'So what do we do?' she asked me.

" 'We wait for help.'

" 'We wait,' she repeated.

"We stared into the day, the shaft of light like an Edward Hopper painting illuminating Fee and dead Mama on the floor. And then a graceful shadow, the sound of doves' wings . . . fabric in the wind, and a soft scream, all followed by a sick, smacking sound.

"Sweet, curious, Zelda Grace had fallen from the upstairs window. We watched her hit the ground.

"Bunny got up in slow motion and walked forward stepping over Mama. She took her time walking off the porch steps. She leaned down and covered her daughter's eyes with her hands and then stood back up.

"I knew what would happen next. I didn't need The Sight for that. I didn't even try to stop her. The day's events were out of my control. Mama knew it was coming. The fortune-teller confirmed it all those years ago that summer day in Playland. It had to finish itself. Run its horrible course.

"Bunny chased the light out into oncoming traffic. The ambulance that was coming to save us killed my sister.

"Fee put her hands over her ears and kept rocking.

"I remember thinking: *Itsy and George . . . Itsy and George.*

"Itsy was living at Mama's house out on Far Rockaway. But it was the middle of the week. She'd be teaching. I had to call her. George was running in through the back door. He tore by me. *Good . . .* I remember thinking. *Someone else will tell him. I'll tell Itsy and she'll come and take care of him.*

"I picked up the phone. The receiver fell, it was so heavy. The air was heavy. I looked at the phone numbers on the chalkboard next to the phone that Mama put up so we could keep track of everyone.

"I dialed Bayside Public School and asked to speak to Itsy. A family emergency if there ever was one. I don't even know how I got out the words. When I hung up the phone I clutched at my belly. I'd forgotten all about the baby. The baby whose family was disappearing by the second.

"My husband Alfred worked in the City with Bunny's husband, Charlie. They'd be home after it was all over. And they did come home. But Charlie packed his things in silence and left. He never saw Bunny buried and we never saw him again. And my Alfred? He stayed by my side. Stayed until I made him leave. But that's another story altogether."

Elly took a long look at her grandmother. It was one thing to know something, another entirely to hear the details. Elly felt the air suck out of her own chest. The things people go through everyday. The split-second spin of a reality gone mad. Elly could clearly picture statuesque Bunny lifting her skirts and stepping into the traffic, her shoulders straight. Her bun still tight and tidy on top of her head. Elly had an itchy, urgent need to paint the whole scene. As if it would purge it from all of them. Mark the moment so they could all move on.

Mimi sat back and relaxed. "Okay, your turn, Elly. What did my sister say to you all those years ago?"

"Well . . . I didn't want to go. I didn't want to leave you and Anthony, the life I had here. I watched the taxi pull up and I gripped the iron bars. Then I ran. Uncle George told me where to go. I ran to my hiding place and found my secret treasure. An old, old smell came out. Lavender like all your things, but stronger and mixed with an odd earthy scent, too. . . .

✦ Babygirl ✦

. . . and then she lifted a heavy folded cotton sheet and found the bones of a tiny baby dressed in a beautiful christening gown too big for her. On the back of the sheet a perfectly pressed brown stain of decay that showed of the features of what would have surely been a pretty little thing.

Fascinated, Babygirl held up the shroud and looked closely at it until her alive little Babygirl nose touched the baby nose imprinted on the fabric. Babygirl saw a flash of light behind her eyes and saw her sad birth and secret burial. Itsy's very own baby!

✦

"Itsy found me there.

" 'What have you found, little one?' she asked me.

" 'Itsy? You're talking!' I hugged her. 'I found your baby. Did you lose her?'

" 'No, I didn't lose her. Not really. I just needed someone else to know about her. I suppose I only needed someone to find my voice. Thank you for finding her. Thank you for sharing my secret. Now, why don't you tell me what is making you so upset, love.'

" 'I don't want to go.'

" 'What should we do about this? How can I help you?'

" 'I wish . . . I wish I didn't remember. If I have to go with her I don't want to remember any of this.'

" 'But why?'

" 'Because it would hurt too much not to be here. And I'm scared of her. I'm so scared of her now that I know what it's like to be with you. I *have* to forget. Quickly! Do you have magic that can make me forget?'

" 'I can try.'

" 'Oh! Wait, but if I forget, then I won't remember your secret . . . and if I don't remember your secret, you won't be able to talk!'

" 'Oh darling, you don't worry about that. It's better this way. So much happened, why should I add an extra layer of sadness onto those I love? Maybe, just maybe it will be a good thing all around. Now come here and let me see what I can do. But first, in case it works, in case you really forget, I want you to know that I love you very much. And that I love your Uncle George, too. The both of you, more than anything, okay?'

" 'Okay.' I said, and Itsy wove her magic spell."

✦

"She had a baby? And we never knew?" Mimi was crying.

"She didn't want you to know. She had to protect George."

"Yes, yes. I see it all now. And so that was the big secret? After all these years? She said she loved you? And then made you forget?" asked Mimi.

"Yes, Mimi, she said she loved me."

"Love should never be a secret and it should never, ever be forgotten."

"It won't be anymore."

35

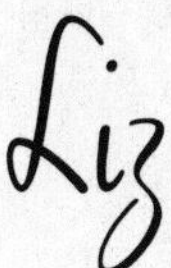

Liz

Elly couldn't sleep. She tossed and turned, thinking about The Day the Amores Died. She checked on Maj, lamenting that she was such a good baby. It'd be better if she was up. At least then Elly would have something to do. She sat in the nursery and rocked back and forth in the ancient chair.

"Elly," called a soft voice, hushed but wanting to be heard. Elly stopped rocking.

"Elly!" the voice called again, insistent.

She went to the window. There stood Liz. Beautiful as ever in the moonlight and wearing a flowered dress. The same dress she always wore when she visited Elly as the "young woman Liz." "I never even noticed . . ." said Elly as she opened the window wider and stepped out onto the fire escape.

"Look, we're like Romeo and Juliet!" said Liz. "But soft! What light through yonder window breaks? It is the East, and Juliet is the sun! Arise, fair sun, and kill the envious moon!"

"Is it really you?" asked Elly.

"Yes. At least I think so."

"But you're dead," said Elly.

"Oh, death. Such a nuisance really. Just another thing to do. Always so much work, you know. Come on down here and sit in the garden with me. The garden's always its most lovely under the moon."

Elly climbed down the fire escape ladder and sat on the bench in the walled garden next to Liz.

"I was always there to protect you. I made a promise to you the day you were born. It was fun, being a kid again. At least I tried—I didn't like playing sardines much," said Liz.

"So did I imagine you, or were you there?" asked Elly.

"You saw me, right?" teased Liz.

"Yes."

"Then what do you think?" She gave Elly a playful shove.

Elly looked at the ghost. Her face in the shadows shimmered from old to young and back again.

Liz leaned forward, whispering a flower of memory into Elly's mind.

"I was a baby," said Elly, "and you came to see me in the hospital. You put yourself inside of me. You told me you'd never leave me, and you didn't."

Liz smiled. "You got it, kiddo! Sometimes you gotta hand it to that Green blood. It helps us accomplish some damn fine things."

"So, you saw it all?"

"I saw you all grown up and beautiful. Your belly full with child. And I saw you dead in the attic. I decided then and there to change it. No matter what Mama and Mimi and Fee said. I wanted to at least *try* to change it, and I did."

Elly sat with her palms open, like Mimi and Fee the night of Itsy's death. Elly understood the real grief now. The enormity of the loss. "Will you stay with me? Stay and protect me still?" she asked trying to be stoic, to hold back the tears. To be an Amore.

"I can't stay, Elly. I'm dead. I only came to say good-bye. I thought you needed to know that *you* can take care of yourself now. I wanted to tell you that it wasn't your fault, not any of it."

Elly let the tears come realizing that this was *really* it. That Liz, Lizzy, Itsy, they were all going away. It was too much. It made Elly remember why she wanted to forget it all in the first place. "Hush now," said Elizabeth Amore, "It's time for me to go. I can't leave you like this."

"Are you afraid? Is it dark?" sniffled Elly.

"Oh no. It's wonderful. Nothing I could ever explain with words. Go back to your family, Elly. Hold your baby. Curl up next to your man. Live the life I couldn't. You owe me that."

"Oh," said Elly feeling lighter. "I owe you, do I?"

"You're alive, aren't you?"

"Please," teased Elly. "You were imaginary for Christ's sake. Some sort of magical Green energy projection or something."

"I wasn't imaginary when I hauled that huge steamer trunk from here all the way to Far Rockaway. I wasn't imaginary then. I saw it, Elly. I saw him come to the building and find you and Anthony in the attic going through my trunk. I saw him kill both of you. I decided to do what Mama hadn't done, what Mimi couldn't do. I decided to try and change what I saw. And see? It worked! Voilà, a whole new fate." Elizabeth reached out, tried to touch Elly's face but there was a crackle instead. "Anyway, I need you to know that the things you see can be changed. Don't let yourself get tied down to one particular road, okay? Promise me."

"I promise," said Elly.

"Oh, and forgive Carmen. I've seen her. She's flawed, but she loves you."

"Already done," smiled Elly. "Liz?"

"Hmm?"

"Why was it such a secret? Why didn't you tell anyone?"

"I had to protect George, of course. If anyone found out he'd hurt me they'd have put him away or something. I swore a solemn vow to Mama that I'd protect him. Forever. And I did. Sort of. Well, I tried. At least I tried."

"You were a good sister, Liz—Aunt Itsy—what should I call you anyway?"

"Call me gone, honey."

A light came from the ivy-covered wall. Dim and then bright.

"I have to go now," said Liz.

A woman—a woman who looked like Elly—walked through the wall and onto the grass. Her steps graceful and tentative. Vines and tendrils grew from where she placed her feet as she walked, delicately, out into the garden. She held her arms out to Liz. Elly could feel the magnetic force. Liz became more of a whisper of an outline and then, she was gone. The woman looked at Elly.

"Take care of them." Margaret Green turned around and walked back into the pocket of light, taking it with her and leaving only the blue of the moonlight in the garden. It was then that Elly saw the vines that grew at her feet were still there, only now those vines were producing the widest, whitest moonflowers, one after the other, that Elly had ever seen.

She was suddenly alone. More alone than she'd ever been. It occurred to Elly for the very first time that pieces of her aunt had lived inside of her forever. *Who am I without you?* she asked the night.

Mimi and Fee found Elly sitting in the night garden with her hands open, palms up in her lap.

"She's seen Mama," said Mimi.

"She's seen Mama," said Fee.

Mimi took one of Elly's hands, and Fee took the other. Together they were three.

"I'm one of you," said Elly.

"One of us," said Mimi.

"Forever and ever," said Fee.

"Amen," said Elly.

Fall

"Stand still!" yelled Fee at Elly's feet as she pinned up the hem of a heavy satin wedding gown.

"Do it. She'll poke you. Just for fun, probably," whispered Mimi, her mouth full of pins as she laced some freshwater pearls into the bodice.

"I'm tired of this. The dress is fine the way it is!" complained Elly.

"No, no. This wedding will be perfect. I know," said Mimi.

Elly didn't want to waste little Maj's naptime with all this fussing. They were in Mimi's apartment with the doors open and the baby monitor on. Elly listened to every sound coming from the baby's nursery.

"Ah! Come *on,* old women! I have so much to do. I *need* her naptime to paint!"

"You are getting married next week. There are things we need to prepare," said Mimi.

Elly smiled to herself. *We were married a long time ago. Long ago on the beaches of Far Rockaway . . .*

A static sound came over the monitor. And then a whisper: *Ohlookathersopretty.*

"Did you hear that?" asked Mimi.

"*What?*" yelled Fee.

But Elly was already on her way, stepping off a low stool as she walked, and then gathering her skirts she ran to her baby. Fee fell over as she tried to keep sewing the hem to no avail. Elly was gone—needles and thread bouncing behind her. She ran out of Mimi's apartment and up the staircase gathering armloads of satin skirting with Carmen's words dangling in front of her, adding steps. *"They'll eat your baby . . ."*

She pushed open the door to Uncle Georgie's apartment, hers now 2B . . . with Anthony. 2A was vacant and up for rent.

She walked through the sunny living room and into the nursery. The windows were open, letting in a cold October breeze. *Did I leave the windows open? Foolish . . .* she went to close them, heard the whispers, again, and turned around to face the crib.

"Oh. My. God," she said under her breath not wanting to disturb the electrified air.

The two children dressed in old-fashioned clothes and holding hands turned to face her. The little girl, hair in ringlets with a bow askew, the boy in short pants and wearing a cap, both seemed to squirm nervously in front of her.

"She's so pretty, Elly," said the little girl, and Elly knew her voice. "She's got your nose, and red hair? Imagine!"

Elly stood very still. "Thank you, Itsy. We love her very much. Please . . . don't take her."

"Don't worry, Elly." The little girl giggled. "I'm not here for your baby. I'm here to collect Georgie." She cupped her hands over the boy's ear and whispered something to him. He smiled.

"What did you say, Itsy?" asked Elly.

The girl was instantly in front of her, looking up and motioning Elly to lean down with her finger. Elly knelt on the floor in front of her old friend.

The little ghost put her hand on Elly's cheek. "I told him it was time to go."

"Oh, Itsy. I'll miss you. Won't you stay? You and George?"

Elly held out her arms to young George who took off his cap and ran into them with abandon. A shock of wild electricity went through Elly as she felt all his sorrow and lonesome days. "I want to go home, Elly," he said. "I'm tired of being here, of crying all the time. When you came back, I started to laugh . . . but you don't have no more time for me, Elly."

Itsy took Georgie's hand. "Like I said, Georgie, time to go. Mama's waiting. Henry, too."

"Henry?" asked George.

"Yes, silly!"

"Well, let's get going then!"

The two children disappeared in a shimmer and reappeared perched on the wide windowsill, the window open once again.

"No, wait," said Elly reaching out for them.

"One, two, three . . . *you and me*!!!!!!!" they shouted, swinging their arms as they jumped out of the window and into thin air.

Elly sat on the floor listening to the quiet and crying softly. They were gone. It'd been Itsy and George all along. Now the walls rang silent. "Loss is a funny kind of thing," she said to the house. "You need to feel it in order to appreciate what you had, right? You can't live without it, can you?" The silence answered its affirmation. It seemed to arch forward and tell her *"What would have been, is simply—what was, only different. It's up to you."*

"It's up to me," said Elly.

✦

After a while little Maj woke up hungry and began to cry. A real cry. Elly went to her, gathered her up and sat in the rocking chair. She pushed down the scratchy, beaded satin of her unfinished wedding gown to breastfeed her baby.

"Let me tell you a story," began Elly as the rocking chair creaked back and forth. "Once upon a time there was a family. A very special family. They came here to America to find a better life, and what they found was hard work and mystical, magical things. The ancients called to them from over the ocean, and those voices carried in their minds and made them a little . . . well . . . strange. But they loved and were loved. And they all love you, even from beyond.

"There was Elizabeth and George the twins, and Bonita who was, like her name, very beautiful . . . there was Filomena your great-grandmother and not forgetting Fiona or the boys, Enzo, Franco, and Dante, all lost in the war. And let's not forget the magical Greens, Faith and Margaret and Ephraim. And then there was Carmen, and me and now . . . you. You are our redo. Everyone deserves a redo, don't they? Sure they do."

1. Facing what seems like an impossible situation, Eleanor decides to leave all that she knows and return to her estranged family in the Bronx. This decision was hasty, but all of her instincts were telling her to go. Would you have made the same choice? Were there any other options that may have taken the story in another direction? How often do you trust your own instinct (instead of logic) when making a decision?

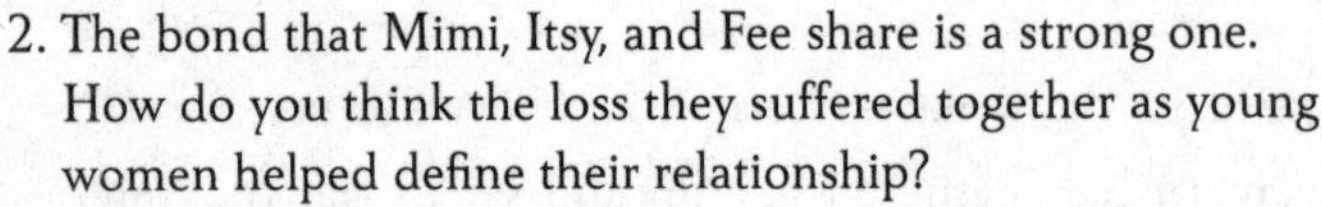

2. The bond that Mimi, Itsy, and Fee share is a strong one. How do you think the loss they suffered together as young women helped define their relationship?

3. Mama, Margaret Green, is the keeper of all the wisdom in the family—but she has many flaws. What are some moments when Margaret was "less than perfect"? Did her flaws diminish her relationship with her children? Why or why not?

4. Many young women suffer from domestic abuse in romantic relationships. The signature of these relationships is that they are difficult to leave. Yet Elly seems to be able to walk away from Cooper without too much internal questioning. What do you think helped her to overcome the abuse so quickly?

5. Though the women in this novel consider themselves witches, what kind of magic do they practice? Is this very far from the traditions, habits, and superstitions that can be found in almost every family? What were some "magical" traditions that you remember from growing up (examples: "Step on the Crack, Break Your Mother's Back," black cats, the number 13...)? How do you think these superstitions or traditions can bring people, especially family, together?

6. Anthony is very sure of his love for Elly. How does he know her so well? He knows her better than she knows herself, and he helps her rediscover the memories that hold the key to her entire personality. In many ways, their love story is the stuff of movies. Has there ever been anyone that you loved, no matter what? How do you think a love like that shapes you? How do you think it shaped Elly?

Discussio
Questions

St. Martin'
Griffin

7. Throughout the novel Itsy has a secret that she holds very dear—a secret that, had her family known sooner, might have changed many things. How do you think their lives might have been different if Itsy had, at the time, added to the Amore tragedies, but in a sense, freed herself of the weight of her secret?

8. Mimi and Carmen have a complicated relationship. Mimi never took care of Carmen emotionally when she was a child because The Sight told her that Carmen would leave one day. Do you think if she had, things might have been different? Or would Carmen have left anyway? Was it in Carmen's nature to be cold and leave, or was that her nature because of her lack of nurturing?

9. Elly changed significantly from the first page to the last. Do you think this was because she recovered all her memories or because she learned what real love—both familial and romantic—is? Could she have become whole with only one or the other? Discuss.

10. There is an unwritten element of the adage "See no evil, hear no evil, speak no evil" with regard to Mimi and the aunts. Do you think this a purposeful theme added by the author, or did it occur organically? And, how does this theme play into the events of the story?

For more reading group suggestions, visit www.readinggroupgold.com.